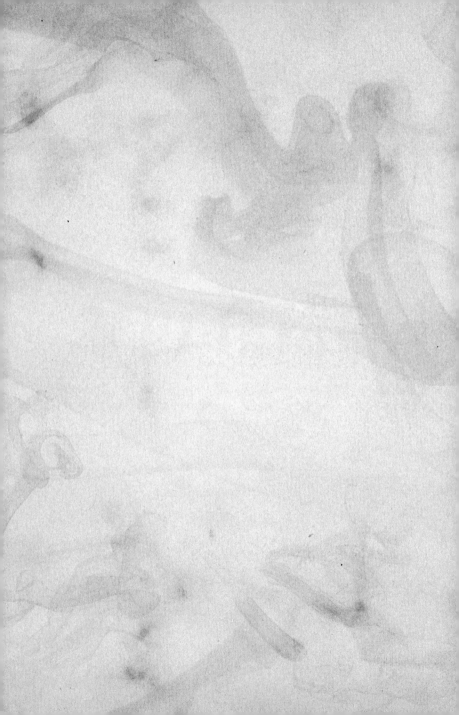

BELIEVE

SARAH ARONSON

🌿 carolrhoda LAB

MINNEAPOLIS

Carolrhoda Lab™
An imprint of Carolrhoda Books
A division of Lerner Publishing Group, Inc.
241 First Avenue North
Minneapolis, MN 55401 U.S.A.

Website address: www.lernerbooks.com

Cover photographs © iStockphoto.com/mattjeacock (shirt);
© iStockphoto.com/spxChrome (burn mark).

Main body text set in Janson Text LT Std 10/14.
Typeface provided by Linotype AG.

Library of Congress Cataloging-in-Publication Data

Aronson, Sarah.
      Believe / by Sarah Aronson.
          pages   cm
      Summary: "Janine is the "Soul Survivor," the girl who, as a small child,
   was the only survivor of a Palestinian suicide bomb in Israel that killed her
   parents. Ten years on, she feels like she's public property more than her
   own person" — Provided by publisher.
      ISBN 978–1–4677–0697–1 (trade hard cover : alk. paper)
      ISBN 978–1–4677–1617-8 (eBook)
      [1. Fame—Fiction. 2. Survival—Fiction. 3. Terrorism—Fiction.
   4. Orphans—Fiction. 5. Jews—Fiction.] I. Title.
   PZ7.A74295Be 2013
   [Fic]—dc23   2012047184

Manufactured in the United States of America
1 – BP – 7/15/13

FOR REBECCA

PROLOGUE

You never really knew me.

I was a photo in a magazine, the cover that made you weep. I was long brown hair, big green eyes, and pale skin—an innocent girl, alone in a foreign land.

I was a moment in time. I was a story. Even now, when people hear my name or see my hands, they tell me exactly where they were the day I became a household name. They like to say it is an honor to meet me. More often than not, I made them believe.

***

Over the years, I have received two hundred and twenty-five teddy bears. I've been invited to participate in four reality shows, and two cable networks will pay my college tuition to make movies about the day Dave Armstrong dug me out of the rubble and saved my life.

Churches and synagogues write to me every year. They want me to talk about hope. And survival. And God and faith and my hands. They all want to talk about my stupid, ugly hands.

You may be curious, but the answer is no.

I don't want to make a statement.

I don't want to pose.

I don't even like teddy bears.

It is hard enough being a sixteen-year-old orphan, living with your mother's sister, making everyday decisions like what looks best with black jeans and if the time has come to have sex with your boyfriend. I am nobody's bastion of hope, and I don't want to make money talking about suicide bombers, holy war, or anything else that has to do with the day I became the "Soul Survivor," America's blessed child, the one and only person to walk away from that Easter weekend bombing in Jerusalem.

Get this straight: I am a victim, not a celebrity. I'm a girl—not that different from any other. My hands do not bear the mark of God. They are not blessed. I like regular things, like making my own clothes and hanging out with my friends. I would rather fade into the woodwork than be famous one more day for something I did not earn or do.

You want the real story? There is none. I am a person—not public property.

ONE

Miriam Haverstraw had beautiful hands.

Long, slender fingers and smooth white skin with absolutely no discoloration, deformity, or any sort of noticeable dysfunction. Her nails were simply perfect—straight on the top and just the right length, not too long and not too short.

She sat curled up in the window seat and rummaged through her faux leather purse for eco-friendly products, never tested on animals, mostly edible. The window seat was always the most coveted spot in my bedroom—cozy and comfortable—but she sat there now because it provided a perfect view of the street below.

"Be careful," I said—pointing to the open bottle of non-acetone polish remover. I had just finished re-covering the cushion she was sitting on. That stuff might be organic, but when it spilled, it left a stain.

Miriam didn't flinch. "Janine, I hate to tell you, but an old lady just took a picture of your house."

I wasn't surprised. Every anniversary, all kinds of people banged on my door, hoping for a quote, an interview, or a photo. "Just do me a favor," I said, taking a break from my work to stretch each of my knuckles, "and don't let her see you."

My hands were ugly. My palms were scarred, my pale fingers bent off to the sides, and my thick nails cracked and chipped. No matter what oil or cream or fruit extract Miriam swore would work wonders, if I didn't stretch them every day, they stiffened up. Stress did not help. Neither did clenching my fists. Or listening to Miriam give me the play-by-play outside.

"Poor thing's dragging her bag up the driveway. She looks like she's having a really crappy day."

Most of the reporters who came here were young. This one, according to Miriam, had gray hair. She said, "She looks sort of sweet. Like a grandma. Maybe she's different."

"Or maybe it's a disguise." It wouldn't be the first time some "hardnosed" reporter tried to trick me into talking.

Miriam dipped her finger into some cream the color of mud and rubbed it into her cuticles. "It's just that . . . under the circumstances . . ."

"No." As far as I was concerned, this was a dead end, a non-conversation. "Can't you see this from my point of view?"

That cream stunk like coffee. "Janine, the farm is in trouble. I'm your best friend. This matters to me. We could really, really use some publicity." She started to pack up her stuff. "I would do it for you."

I hated when she begged, when she made me explain (again) why this was not the same kind of favor as getting her an invitation to a party (*that* I would do) or going to some event (which I knew she did all the time, even when it was the kind she found boring). This wasn't a football game. It wasn't a study session or a chance to meet some cute guy. "You know what'll happen. She'll listen and make conversation until you say something you shouldn't. Think about it. She wants a story about me. She doesn't care about your farm."

Miriam's farm was a two-acre plot stuck next to an old, half-empty nursing home, not too far from school. For as long as I could remember, the town's supervisors had leased it (for one dollar) to a bunch of professors so they could plant vegetables and teach nutrition. She thought it was the most beautiful place in the world. It was an essential part of our town's future sustainability and growth, proof that good people (like herself) could come together and make the world a better place—a lesson for other small towns to learn from. It had to be protected at all costs.

Personally, I thought it was a piece of land—nothing more. It was nice that the town let people plant their vegetables there, but the truth was it didn't even get much sun. But I couldn't tell her that—especially not now. The trustees from one of the local colleges had their eyes on that property. They'd already offered the town a whole lot of money plus a bigger farm (but on the outskirts of town) for it. They wanted to build dorms. Or a research lab. Or offices.

Normally, the town's board of supervisors would have jumped at this deal. It was a lot of money. The new farm would be bigger and better. It was smart to work with the college. Win–win.

But in this case, no deal yet. That was because of the giant oak tree in the corner of the property—it was the biggest one for miles—possibly the oldest in the area. People were crazy about it. When the trustees couldn't promise to protect it— their issue was safety (it was a really old tree)—protests and arguments flared. The newspaper had already run at least ten letters to the editor.

The whole thing annoyed me. Every letter or comment made that tree out to be a symbol for some over-the-top concept like freedom or life or the power of the people. And that was wrong. That kind of talk blew everything out of proportion. It's not like you could argue over something like freedom.

It made me feel sorry for the tree.

But it also made me feel a whole lot less guilty. Because of that tree, the farm was safe. Miriam didn't need to talk to that reporter.

Outside, she rang the doorbell once, then two more times. "Are you sure?" Miriam asked. "Just this once. I'll never ask again. We could really, really . . . "

"No. Finish your toes. I am totally, one hundred percent, absolutely sure." Miriam put up with a lot from me. But this was too much, too risky; I didn't need this stress. I had more important things to do.

I hunched over my prized possession, my brand-new Brother Quattro. If I was going to finish this dress for my official portfolio, the hem had to come up. The bodice needed a little more bling. Miriam was going to have to stop telling me to come to the window.

"What is it now?" I asked, mid-seam.

"Abe is here. He's talking to the lady." I stopped sewing and walked over to the window. This was not cool.

He could be telling her anything: what I like to eat, what I do in my free time, that sometimes, for no reason whatsoever, I turned sullen. He could be telling her important stuff—like how I have a hard time sleeping. Or stupid stuff—that my aunt, Lo, and I had lived here since I came here from Israel; that my bedroom was in the loft; that last year I'd created a series of silk-screened T-shirts called "A door of one's own." Because I really wanted my own way out.

I glared at Miriam. If we tried to get his attention, that reporter would figure out we were here. If we didn't . . .

"I thought you told him we were having a girl's day."

She pressed her nose to the window. "You know he never takes a hint."

Some days, nothing went right.

When Miriam first introduced me to Abe, I was skeptical. I told her a tripod relied on three strong, equal legs. "I don't believe that guys and girls can ever have completely mutual, platonic relationships," I'd explained. One person always wanted more than the other.

But he hung around. So, after a while, we made an official pact. Friends only, nothing more, no matter how "right" it felt. No discussion whatsoever about God, faith, or anyone who became famous because of reality TV. I told him that everything I said must be kept absolutely confidential—no exceptions—especially when it came to the press.

I figured he'd balk. Or at least tell me I was unreasonable. But he agreed to everything. Same as Miriam, he said, "That's what friends do. They trust each other completely." Then he held out his hand—a perfectly nice hand the color of caramel, no exfoliation or moisturizer necessary. "You want to prick me? Share blood? Take an oath of brotherhood?"

Now I hoped he meant it.

Now I had to trust him.

TWO

Four and a half minutes later, Abe walked the lady to her car. When he turned around and headed for the back door, I collapsed over my machine. "Would you let him in?" I asked Miriam. "Keys are in the door. Make sure to relock." It was a risk—you never knew if someone else might show up—but I needed a minute to cool down—alone. I didn't feel like climbing down two flights of steps only to come back up.

Miriam practically flung herself over the banister. "Sure. Be right back." As she sprinted down the steps, a sudden patch of sun shone through the skylight.

Having a skylight was both a plus and a minus. It made the room too bright too early, but at night, if I kept the glass clean, I could see the stars. But that wasn't why I loved my room. I chose it over the room below because the loft was the biggest room in the house, with space for a makeup mirror, a workstation complete with sewing machine and dress form, two big closets, and three shelves for books, photos, and a few mementos.

My bedroom might not have had a door, but it was private enough. Lo almost never used the guest room below. The only real inconvenience was climbing all those stairs.

"Can I get you anything?" Abe called up.

He felt bad. Or he knew I was feeling lazy. "No, thanks," I screamed. "I'm good. Just come on up." I listened to them climb the steps.

Miriam was fast—a light pitter-patter. Abe took two at a time. As he clomped, he sang the first line of a song I liked last year.

I tried to keep sewing, even when I could feel him standing behind me, staring at me, waiting for me to turn around. Then he sang the same line again. That was the funny thing about Abe. He sang random lines from random songs, sometimes in the middle of a conversation, often over and over again. I used to take it personally—I was sure they were subliminal messages—but he swore it was completely spontaneous—just the last song he had heard. Stuck in his head. Top-40 Tourette's.

When he sang the line a third time, I lost my concentration. My seam went crooked. I stopped sewing, ripped the dress out of the machine, and started tearing out the bungled stitches. Abe didn't wait for me to blame him. He leaned on my dress form—whom he'd long ago named Annie—and addressed her like she was a real person. "What did I do? Why is Janine so mad? That lady was nice. I told her nothing. She isn't going to write anything mean." Thanks to Abe, Dress-Form Annie had painted red lips and big blue eyes with falsies for lashes.

She looked happy. Like she was smiling. The little orphan Broadway Annie. I shouldn't have to remind him that reporters always seemed nice—at first. That's how they got you to talk.

I shook the dress in his face. "Can you be quiet? I need to finish this. My portfolio review's on Monday."

I cut a few stray threads, made a note to add some gathering in the sleeve. "I think it's gorgeous," Miriam said, back in the window seat. She yawned. "A total winner. You are going to blow everyone out of the water."

Two seams later, she yawned again. Abe freshened Annie's lipstick, so that her lips looked pouty, a lot like Miriam's. He said, "I was thinking we should get out of here and get gelato."

He did not understand what it was like to be me. "You know I can't go."

Five years ago, reporters hid in the bushes. Three years ago, they cornered me at school. Tomorrow, *Time* was coming out with a ten-year retrospective. "Go without me," I said, motioning to the stairs. "I don't mind. Have fun."

Miriam didn't want to go unless we all went. "They shouldn't be able to make you a prisoner." She took the tripod thing a little too seriously.

Abe always stuck up for Miriam. "What if I inspect the entire yard?" He said he'd check the front and back yards as well as the rest of the block. "We'll take every precaution. We won't leave the house unless we are positive it's absolutely safe."

It was tempting. On weekends, the gelato place made citrus cream. And double chocolate with hot pepper. My favorites. Together, they tasted like one of those chocolate oranges everybody brings back from England.

Miriam was right: I should be able to go out any time I wanted to. This was my life. These were my friends. I shouldn't have to hide.

"Okay," I said. "But if you see anything suspicious . . ."

Ten minutes later, he swore on a stack that the coast was clear. "I looked everywhere," he said. "The entire block is empty."

I trusted him. Mostly. We walked downstairs and stood at the door. "Just to be safe, you go out the front." This was a trick Lo and I had perfected when the press used to ambush me on a regular basis. "I'll wait one minute. Then, if no one jumps, I'll come out the back."

They got into the car. Nothing.

I walked around the living room—then I opened the back door. Still nothing, but something made me hesitate. It was a feeling I got when I knew someone was watching me or I had drunk too much coffee or made a seam that I knew had to be removed. But Abe promised he checked, so I shook it off. I told myself there was no one hiding in the bushes or the tree or the garage. I was just being silly. Vain. The whole world could not be *that* interested in me.

I reopened the door.

I stepped onto the back stoop, looked both ways, and closed the door.

Click, click, click, click, click.

A tall man rushed toward me. Behind him was a woman with stick-straight brown hair and a blue-and-white pinstriped suit. She was wearing those plastic ugly/chic glasses that may be the rage, but as far as I could tell, they flattered no one. "Janine Collins!" She shoved a fat, brand-new *Time* magazine into my hands. The retrospective. "Do you ever think there'll be peace in the Middle East? If there's a treaty, would you ask to attend the signing?"

I dropped the heavy magazine on the porch. "I'll tell you the same thing I told them—no comment." Sure, I wanted peace in the world, just like everyone else. But this wasn't about the world. She was here to get me talking.

I scrambled for the door, but when I tried to close it, she was too fast—she stopped me with her polished cherry-red peep-toe pump.

We stood face to face.

Click, click, click. "It's been ten years since the bombing," she said, holding her pen so tight her fingers blanched. "How have you changed? Do you still have nightmares? What do you want the world to learn from your tragedy? What do you remember?"

I remembered glass breaking, people screaming. I remembered feeling pain from my head to my hands to my stomach. I remember crying for my mother. But what woke me up at night was the one image I will never talk about or forget—the face of the boy named Emir. It was a pretty face. An innocent face. When he walked into the synagogue, he stopped and looked at me.

I saw him.

I saw his face. I looked into his eyes. He looked back at me.

You don't forget eyes like that. You can't. Believe me, I've tried. Eyes like that—they give you nightmares. They wake you up. When you least expect it, they make your hands burn.

If I wasn't going to sell that detail to *Time*, there was no way I was going to tell her.

The reporter spoke quickly. "Janine, I just want five minutes. I want to tell your story—paint the picture you want. I want to know what you believe." When I didn't take the bait, she said, "Do it for your mother." She grabbed my hands. My hands. No one grabbed my ugly, crooked hands.

I shoved her as hard as I could, and she stumbled backwards. I said, "I don't believe in anything. You don't have the right to bother me. Not today. Not tomorrow. Not ever."

Click, click, click, click, click, click, click, click, click, click, click, click.

I slammed the door shut and ran upstairs. Next to my bed was a fuzzy eight-by-ten from the Dead Sea, the last picture taken of my family. My six-year-old belly stuck out like a big red balloon. My eyes were closed—my smile was that big. Mom sat up straight in a bright red bikini. Her tummy was flat. Dad wore a ripped University of Pennsylvania T-shirt and long cutoff shorts. Our skin sparkled, toasted by heat and the minerals of that magic water. He held rabbit ears behind her head.

We looked happy.

Lo, my mother's sister, my guardian, took that picture. She said we were instant friends, but unlike the pain and the eyes and the screaming and the glass, I don't remember that. My first memory of her was in the hospital, when the second wave of pain began.

The operations. The therapy. The constant stream of reporters.

They should know by now: My tragedy was history. God did not destine me to live. Every day, new suicide bombers blew themselves up. Dave Armstrong can call me his miracle, but he did not see stigmata in my hands. No matter what anybody says, I am not superhuman. I cannot change the world.

Because if I could, the boy named Emir would have stayed home. My parents would be alive. This dress would be perfect, and reporters and photographers would not be ruining my life.

And if not that, at least, I'd have beautiful hands like Miriam Haverstraw.

THREE

I took out my frustrations on a pint of store-brand French silk. It wasn't gelato, but at least my freezer was free of photographers.

Miriam sent me six texts and left two voicemails. They all said the same thing. We are so sorry. And We feel just awful. And You know Abe just made a mistake. Can you let us back in? We can get your flavors to go.

I wrote back, "No thanks." Texting more than that made my fingers ache. She might be sincere, but I was mad. I didn't want to ask Abe how he could have missed a guy that size. I didn't want to think he hadn't bothered looking . . . on purpose. Instead, I opened the door a crack and grabbed the retrospective.

I had to give them credit; the cover was provocative. Across most of it was a photo of the Israeli flag, pumped full of bullets. Dark block letters asked, *Are We Any Closer to Peace?* In the upper left-hand corner—the space reserved for special features—were red letters asking, *Where are they now?* and next to that was the picture that made me famous: me in Dave

Armstrong's arms, covered in soot. In that moment, I stared straight into the camera. Wide eyes. Broken hands.

That photographer won a Pulitzer. I flipped past the ads to the table of contents.

There were sections for real news (as opposed to reality/celebrity news), editorials, glossy color pictures of Israel over the last ten years, a few pages of history, and of course, the stuff that sold the whole thing: the tragedy. The heartbreaking story of the everyday people. My story. It was all there.

My phone rang again. It was my boyfriend, Dan Snyder. This was no coincidence. "Hi," I said to Dan.

He said, "What's up?"

I obviously didn't like Dan because he was the greatest conversationalist. But he did have great hands and great lips and a pretty good sense of humor. And it wasn't every day you met a guy who cared about style, who understood the merits of pants with minimal break on a shorter physique, who knew that a jacket fit when your knuckles (arms extended, not flexed) lay even with the bottom of your jacket. He even liked talking about *Glamour* do's and don'ts.

I said, "I guess you saw the retrospective."

If he were smarter, he would have said, "What retrospective?" Instead he said, "I heard you were having a rough day. You want me to come over?"

Dan Snyder might have been the first varsity shortstop with an eye for good tailoring, but he was just like every other guy when it came to getting a girl to possibly say yes.

Eight minutes later, he was sprawled across my couch. Two minutes after that, he had his hand on my bare shoulder, two buttons undone, and the retrospective open to a list of all the journalists and photographers who had lost their lives covering the wars of the Middle East.

There were a lot of them. From a lot of different countries.

Dan kissed my neck. His hair tickled. He smelled like a combination of sweat and excitement and cinnamon donuts. "She's here somewhere." He scrolled down the smiling headshots until he found the picture of my mom. "You look a lot like her."

Yes. We had the same forehead. Same nose. Lo thought I was stubborn like my mother, too. She said my mother was really passionate; she turned into a Hulk when she saw any kind of injustice.

But I wasn't just a carbon copy of my mom. My chin and eyes came from my dad's side of the family. According to Lo, so were my feet. Fallen arches. Second toe bigger than the first.

Dan asked if I'd read the section about me. "No. And I'm not going to." I sat back and tried to look sexy. "Is this really what you want to do?"

He threw the magazine on the floor and kissed me again, this time harder. But the sad/funny thing was, the longer we kissed, the less interested I got, the more sure I was that I didn't want to have sex. Not here. Not now. I may not have believed in waiting for "the one," but I wanted dinner first. And something besides this itchy couch.

Today was not the right day. It didn't matter how cute he was. No doubt, if I got naked, Lo would walk in the door.

My lips were numb when he finally got the hint and gave up. "Can I show you the new dress?" I disengaged. "If you want, you can come up."

He looked at the front door. I was pretty sure he thought

that was code for something else. "Sure." He followed me up the stairs.

In my room, we slipped the brown dress onto Dress-Form Annie and examined her from all sides. He said, "It's cute and it's got a lot of great movement, and I think you'll get into every school in the universe." He took a few pictures, then reached around me and felt under my shirt to the small of my back—just in case I'd changed my mind. "But I also think you can do more. I think if you put your mind to it, you could make something really spectacular."

Annie's lips looked lopsided. "This isn't spectacular?"

He unsnapped my jeans and fumbled for the zipper. "If you want to be spectacular, you have to push the envelope. You have to trust your instincts." When he had it open, he rested his hands on my hips. "You have to let yourself be vulnerable." It was a pretty intense thing to say.

It hit a nerve.

He kissed me again. Pulled me so close I could feel every single part of him. He whispered, "What about that other dress you sketched?"

I almost stopped breathing. He meant the one inspired by an old picture of my parents. He was the only person who'd seen it.

He said, in a very soft voice, "That dress would blow Parsons away." He put his hand on the small of my back again (crap), and I couldn't be sure if he believed this or if he realized that now he actually had a chance. "It's more exciting. It's definitely more you."

I hesitated. "Definitely?"

He smiled. Maybe he did. "Definitely."

If this had been a sitcom or even reality TV, I'd have ripped off my jeans right here. But it was my real life. Which meant that just when I thought I wanted to do it, the door downstairs beeped. Lo was home. I guessed that settled that.

She must have recognized Dan's car, because instead of coming straight up, she clanged around the kitchen for a good five minutes. In this way, Lo was very cool. She talked to me about safe sex and drugs and drinking, and when it was just us, she gave me a sip of wine. She took hot yoga three times a week. She and her girlfriend, Sharon, would probably get married if Pennsylvania would ever join this century and make it legal.

But that didn't mean Lo was what the tabs call a "modern woman." She never wore a skirt above the knee—even on dress-down days—and she didn't seem to understand that baggy clothes did not make you look smaller. She had worked at the courthouse for five years, but she never came home with juicy stories. She and Sharon had decided not to live together. I'd only seen them kiss twice.

Maybe Lo thought she needed to act like all the other moms. She walked into the guest room and reminded us that Dan was not supposed to be above ground level and that if we knew what was good for us, we'd better both be decent. Then she came up. Slow, heavy steps. "I'm surprised to see you, Dan. I was under the impression that Miriam and Janine were going to spend the day doing homework."

He knew better than to argue with a former first lieutenant of the Israeli Defense Forces. He made an excuse and headed out the door.

"We didn't do anything," I told her.

"Not this time." She didn't trust Dan. Or Abe. Or any guy she thought might someday want to have sex with me.

It really wasn't fair. I said, "I'm sorry you were surprised, but I was having a rough day." I gave her the retrospective and told her about the reporter. "They took pictures. I got mad. I didn't even want to go out. The whole thing blew up in my face."

She took two big *kapalabhati* breaths—the breaths of fire—before barraging me with I-told-you-so's. "I told you not to leave the house. I told you ten years is a big anniversary. These reporters—a lot of them knew your mom. They admired your father." She paged through the magazine, stopping at the section about me. "How did they get this?" she asked. There was a school picture for every year from then until now.

"How am I supposed to know?"

I told her what the reporter said about my mother. She shook her head. Working for the DA reinforced her distrust in the press—as well as casual acquaintances. "You didn't make a statement, did you?"

I sighed. "I didn't tell them anything."

That was Lo's number-one rule. No statements. No confessions. We never talked publicly about the past, especially the day I was buried alive, when the rubble dirtied my hair and stung my eyes, when my throat closed and I almost died. We never told anyone that my mother didn't die right away, that she talked to me the whole time.

She said, "You are strong." And, "You can do this, baby. Keep talking to me, don't be afraid, and I'll stay here with you." When I started to sleep, she told me over and over again, "You have a holy soul. You have so much to look forward to."

Lo said that was love.

I knew her voice kept me alive.

It was also the hideous punch line to my story. That day, the microphones could have helped me. The cameras should have found her. Dave Armstrong heard my voice, and at the same time, she stopped talking. I told them, but nobody listened. By the time they were done cheering, my mother was dead.

FOUR

There were some days that weren't meant to be sunny.

In the morning, my fingers felt cold and stiff. My joints ached. It was one of the not-so-great side effects of all those hand surgeries. If I sewed for too many hours, my hands went numb. I couldn't text with accuracy. If there were a game show called *Predict the Weather*, I'd probably win a million dollars. When rain or cold approached, I felt it in my knuckles.

Heat helped, but the problem was, too much of it made me feel claustrophobic. Lo said it was the PTSD. She said that, even after years of therapy, I would always hate feeling covered; loud, sudden noises would freak me out. I'd probably always have nightmares.

She called up from downstairs. "Are you awake?"

"Come on up."

On the anniversary, there was no work, no sewing, and no yoga. Instead we talked. We went to the cemetery. At some point we looked at old photos—the ones nobody had ever put in print.

I had two favorites: the first was of my dad and me. We were sitting under a tree, and I was pointing up at the sky. The other was taken two years before they died, right after my mom won some local journalism prize. In that shot, she leaned back in her chair, her feet up on her desk, her sandals dangling from her toes, a big smile on her face. Her T-shirt said in big black letters, "Face your fears." According to Lo, that was one of her mantras.

I kept them both next to my bed.

The phone rang. Private name, private number. Lo ignored it. "I have something for you," she said. "It's from your grandparents. They asked me to give it to you today."

I loved getting presents, but my grandparents didn't really know me that well. They lived in Tel Aviv, and in ten years, we had never gotten together once. We talked for two minutes every other Monday, and in between my grandfather e-mailed me articles about Judaism and/or Israel. They sent me things I did not want or need: a piece of Roman glass, halvah, or a T-shirt, usually too small.

Lo reached into her pocket and pulled out a small, square box. "Open it," she said without excitement. "They were very insistent."

In a small box was a black satin bag with a black drawstring. A tag taped to the bag said, "This belonged to your mother."

As fast as I could, I untied the string and dropped the necklace into my open palm. When I saw the charm, I couldn't move. I couldn't breathe. If it hadn't been my mother's, I would have thrown it across the room.

It was a hand. Three round fingers and two tiny ones flaring out on either side. There was a blue stone in the middle of some beveled silver that made it look a lot like an eye. A yellow piece of paper stuck to the bottom of the box:

The hamsa is an ancient symbol used as a protective amulet by both Jews and Muslims. It is usually worn around the neck or hung on walls or over doors as protection from the evil eye.

Lo took it from me and clasped it around my neck. "I remember this. She used to wear it all the time."

I was confused. "My mother hated religion." My mother wrote about politicians who claimed to be faithful but didn't vote or act that way. She wrote about religious strife all over the world. Her most noted series focused on the many soldiers who had sacrificed their lives for causes that were rooted in religion. You didn't have to read between the lines to infer that she blamed religion for America's interest in Iraq, Iran, and Afghanistan. Or 9/11. Later in her career, when newspapers began printing her columns, she didn't mince words: religion was a hoax/a business/a conspiracy—at worst, a lie. She was 100 percent sure that religion was going to lead to the destruction of the world. "Are you sure?"

Lo nodded; she handed me the phone. My grandfather picked up on the second ring. He asked, "Will you wear it?" (as opposed to "Do you like it?"). His accent was heavy, hard to understand.

I said yes, but the connection was spotty. I didn't think he heard me. He said, "The hamsa is for protection, so you shouldn't take it off. Not even to shower. It encompasses the four areas of healing: heart, soul, mind, and world."

I didn't care what it was supposed to encompass. It was hers. She wore it. For that reason alone, I promised to wear it every day.

My grandmother said, "When your mother was a little girl, she used to have this dream—that the whole world was linked, hand to hand to hand to hand. We gave it to her when she was your age—when we came to Israel. Even though we know that the hand as a symbol might be . . . complicated for you, we thought you should have it now. Because we know—you must have dreams too."

I did have dreams. In every one, my mom skipped the assignment. We were just like those people who didn't go to work on September eleventh or missed their connection on a plane that later crashed. In my dreams, she finished her work and we went to the beach and then we left Israel and lived normal lives. Many nights I've dreamed that, on this one day, the story was about someone else. In my dreams, my whole family let go of her stupid chain of hands.

My grandfather asked if I had questions.

In my head, I said, "A million." In my head, I yelled at him.

Out loud, I didn't dare. I didn't ask: "Why now? Does this mean you're sorry? That you have regrets? Are the Land of Israel and all your opinions not as important as you thought they once were?" But this day was already hard enough.

Instead, I said, "Not now." And "Thank you." I asked them if they had anything else they could send me. An old picture of her. Some of her letters. More of her jewelry. They said they loved me, and "We'll put something together. We'll put it in the mail as soon as we can."

One awkward pause later, I gave Lo the phone. Whenever she spoke to her parents, she spoke in Hebrew. Today sounded a lot like other conversations. First soft. Then loud. Then louder. Thirty seconds later, she hung up a little too hard.

"You're mad," I said.

"It's complicated." She walked to the window so I couldn't see her face. "We must accept our lives the way they are." This was yoga talk for "Stay out of it." She walked out of the room. Today was not the day to talk about why my grandparents didn't get on a plane and visit me.

This is what I knew:

They moved to Tel Aviv when my mom was sixteen. For Lo, it was an adventure. She was eleven. For my Zionist grandparents, it was a dream come true—the fulfillment of a lifetime of yearning and saving. For my mom, it was a nightmare.

According to Lo, Mom missed her friends. She didn't feel like she belonged. Nothing was right. She hated the heat, the food, the traffic, and she never could figure out paddleball, the game that everyone seemed to be playing. When she left the army after serving the minimum, my grandparents begged her to give Israel one more chance, but in the end they packed her up and sent her off to Douglas College in New Jersey.

That's where she met my dad.

He was a journalism professor, a semifamous photographer, a newspaper man. She became his star student. Then they fell in love.

The event that Lo never talked about happened the summer before my mom's senior year. She went back to visit. She brought my dad, and it did not go well.

To my grandfather, my future father was way too old. Worse than that, he was not Jewish. And that meant he was not the kind of man he wanted my mom to marry. When she wouldn't back down, he called her terrible names. He reminded her of relatives that had died in the Holocaust, that Jews had a responsibility to pass down their traditions, and that he would never never never approve or condone or acknowledge their marriage or children. No matter how Jewish or not Jewish you were, there was nothing worse than that. For a while, she wrote about "his betrayal" whenever anything good happened.

Which was a lot. Because the rest was as close to a fairy tale as real life got.

My mom chose my dad. They went home, got married, and my dad left the college to work on his fine-art photography. My mom worked freelance. They settled in eastern Pennsylvania— halfway between New York and Philadelphia. In one very angry journal entry, my mother noted the irony: "Jewish girl abandons Israel to settle near towns called Bethlehem and Nazareth." She wrote, "How funny is that?"

Maybe it was, maybe it wasn't. My mother might have never forgiven my grandfather, but I was pretty sure she wanted him to forgive her. The way Lo looked at the hamsa, I bet she felt exactly that way now.

There should be a law. If you cared about someone, just say it. Tell the truth and don't play chicken. Life is too short to be so ugly. When Lo said my grandfather was proud, she meant he was religious.

I suspected she meant he didn't accept who we were either.

As the phone rang for what felt like the fiftieth time, Lo returned with the local newspaper, folded back. There was a picture of me, shaking my fist at yesterday's reporter. The headline was bolded: "Soul Survivor Won't Talk." Lo acted like page three was no big deal. "The good news is, you actually look quite pretty."

My hair did look pretty good. And the camera angle made me look like I'd lost weight. "You know, when I make a fist, my hand looks normal." Lo half-smiled. I wasn't fooling anyone.

If that reporter really did admire my mother's work, she would have known that Karen Friedman would never have taken such a stupid assignment. She'd never use her death to ruin my life. She would know that my parents would never have wasted their time writing this crap, asking the questions that have no answers. I couldn't understand why anyone cared to read this one more time.

But they must. Because the phone wouldn't stop ringing.

"Can you run interference?" I asked Lo. "Or take the phone off the hook?" For at least a few minutes, I wanted to be alone. No noise. No interruptions. No conversations. I tossed the newspaper onto the floor.

Lo walked downstairs to the guest room, picked up the phone on the very next ring. "Yes. No thank you. Please respect our privacy." She had long since memorized her lines: "At this time we choose not to make a statement."

FIVE

After Lo left the guest room, I got out of bed and grabbed some of my mother's journals. These were the only stories I felt like reading. They were the stories that kept her alive.

I'd bookmarked all the highlights: the day they got married. The night they found out Mom was pregnant. When I was six months old, she took me to the Museum of Modern Art in New York City. I laughed at all the Magrittes, especially the one with the man with an apple for a face. She wrote that this was a sure sign that I was the most intelligent baby in the universe. When I was seven months old, I said my first word: "Shoe."

There was only one volume I hadn't read. That was the last one, the one she took with her to Israel, the one the search and recovery squad found in her purse under a pile of crushed rock. I called it The Book of Death.

Lo kept it hidden. She said it was mine—that I could have it whenever I wanted. All I had to do was say the word.

I wasn't ready yet. There was something sacred about a person's last words.

After a while, Lo returned with Sharon. Sharon had a lopsided gait—she'd broken her leg in college, and when it healed, she was left with a pretty intense leg-length discrepancy.

They looked uncomfortable, like their shoes were too tight, like maybe there was something more to discuss. I asked, "What is it now? Did something happen? Why was the phone ringing off the hook?" I imagined the worst possible scenarios—another bombing in a synagogue. More death. More pain. It wasn't out of the realm of possibility—or even all that rare. In ten years, the Middle East political situation hadn't changed that much.

Suicide bombers—unless they killed a whole lot of people or ruined a landmark—or left one lone survivor—didn't cause a stir like they used to.

Or maybe it was just my picture in the paper.

"What's the problem?" Today was going to be bad enough. "You look like someone died."

Sharon picked up the newspaper off the floor. She handed it to Lo. "You need to show her."

I wasn't in a reading mood. I hated playing games. "Can you just tell me?" I asked. "Whatever it is, it can't be that bad."

Lo shrugged. Sharon read, "Scholar-pastor to offer lecture about the rise in religious fundamentalism in government."

I didn't see what the big deal was. "Must be a slow news day." I rolled over and stared at my stacks of sewing books, my piles of patterns, and of course, Dress-Form Annie. The bright red lipstick made her look a little manic—like she was laughing at me. "Can we talk about something else?" I buried my face in my pillow. "Scratch my back."

"Sure." She found the itchy spot right away. Lo clearly didn't want to talk about Dave Armstrong any more than I did.

Before he became an internationally known pastor with an online congregation and a weekly televised address, Dave had been a professor of political science. He was visiting Israel to witness some of the same events my mom was covering. But the morning of the bombing, he couldn't get into the synagogue. Maybe he wasn't influential enough. Maybe he needed a ticket. Maybe he was just lucky.

Maybe I was.

When the blast erupted, he was two blocks away, killing time in the marketplace. He said it felt like an earthquake. While most people ran away, he was drawn to the explosion— *compelled* to go see what had happened. Later, after he found me, he claimed this was a direct message from God.

Lo has never believed him. She thought he was an opportunist who one day in his life did the right thing. She thought his entire ministry—and she used that word lightly— was about money. And fame. And the worldly benefits that went with speaking the gospel to desperate people in desperate situations.

Hypothetically, I had no problem with him using this day for donations. That day, there were a lot of people searching for survivors, but he was the one who heard my voice, who lifted the final rocks, who uncovered my hands and found me. He was the man who sat by my side every single day until I could move my fingers. He read me stories. He sang to me. I knew it sounded cliché, but for months—almost a year—he made me laugh when all I wanted to do was cry.

Bottom line: I couldn't hate him. Even though his mission seemed a little too vague and even over-the-top, I thought he was basically a good guy. He had the right to make his speeches, to offer prayers to the world, to try and bring peace and health and happiness to the world. He was the man holding me in the picture that won the Pulitzer. Technically, it was his story, too.

I just wished he could leave me out of it.

I pointed to the small of my back. "A little higher." When Lo found that spot, too, I finally let my arms and head and shoulders relax. She was the best back scratcher in the world.

Too bad Sharon would only drop the subject for so long. "I think we need to talk about this. Janine needs to consider the implications." Her voice turned whiny/screechy. "She's sixteen. You have to stop protecting her."

That was enough for me. I got out of bed and booted up my computer. Dave must have made some really obnoxious statement for Sharon to react so strongly.

It was all there on CNN.com. Thanks to an anonymous donation, Dave Armstrong was going to visit small colleges to give a series of lectures about politics and religion.

"I don't see what the big deal is."

"Watch," Sharon said. Maybe she was more uptight than I'd realized.

I clicked on a seven-minute clip of Dave speaking—the shortest of the three. It was filmed early this morning. Dave Armstrong's thick white hair was slicked back; his voice was deep and clear and careful.

The clip already had 2,832 views.

"Many times, I have spoken about the extraordinary events that occurred ten years ago this day. I have talked to you about the serendipitous moment when I became part of an army of men and women determined to find survivors. I have also shared my secular past and personal awakening and call to serve our Lord. Every year on this day, I have recounted my joy and gratitude that I was the one who first heard Janine Collins's tiny voice and touched her broken, bleeding hands." I had to admit, Dave was a charismatic speaker. But he also had only one note. He tended to use words with vague implications and not much else. But he knew when to raise his hands toward his face. He knew when to bow his head. He knew how to connect with the audience. "When I touched her hands, I felt euphoria. Warmth. Peace. I knew God was with me. I was not alone, and I never would be again. In that moment, the Lord made it clear I had to do something more with my life. I needed to tell the world miracles were possible. I'm looking forward to talking about the world today and why the time is right for a greater thrust toward faith."

I muted the video when he started praying and quoting Scripture. "I still don't understand why you're so upset." Dave Armstrong, like a lot of people, believed that my story had biblical, spiritual implications far beyond bad or good luck. "So what? He pretty much said the exact same thing last year. And the year before that."

Sharon shook her head. "It's not the *what* that bothers me. It's the *where*."

I looked again. The background did look familiar.

"He's here?"

"In Bethlehem. At Moravian College."

That was odd, but it didn't necessarily have anything to do with me. Moravian College had a theology department. He *was* a professor. And, all things considered, he was a high-profile one. This time of year, in and around the Lehigh Valley, you could hardly walk a block without stumbling across a pastel Easter display or some announcement for a service or a religious discussion. On top of the mountain, three hundred and sixty-five days a year, was a huge "Star of Bethlehem." You could see it every night of the year. Dan and I tried to make out there once, but the cops wouldn't let us get near it.

Dave being here made sense. Sort of.

Lo asked me to turn off the computer. "Sharon's afraid he's going to try and ambush you." She paused when Sharon cleared her throat—a clear sign they had agreed to some sort of compromise. "We think you need to be extra cautious."

Sharon picked up the new brown dress, crumpled on top of the sewing machine, and smoothed it out. In the light, there were wrinkles. Flaws. I saw a pucker in the collar, a thread hanging from the hem. The phone rang again. She told Lo, "If I were you, I'd talk to Robert."

"No." Lo never asked her boss for help. Too much testosterone. She didn't like to owe him favors. She said, "What could he do? Armstrong has a right to speak here. He has an invitation. We may not like him, but he's never threatened Janine."

Sharon hated when Lo rolled over and played dead. "You don't call this threatening?" The last time she'd looked this aggravated was when Lo wouldn't spill a single detail about the town's last murder trial. "I wish you'd stand up for yourself. Take the offensive." She shook my dress in Lo's face. "What have you got to lose?"

Now I saw an uneven hem. A pointy dart.

I snatched the dress out of her hands. Yesterday, I thought it flowed, but now I hated it. The details were tacky. The handwork a mess. This dress was supposed to be part of my portfolio, to show the colleges what great work I could do. It was supposed to display my potential.

It looked like crap.

I grabbed a pair of scissors and tried to catch a loose thread, but I was frustrated and not careful, and I snipped too far. When the hem tore, Lo tried to snatch it away, but she was way too slow. She said, "You don't want to destroy it." But I did. I wanted to destroy it. This dress was a rag. I tugged at the tear.

I hated when they fought.

I wanted them to be quiet.

I stabbed the cloth with the scissors, then gathered it into my palms by the ends and pulled as hard as I could. Yes, it was a miracle that I lived, but I would know if my hands were blessed. "It's my dress," I shouted. I made it. And I was going to destroy it.

I didn't stop tearing and tugging until all that was left were some gathered strips of shiny brown cloth. A dismembered sleeve. Four blue buttons. I could never understand why I was the only one who lived or why I didn't remember anything about my parents that wasn't written in a book or found in a photo.

Through the skylight, the clouds looked dark. Out the window, two joggers ran by. Miriam's car pulled into the driveway. Her engine sounded like it was about to give up and die, but she left it running and walked in the front door with a brown grocery bag. She said, "I hope I didn't wake the neighborhood."

I checked out her outfit. "You're wearing the shoes."

Miriam nodded. "They're killing me." She didn't dress up often.

Her dress was simple, which drew your eye to the obscenely high platform Mary-Janes I'd talked her into buying, even though they were totally impractical. She had needed something for some interviews. The salesgirl was a sister of one of the most popular girls in our grade. "Even Melissa can't walk in those," she'd said. Sold.

We sat down at the kitchen table so she could give her toes a break. Miriam saw the hamsa straight away. "Did you just get that? My aunt has one. She wishes on it all the time." Miriam reached into a brown bag and pulled out a box of cinnamon buns. "Doofus out there will bring the coffee." She rolled her eyes. "He'll come in as soon as his song is over."

Five minutes later, Abe appeared, balancing five steaming paper cups on a cardboard tray. When he put the cups on the table, a little bit of foam bubbled out of each lid.

He gave me a long, overly formal hug, the kind that meant *I'm sorry about yesterday* and *Whatever you need* and *I'm not totally comfortable hugging you in front of your aunt*. It was a reasonable response—I was still in my pajamas. I wasn't wearing a bra. If he didn't let go of me soon, Lo was going to have a heart attack.

I pushed him away. "Did you see the paper?"

Abe gave me a coffee. "I bought four copies." When I didn't laugh, he said, "Come on, J. Have a sense of humor. I'm joking." He sighed. "Only two."

Before I reminded him that this was all his fault—he was the idiot who hadn't seen them hiding—Miriam raised her cup. "To your parents, Karen and Martin."

Lo nodded. "Their memory should be a righteous blessing."

I didn't know if my memories were righteous or not or, for that matter, even mine, or if they had all come from stories I'd heard a million times. What I was sure of: Time was supposed to heal all wounds, but this one was too big to fix. This was the day my parents died. It was the day that changed the rest of my life, the day that made me famous. If Dave Armstrong wanted to believe that I was a miracle, there was nothing I could do.

I needed to get dressed. It was time to go to the cemetery and pay our respects.

SIX

I settled on a navy blue dress with white collar and cuffs that I made last year for a Social Studies presentation. It had an empire waist. It wasn't too tight. I could wear it with flats. "Your hamsa is really pretty," Miriam said. She stood back to look at me. She thought the dress made me look "mature."

"Is that another word for fat?"

"It's another word for let's go." She held on to the rail as she walked one half-step at a time down the stairs toward her car.

"Sorry about the mess," Miriam said, like her car wasn't always scattered with junk.

There was a science journal and four weeks' worth of *The Economist*. The *New York Times* crossword puzzle—completed in pen. The floor was covered with crunched-up brown bags and a lot of dirt, courtesy of an old pair of rubber boots, two shovels, and a dozen green containers. Miriam liked to say that during the growing season, she lived out of her car. "The other day, I planted beets and carrots and I didn't have time to straighten up." Abe added,

"Tomorrow after school we're going to put in some turnips and onions. You want to help?"

I said, "If I have time," but I knew neither one of them expected to see me there. I blamed my portfolio—the ruined brown dress—but the truth was, this was their issue, not mine. Philosophically, I agreed with their mission, but that didn't mean I wanted to play on my knees in the mud.

Miriam pulled out of the driveway, and Abe cranked up the music. I slumped as low as possible so no one outside could see me. "Could you turn it down?" I asked. "You're practically begging for attention."

Just to get on my nerves, he played a very enthusiastic air guitar until the chorus was over. "Do you honestly think anyone's going to bother you at the cemetery?"

After yesterday, I couldn't believe he had the nerve to ask me if there was a chance there might be reporters at the cemetery. Reporters came to my house. They showed up at the school. They wrote retrospectives about me. Why wouldn't they show up there? If there was a story my mother wanted, she'd have had no problem crashing a funeral to get it.

That was the job.

As Miriam parked the car, I knew they could be waiting in the parking lot. Or on the sidewalk. Or near the mausoleum at the center of the cemetery. They could be photographing me right now.

We walked down the path, and I kept my eyes open. I checked out the couple by the bridge and the woman with the stroller. I pointed out an old man and lady who looked at me a second too long. I asked Miriam, "Do they look familiar to you?"

"Not really," she said not-so-sympathetically. When I looked again, I knew she was right. I didn't know them. They didn't know me. They had their own problems. Their own dead person to visit. When I looked closer, I could see they were crying. Now I felt even worse.

I never cried. Not for my parents. Not for myself. Not for anything.

Lo thought this was abnormal. To get me to cry, she took me to therapists; we tried every kind of yoga there was, meditation, and even hypnosis—but nothing worked. One expert said, "If she could cry, she would feel better." Another one blamed anxiety. "If you would take your medication, you might relax." The last guy I saw told me that I was repressing my memories, maybe for a good reason.

That made me laugh. "You think?"

Dave Armstrong and his posse would say that I should pray for tears, that the absence of saltwater proved that I needed to get in touch with God. Of course, he would also say that my parents died for a reason—that tragedies like mine did not occur in a vacuum—and that we should trust in the Lord because bad things happened to good people every day. He probably believed they were happy in heaven, like it was some kind of party we all got to go to.

On every anniversary, Dave Armstrong had a lot of things to say about how I should be feeling. He had a whole lot of opinions about memories that were supposed to be mine.

Now my dry eyes stared at my parents' epitaphs. My father's, in small block letters: "Beloved husband, father, and son. Blessed are the pure of heart." The letters on my mother's gravestone said "Wife and Mother." Some Hebrew at the bottom. I also counted twenty-eight tiny stones on the top of my dad's marker, thirty-two on my mom's, which meant that three people visited since I came here last.

"You think Armstrong showed up?" I didn't want him coming to this place, standing where I was standing now, marking his visit with a rock and a televised statement.

Neither Abe nor Miriam thought he'd have the nerve. Lo didn't care. She just wanted to go through her rituals. She reached into her bag and handed us each a five-by-seven laminated card, the one with Hebrew on the top and transliteration on the bottom. Every year, we recited the Jewish prayer for the dead, because Lo couldn't imagine not saying it. The explanation at the bottom said that reciting Kaddish allowed a soul to climb to the next level or world.

I held the card at my side.

"Yitgadel, v'yitkadash, shemay rabah." I memorized these sounds years ago. But that didn't mean I got it. I didn't understand how this prayer of all prayers became the one we say now.

The last line made me angry: "May God who makes peace in the heavens, bring peace upon us, and upon all Israel; and say Amen."

Attention: God who made peace—if you're really out there—if you really wanted me to come to terms with this—I was here. Waiting. Still looking for a little bit of peace. Still looking for an explanation. A justification. A reason why so many terrible things have happened.

I'm waiting for a sign. I may not cry, but I'm open to anything you've got!

Totally by coincidence, the wind picked up. We held down our dresses, and Sharon pulled me, Miriam, and Abe into a close circle.

"Don't look now," she said, so we all looked. Near the bottom of the hill stood two men and a woman carrying a purse big enough to hold three cameras. All three of them wore khakis—it was obvious they were on the job.

Sharon ripped off her vintage red bomber jacket and pushed it in my face—it was a pretty obvious ploy, but maybe it would work. I took Lo's umbrella, too. They told me to walk as fast as I could in the opposite direction. Sharon zipped up my jacket and tried to pose the way I stood. "If we're lucky, they'll think I'm you and you're me. You'll have time to get away."

SEVEN

Abe thought we should run. "Just to be safe."

I said no, we should stick to walking. Running attracted attention. It was the worst thing we could do.

Miriam didn't care what we did as long as she could take off her shoes first. She leaned against a mailbox. "I already have a blister," she said. "Why don't we just hold our ground? If you tell them no comment, what can they do?"

I wished it were that easy. (It irritated me that she'd ask this.)

To them, "No comment" was just the first thing I said before they took my picture. "No comment" was just a line; it was part of a script or a dance. It was the challenge to get me to say more. "No comment" was pretty much the same as saying, "On your mark, get set, go. Exploit me."

Miriam was naïve. Being the subject of a story was an invasion of privacy. It was not flattering, not fun, not exciting. It never ended with "No comment."

For a few steps, Abe turned around and walked backward.

He stared at the street behind us.

I had a bad feeling about this. "Where are they?" I asked. "Do you see them? Tell me the truth."

"They're two blocks back. I told you we should have run." I turned around and looked. That was a huge mistake. I saw them, and they also saw me.

"Janine! We'd like to talk to you."

"Janine, turn around."

"Janine, just one moment. This isn't just about you."

Now we ran. Abe first, then me, then Miriam. We passed storefronts and a kid on a skateboard, and Abe practically plowed into a couple of people from my history class.

We didn't stop. Miriam threw her shoes like grenades. Now four strides ahead, Abe pointed to the big white church just across the street. It wasn't our turn to walk, but he leaped into the intersection anyway. I heard him say, "Come on, J. We can make it."

But I stopped. Because at the same time, there was a car.

In reality, the whole thing probably took three seconds. But like all disasters, it felt like it went on for hours. The problem was, there was nothing I could do to stop it.

One.

Miriam came from behind me and yanked me back. We hit the ground hard, and brakes squealed. Abe looked at me and for that one long second, we both knew what was about to happen. In the background, the church's electronic bulletin board announced the schedule. *Services are held every Saturday and Sunday. All are welcome.*

That blinked in my eyes.

Two.

Glass shattered. People screamed. Abe took flight like an angel, his arms out, his legs straight. When he landed, he made one sound.

Thud.

Three.

For one moment, one endless moment, there was silence, like a vacuum. It was the same kind of silence I heard just after the bomb went off, when I wasn't sure if I was alive or dead. This kind of silence made time stop.

It made me feel like I was walking through water.

And I couldn't speak.

Just like before, I was suffocating. I was alone. My hands curled up and sent sharp pains to my neck and head. But this was not rubble, and it wasn't Jerusalem either. I was not fighting for my life.

This was Abe.

He was in the middle of the road.

Miriam called 911. "Our friend was hit by a car. In front of the white church. No I don't know if he's breathing. I don't know if he's got a pulse."

Somehow I stood up, and my legs worked. Somehow I was able to walk into the street, and kneel at his side, and check his pulse and his breath, and even though it sounded weak, it was definitely there. I shouted, "Abe. Can you hear me?" There was blood pooling under his head. His eyes didn't look like he saw me. I knew I shouldn't move him, but his head was bleeding like crazy. Somehow I remembered to press my hands against the wet, hot wound.

And wait.

I listened for the sirens. They seemed too far away. I looked up at the clouds. A camera captured the moment. *Click, click, click, click, click.*

I didn't care how many pictures they took. This was Abe. I begged him, "Don't die." *Click.* "Please, Abe. I know you can make it." *Click.* "You cannot die right here in the middle of Marsden Avenue."

Click, click, click, click, click, click, click, click.

There were more people now, and they all shouted and cried and gave me advice at once. I focused on Abe, on his blood and his breath. I felt Miriam standing near. I told him, "We have tickets to three concerts. And I need you to help me with chem. I thought we were going to go somewhere crazy this summer."

"Stay calm, Janine. Help is on the way."

I wondered if I was going insane. That sounded like my mother—here—in this crowd—telling me all the things she said ten years ago. I looked around, but of course, she wasn't in the crowd. Only when I looked at Abe could I hear her:

"You can do this, baby."

"You are not alone."

"Hang on, Janine. You have a holy soul."

I understood I was imagining this, but it was nice. It felt good. Like there was hope. For a moment, I let myself smile. *Click.* Because my mother was here, I sincerely believed that Abe was going to make it.

As the ambulance pulled up to the scene, a woman shouted, "That's Janine Collins—the Soul Survivor. We're witnessing a miracle. Look at him. She's healing him with her hands."

The medics didn't care. They ran toward us and pushed me away. I fell on the ground, on my knees, onto my hands. I listened for my mother to tell me what to do next, but she was gone. All I heard were the medics. They said, "He's in trouble."

Click, click, click

The cameras were all around me. A Nikon D4—the camera of choice for many photojournalists—is capable of shooting eleven frames per second. (After having enough of them shoved in my face, I looked it up.) If these guys had held their fingers to the shutter, they'd have close to a thousand frames by now.

Of me. And Abe. He wasn't going to die. Not if I could help it. This was not his fifteen minutes, I promised myself.

I looked up at the clouds and bargained: If he gets better, I will work harder. I will be nicer. I'll help Miriam with her farm. If Abe will just get through this, I will try and be a better person, too. I will do interviews. I'll talk to Dave. I'll face every single one of my fears.

Click. Click. Click.

Click, click, click, click, click.

EIGHT

After the paramedics drove away, the policeman thanked us. (I assumed he was just trying to make us feel hopeful.) "I hope your friend makes it. You did a good job. Like a pro."

During a disaster, average people have documented performing extraordinary acts of strength and will. Most weeks, you could read about it while waiting in the checkout line at the grocery store. A mother lifts a car to save her child. A man tackles a full-grown polar bear. It's called hysterical strength. Dave Armstrong thought that this happened to him. Right before he saw my hands, he lifted very large rocks that normally he could never have budged.

I said, "Do you think he's going to make it? Do people like him—people who get hit by cars—what are their chances?"

The policeman looked alarmed. My hands. They were shaking. "Are you okay?"

My hands were bloody, shaking, spiny, crooked. They looked like old leather gloves that someone found in the bottom of a drawer. (Even people who recognize my face are shocked when they actually get a look at my hands up close.)

"Yes. I'm sure. I'm fine." When he offered to drive us to the hospital, I told him, "We have a car. My hands always look like this."

After he left, we sat on the corner of the curb. We watched the police take a few pictures of the car before some guys came and towed it away. A cleaning crew came in and swept up the glass. Still, we didn't talk. We didn't move. If this had been on TV, and we'd been playing friends, we'd have rushed to the hospital. We might have even jumped into the ambulance.

But this was real.

We were left behind.

Moving and driving and thinking and talking did not seem possible.

Finally, when our legs and the street and the traffic seemed back to normal, we got up and walked. Miriam said, "You know, this isn't your fault. Those reporters—they did this." She had a skinned knee. There was gravel stuck in her palms. "That lady was crazy. Nobody really thinks you healed him with your hands."

"I know." I did not heal him. My mother wasn't there, and she wasn't talking to me. I was just hallucinating. The PTSD. Halfway to the car, I confided, "You know, when I was holding his head, I heard my mother."

Miriam stopped walking. She looked scared. "What do you mean, you heard your mother?"

Now I felt stupid. "I mean I thought I heard her. Like she was sitting right next to me." I grabbed her elbow. "She said all the same things she said right before she died." I waited for Miriam to respond the way I wanted her to. "Crazy, right?"

"Crazy." She was my best friend. She would be the first person to tell me if I'd lost it. "But to be honest, I'm not surprised."

"You're not?"

She looked away, resumed walking. "You're sad. It's the anniversary, and you were just standing in front of your mother's grave. You're in mourning. Then we get chased by idiots and our friend was hit by a car. It's really not that surprising that you heard her voice . . . that you freaked out." She pointed to the sidewalk. "Look at that. My shoes. No one stole them." We both laughed, even though it wasn't all that funny.

At the car, someone snapped my picture then ran away. Miriam shouted, "Loser!"

I said, "Don't waste your breath. They're cowards. I think I turned away in time." There were eleven business cards and a folded piece of paper under the windshield wiper. I gathered them up and balled them in my fist.

On every one, scrawled handwriting offered different versions of the same thing: *Call me. Let's talk. I would love to meet with you. I will be brief.* "So much for them leaving us alone on this *sensitive* day."

Miriam took them away. "We should give these to the police, in case Abe . . ." She didn't finish the sentence, but I knew what she meant. If Abe died. We could blame these people. They were the ones chasing us. We could get our revenge.

This was their fault. Not mine.

She turned on the ignition, and Abe's iPod flipped on. It was a song about love. She yanked it out by the cord, tossed it into the backseat, and stepped on the gas. She took a corner too hard and rolled over the curb.

"Stupid song."

No. It was my fault.

I told her to slow down. "He is going to be okay. I'm sure of it. He was breathing when they took him to the hospital." She accelerated through a yellow light. I reminded her, "When I held his hand . . ."

"You don't know that." She sped past a stop sign. "I told you we shouldn't have run."

Now it seemed so obvious. I should have held my ground and said, "No comment." Or for once I could have listened to their questions. It's not like they ever asked questions that had actual answers. It was one of the things that made talking about faith so irritating.

There were just words. No proof.

If I had posed for pictures, Abe would be sitting where I am now. He would be singing some sappy song and getting on my nerves. Miriam would not be driving like a lunatic.

My phone beeped. There were three messages from Lo— all minutes after we split up. She wanted to know where I was. "Are you okay? Please check in." Dan called, too. His messages were always a little awkward. He asked, "How was the thing?" And then, after five seconds of dead air, "You know you can call me. Okay? Bye!"

As the first raindrops hit the windshield, I left Lo a purposefully vague message: *I'm fine. Don't worry. Will call you later.* Miriam flipped on the wipers to the fastest speed. "You're not going to tell her what happened?"

"No." I shook my head. "You want me to tell your mom?"

"I'll call her later." Miriam didn't have to elaborate. I understood too well. If she told her mom, it would make it real. If we talked any more, we'd need an explanation. When lightning flashed, she pumped the brakes. She drove extra slow.

As long as I'd known her, Miriam had hated driving in bad weather. Her greatest fear was being hit by lightning. She was spooked by it. I had no idea why. It wasn't like you heard about people dying from lightning strikes on a regular basis.

Two minutes and three thunderclaps later, she pulled into the parking lot and stopped the car. We were at the hospital. Abe was hurt. The water rushed over the windshield.

"What if?"

"Don't say it."

"But what would we do?"

The rain fell harder. Neither of us moved.

(This is what it feels like to be in shock.)

Lightning flashed, two sticks at a time. I tried Lo again, but now her phone was out of service. Miriam gripped the steering wheel. I said, "We're safe in the car, right? Because of the tires. The rubber."

She stared straight ahead. "Yeah. I think so." We sat still and watched the rain. It was all we could do.

I heard my mother.

I was sure Miriam didn't believe me.

I said, "She did sound very real. Very alive." At the same time, lightning flashed a split second before the thunder sounded.

Miriam looked confused. Then she looked mad. "Do you really think that's important?" Then she opened the car door, and even though she had to be terrified, she stepped determined into the storm and started running.

NINE

"I hate hospitals."

Miriam crossed her arms over her chest. Her teeth chattered. "That's understandable."

I hated the smell. I hated the lights, the doctors in their white coats, and the nurses who smiled, even when they knew they were about to hurt you. Miriam didn't know what it felt like to be told that everything was going to be okay, when that was a lie.

But now Abe would.

The emergency room was full of wet people. Every seat was taken. The line to the receptionist was long. We grabbed handfuls of brown paper towels and took our spot behind a bunch of old people, a young man who smelled like he hadn't showered in three weeks, and a man and woman with a young kid. She held him next to her and pressed a towel to his ear. He screamed in pain, but nobody in line seemed to notice.

"What happened?" I asked the lady, trying to dry off my arms and legs as fast as possible.

"You don't want to know." That was probably correct. As I stood shivering—it was unnaturally cold in this waiting room—the red on the towel spread. It was looking bad. I didn't understand why they didn't go to the front of the line. That ear could be falling off. Or his brain could be bleeding. You heard about things like that. The parents thought they were doing the right thing, or being polite—maybe they thought those were the rules—but the whole time, the kid was in trouble.

I told her to speak up. "I don't think anyone would mind." As the towel got redder and redder and redder, my head turned hot and my palms sweated and tingled, and for the second time today, I tasted dust. I was soaking wet. My ears rang. I imagined my parents, covered in blood, dying under the rubble.

First my ears. Now my eyes. I told Miriam, "I need to sit down. I think I'm going to be sick."

There was blood on the floor.

There was also blood on my hands. Not figuratively—literally. In the middle of my palms—a dark splotch of blood in the center of each palm—just like Dave Armstrong had described. Look at it one way, it's a splotch. Look at it another way...

I stuffed my hands in my pockets. I didn't want anyone to see them. This was just the kind of thing that made people freak out. If they saw the blood, they'd photograph my hands. They'd make assumptions. Then they'd write stories. That was how the media worked.

How the ER worked: When the kid with the ear passed out, he finally got some attention. They wheeled him away. Two groups of sick people later, we made it to the front of the line, but we still had to wait. The receptionist told us there was another emergency. "Just a moment," she said, reaching for the phone. "It's been a crazy day."

I shoved my hands in Miriam's face. "Look."

Miriam looked at my hands like they were perfectly clean, like I was hallucinating everything. "What do you want me to see? They look the way they always look." Two minutes later, we watched an ambulance pull up to the door. There was a lot of commotion. We couldn't see it, but we could feel it.

Someone said, "The rain is causing a lot of problems."

Although in reality it was less than half an hour, it seemed like an eternity before the receptionist was ready to talk to us. Miriam took the lead. "We're here to see our friend, Abe Demetrius." She spelled his name three times. "An ambulance brought him here. Not just now. A while ago." She whispered, "He was hit by a car."

The woman stared at her computer screen. "He's in surgery. I'm sorry. Only family can go back." She gave us directions to the chapel, the cafeteria, the waiting room, the ladies' room, and the gift shop, but other than that, there was nothing we could do but wait. She wasn't really sorry. It's like when people tell you that everything will be fine. It was just something they had to say when things suck.

Miriam, however, was not in the mood to take no for an answer. "Please? We were there when it happened. We feel terrible. We're his closest friends."

I almost thought it might work, but the answer was still no. The receptionist simultaneously typed and talked the way some people patted their heads and rubbed their stomachs. (It was actually very impressive.) "Please take a seat. Or go home. Wait for his family to get in touch."

As the next person pleaded her case, I told Miriam we should take the woman's advice and get out of here. But Miriam wasn't leaving. She grabbed me by the elbow and dragged me to the ladies' room. In front of the long mirror, she washed her face with a small mountain of cool foam soap. Between the two of us, the only makeup we had was one tube of lipstick. She put it on, then wiped it off, then applied it again. On off, on off, she was getting a little bit manic.

She muttered, "He better be okay. He has got to be okay. That lady didn't have to be so rude."

I grabbed a paper towel. I rubbed my hands. In the fluorescent light, they looked clean. The soap made my face feel tight. It burned my eyes. When I closed them, all I saw was blood and death. The boy with the bomb. Abe lying on the ground. The kid with the ear. I wondered if everyone had it wrong.

I wasn't blessed. I was cursed.

My mother was dead. She wasn't there.

My hands were clean.

I looked at my phone. It was almost out of power.

***

Two hours later, a youngish man with a thick beard and a huge tattoo of an eagle sticking out of his collar took over. Miriam practically ran to the desk. "Abe Demetrius?" she asked, like it was a question. "Can we see him? Can you tell us how he's doing?" When this receptionist looked no more moved than the last one, she stamped her foot and waved me over. "Do you know who this is?"

This was not a good idea. "Miriam!"

"What?"

"Don't go there."

"Do you want to see him, or not?" I started to walk away, but she grabbed me by the sleeve. "This is Abe's friend, Janine Collins. Look in your newspaper. Or better yet, check the magazine rack. You can read all about her."

He began to laugh. "I knew you looked familiar." He rummaged under the desk and pulled out today's newspaper. "Some of the nurses were just talking about you. They could still remember exactly where they were when you were . . ." He paused.

I hated moments like this.

"She's the Soul Survivor." Miriam smiled, like she'd just won a bet. "Now can we see him?"

The receptionist reached for his phone, and the eagle on his neck stretched out. "How cool is this? The little girl in the rubble. You still look the same!" He pressed a few numbers. "Hold on a minute. I'll tell the family you're here."

I never understood why anyone liked tattoos, especially big ones, and even more than that, big ones you can't hide. "Sixth floor of the main hospital." He pointed to a box full of masks on top of his desk.

"Do we need to wear them?" Miriam asked.

"Hospital policy," he said. "But could you sign one first? To Lydia." He turned a little pink. "My mother is a huge fan."

After I had signed four masks and a prescription pad, we walked through the crowded lobby, past the TCBY, the Sbarro, and the gift shop, which had a huge stack of the retrospective issue. An oak door was marked Chapel. Underneath: "He who gives his life for the holy cause will have his sins forgiven and a place reserved in paradise."

Miriam grabbed my arm. "That's not good, is it? That they admitted him."

I said nothing.

Instead, I pushed the elevator buttons. Up. Close. Open. It was all too slow. When the door finally opened to the sixth floor, we faced a little kid in a wheelchair and a family and six balloons. "Get well soon" and "Happy 6th Birthday." Miriam started to cry. I wanted to throw up. Behind them, there was a big whiteboard behind the nurse's desk. Demetrius, 611. Abe's door was open.

This time we didn't ask for an invitation.

TEN

He looked dead.

Abe's parents stood at either side of the bed, hands cupped, heads down. At the foot of the bed, with his back to us, was a man in formal black pants. Abe's parents nodded and swayed as the man spoke to them about the greatness and mercy of the Lord.

They didn't see us.

"Dear Jesus, Divine Physician and Healer of the Sick, we turn to You in this time of illness. O dearest Comforter of the Troubled, alleviate our worry and sorrow with Your gentle love, and grant us the grace and strength to accept this burden. Dear God, we place our worries in Your hands. We place our beloved Abraham under Your care and humbly ask that You restore Your servant to health again. Above all, grant us the grace to acknowledge Your holy will and know that whatsoever You do, You do for the love of us. Amen."

Then they all stood very still with their eyes closed. And prayed.

The man told them to lean on God. For support and guidance. For strength. He said in a low voice, "You are not alone."

Dave used to say that all the time, too, especially when I was crying in pain. When I was struggling to move my fingers or just plain upset that my parents were dead, he used to say, "The Lord is with us when we need Him."

That always got on my nerves. It didn't make sense. By definition, anything that kills your parents or gives you excruciating pain is not sitting by your side.

I touched Miriam's shoulder and motioned to the elevator, but Miriam didn't move. "Let's go," I said as loudly as I dared—I wanted to get out of here—but my voice carried, and they all looked up.

"Girls," Mrs. D. said, extending her hands to us and pulling us into the circle. "Come in. Join us. We're so happy to see you. We're so grateful for everything you did."

This was not what I was expecting.

We walked up to his bed and the machines and stood over him. This was so wrong. His face was too slack. His skin didn't look right. There were too many tubes sticking into his arm and nose and I didn't want to know where else. At least one machine beeped regularly. Another one hummed. The whole thing made no sense. What did he ever do to deserve this?

Mr. Demetrius said, "We heard you were brave."

Mrs. Demetrius agreed. "We heard you did all the right things."

They held our hands. "It is such a blessing that you were there. Such a blessing that the Lord was listening."

I couldn't believe they were thanking us—how they could honestly use the word *blessing* when Abe was so obviously messed up? I wondered if something went wrong during the surgery, because he could breathe when he was lying in the street, but now he needed a machine. On the street, he looked hurt, but he didn't look so gray.

I grabbed his hands. "Abe! Open your eyes! I know you're in there. I just know it. You're going to be fine."

The priest looked horrified. He tried to pry my fingers off Abe, but Mrs. Demetrius told him to let me pray the way I wanted to. "She's the girl we told you about. His friend. The one who survived the bombing." She outlined the highlights of my biography. "Today is the tenth anniversary of the day she survived."

One machine beeped faster. "Did you hear that?" I asked. I went to find the nurse. "Did something go wrong? Is he in any pain?" I needed to know. "Why is he hooked up to all this stuff? He was breathing on his own when he got in the ambulance."

The nurse told me to calm down, that we needed to be patient, that with all emergencies, you had to wait and see. The doctors did everything possible. Every test. Two surgeries already. She explained that they had to sedate him, but that this was only a temporary measure, a solid medical decision, nothing that unusual under the circumstances. Abe's father butted in to say that there was no doubt the situation was grave—Abe lost a lot of blood and hit his head really hard—but there was also no reason to believe he wouldn't wake up.

Mrs. Demetrius took my hand and put it back on Abe's. The priest said in a formal voice, "We were just about to read some Scripture. If you want to, you could join us." He handed me a Bible. Mrs. Demetrius said, "We would love to hear you read. After everything you have lived through, it might make us all feel better."

Saying no would be wrong.

Saying no would be selfish.

I held the book open to the page she wanted to hear. It had been read before, many times. The corner was almost torn. The page was slightly crinkled. "Behold, I send an Angel before thee, to keep thee in the way, and to bring thee into the place which I have prepared." Abe's parents closed their eyes and listened. I kept reading. "Beware of him," I said, clearing my throat, "and obey his voice, provoke him not; for he will not pardon your transgressions: for my name is in him."

Abe's mom squeezed my hand. "We know Abe can hear you. We trust that the Lord will heal Abe's body."

I didn't agree. The Lord—these prayers—they didn't work. But there was no way I could stop now.

"But if thou shalt indeed obey his voice, and do all that I speak; then I will be an enemy unto thine enemies, and an adversary unto thine adversaries." There is stuff about an Angel and some people who may or may not believe. The machine beeps. I feel lost. These words make promises, but I don't understand why anyone thinks they can help. I don't know who is ye and thy and thine. "And ye shall serve the LORD your God, and he shall bless thy bread, and thy water; and I will take sickness away from the midst of thee."

I felt trapped.

Tricked into saying words I did not understand or buy.

I gave her back the Bible and grabbed Abe by the shoulders.

"Abe. Please wake up. Please. Just open your eyes. I know you're in there. I know you can hear me."

His mother cried. She grabbed me and held me in her arms. Her body shook with fear. "Janine, we know you're scared. We know you're suffering, too."

"This is not your fault," Miriam added. "You did not cause the accident. What you're doing right now . . . it's all we can do."

That's what made me mad. There had to be something else to do.

When Mrs. D. pushed the Bible back into my hands, I gave it back. I couldn't fake it. I was scarred, broken beyond repair. These words made promises that never come true. I leaned over Abe, gave him a hug, and walked as fast as I could to the elevator. I said to no one, "I'm sorry, but I can't do this. I need to go."

The Demetriuses thought that praying helped, but they were wrong. It never did. It didn't take sickness away. It didn't save anyone.

Outside, I walked faster. The air had that after-storm smell—fresh and cold and light—but I couldn't calm down. They believed that God was going to take care of Abe, but I knew that doesn't always happen. Sometimes, bad things happened. Sometimes, no matter what you wanted, God did nothing. They could keep praying, but they'd never convince me that anyone or anything was listening.

When I got to Miriam's car, I called Lo, but no one picked up. Then Miriam called. Probably to tell me I wasn't going anywhere without her.

"Janine?"

"What?"

She sounded like she'd been crying. "You have to come back. Right now, J. Come back."

"Why?"

It took her a minute to calm down. "After you ran out the door, Abe held up his hand. Then he nodded. And when I said your name, he smiled. Janine, Abe is going to be okay. The doctors are with him. Come back, so you can see for yourself. They are calling it a miracle."

ELEVEN

Abe held up two fingers; he wiggled his toes on command. He could blink, too, one for yes and two for no. If he didn't have a tube in his mouth, he would probably start singing one of those sappy ballads people use for prom themes and ad campaigns.

Seeing was supposed to be believing, but in reality, when it stared you in the face, seeing was confusing. These were not hard things to do, and yet, right now, after everything that had happened, they seemed impossible. The doctors patted each other on the back. Miriam practically danced around the room. "I told you it was a miracle."

I hated that word, but I refused to be unhappy. "Yes! This is wonderful. It's a miracle of medicine."

Mrs. Demetrius clutched her Bible to her chest. "No, no, no. She meant it was a miracle of faith." She introduced me to some of the doctors, like I was some sort of miracle-diplomat. "This is the girl we were telling you about. Janine Collins."

They looked like they found me amusing. It was sort of embarrassing. Maybe they knew who I was; maybe they didn't.

When people thought they should have heard of you but didn't, they always acted a little funny.

Most people needed less than twenty seconds to figure it out. But once, someone thought I was the daughter of the plumber. Today the doctor snapped his fingers after less than six seconds. "Oh yeah. Wasn't I just reading about you somewhere?"

Mr. Demetrius reached into his bag for the retrospective and waved it in his face. "She is the *Soul Survivor.*" When they all started nodding—*oh yeah, of course, I remember you—the kid in the temple, right?*—he told the group, "At the scene, she held him. She prayed for him. Right here—right before he woke up—she read him Scripture. Every word she said, I could feel him getting stronger. If you ask me, that girl healed him right in front of our eyes."

"For a long time," Mrs. D. said, "people have wondered about why Janine lived, when everyone else in that synagogue died. Now we know. She has a gift. A quantum force."

Quantum force? I almost laughed out loud. Religious people came up with the craziest things.

The doctors must have agreed, because they talked about things like friendship and family and the healing power of touch, which were the only logical ways to deal with the questions with no answers. As they rationalized, I looked at the floor, the door, anywhere but at their faces—I was sure they were laughing at me. I worried they were thinking *fame whore.*

Freak.

Or maybe they were hoping to give a press conference.

After they left, Miriam excused herself. "I need to go call my mom." She shrugged. "She's left about ten messages."

"I should call Lo, too," I said, following her out the door into the hall. The power must have still been out, because all I got was an off-key tone and message. Luckily, Miriam got through, but when she was done talking, she looked really upset.

"What's wrong now?"

She said, "We need to get going."

The doctor thought this was a timely idea. "I think we've had enough excitement for one day. We don't want Abe to overdo it."

Outside, Miriam walked fast. The air still had that cool, saturated feeling it had after a big storm. The rain had passed, but Miriam still looked miserable.

"So are you going to tell me?"

She kicked some gravel. "The tree was hit by lightning."

I didn't have to ask what tree. There was only one tree that would make Miriam's face turn white.

***

This time, Miriam couldn't drive fast—there were too many branches in the road. Too many detours. Orange cones blocked streets. Many houses were dark.

She took a sharp right past the school. "It was hit by lightning. My mom says it looks bad."

"Wow. That's terrible." There was no point saying sorry. Miriam loved that tree. She loved that farm. It wasn't the right time to tell her to put it in perspective.

Sometimes the best thing a friend could do was say nothing. Even I knew that.

The road was closed. Bright lights illuminated the damage. Trucks blocked the road. They beeped loud warnings. When we didn't pull a U-turn, a man in a hard hat jogged toward us, waving us away. He looked annoyed.

"We're closing down the block," he said. "You need to go another way. We're fixing these lines."

One huge bough lay strewn across the road. Its branches looked like broken fingers, splintered and disjointed at unnatural angles. At the break, the trunk's white middle was exposed.

Miriam asked, "Is it dead?"

"I don't think so," the man said. "At least not yet. We'll just have to wait and see." Miriam nodded her head and stared at the broken tree. He said, "That old tree has survived a lot of storms. It was due for something like this."

The tree looked lopsided, deformed, like it could topple over at any moment. He should have been able to tell us definitively. Was the thing dead? Or was everything going to be okay?

Without this tree, the land was not special. It could be any piece of land on any street in any town. If the tree died, there'd be no reason not to sell the land and there'd be nothing anyone could do to stop that. For the second time, I felt bad for the tree. It didn't ask for this. It was just trying to be a tree.

I started to say something to Miriam, but she didn't have time for an existential discussion about trees and life and responsibility. She started calling the other people who cared about the farm. I redialed Lo, and this time she picked up. The first thing she said was, "Thank God you're okay." She sounded like she'd just run ten miles. The second thing: "When I got your message, I thought I was losing my mind."

I gave her the extended version—what happened, and where I was now. "It looks like he's going to completely recover."

She started to lecture me, but then stopped, like she didn't know whether to be mad or sad or furious or relieved. I said, "Can you come and get me? I'm confused. Something big happened. I need to figure out what to do next."

TWELVE

On the way home, Lo picked up a big bag of individually wrapped chocolates, Diet Cokes, and baskets of strawberries and blueberries, even though all they had were the fancy organic kind. And they were out of season. White in the middle. Taste-free.

She chopped the strawberries with more force than necessary, then doused them with sugar. "You are not a faith healer, if that's what you're worried about." Not really, but hearing her say it made me momentarily less sure.

I went straight for the chocolates. I unwrapped two, crinkled up the foil, and stuffed them in my dry mouth. Sharon picked out the blueberries, one by one, feeling them first to make sure they were firm. For some reason, when she was stressed out, she preferred fruit.

While we ate, I told them every single thing that happened, every detail, every sound, every second. I told them I heard my mother and that Abe woke up after I touched him. And even then, they didn't waffle, not one iota.

I was not a faith healer.

I had nothing to do with Abe getting better.

I should have come home.

"The accident was all over the news. Your message was too vague."

When only shriveled blueberries were left, Sharon started on the strawberries. "Tell us what you heard your mother say." She reached out to hold my hand. There was red juice under her nails.

I took a long breath. This was a little bit sad, a little bit embarrassing. "The same words she said when we were buried alive. You might think I'm crazy, but it wasn't that bad. Hearing her voice made me feel like Abe was going to be okay, even though he looked almost dead."

Lo walked into the corner and poured herself one drink and then another. She blamed herself. She never should have let me out of her sight on such an emotionally packed day. "Do you want to talk to someone?" She meant a shrink. "It helped before."

"Not really." I hated sitting on the couch with my "paid best friend." I was pretty sure it wouldn't help me now.

She didn't fight me. "You could come by the studio and take a few classes. Maybe a thirty-day challenge." Lo believed that Bikram yoga was the answer to 99 percent of the world's questions. When I shook my head no—to me, thirty days in her hot room was the equivalent of a torture chamber—she frowned. "Maybe you should do some research. You know—in the name of understanding the other side." Lo's favorite yogi worked at the used bookstore—right near the white church. Many times, she'd asked me to check out the section on medical and spiritual health. "You know, the Demetriuses are right about one thing: the body heals itself in all kinds of mysterious ways. You can call it God. Or just nature. Reading about alternative medicine might be helpful."

"Alternative medicine?" I almost laughed. I'd rather blame my PTSD.

Sharon had other concerns. "What does Abe think? Who else knows?" She turned to Lo. "Now will you talk to Robert? With Armstrong in the area, things could get messy fast."

I sighed. Yoga wasn't the answer. Neither was the law. "My friends will not sell me out. They won't go to the press. They definitely won't talk to Armstrong." I held up my hands to stop them from interrupting me. "When I told Miriam about my mom, she said the same thing you did. That I was stressed out. It was just bad timing. I heard her because I was scared. And because of the timing." I stood up and headed for the stairs. I had nothing more to say.

Up in the loft, remnants of the brown dress lay scattered on the floor. The retrospective sat on my bed. I opened it. Then I closed it. I thought about tearing it into pieces or throwing it across the room with the rest of the mess. But after everything that had happened, I had to admit—I was curious. I didn't know what they could have said. It had been years since I had given an interview.

First I flipped through the magazine. It was printed on high-quality glossy. There were at least thirty pages of ads. It felt heavy.

Then I scanned the sections about Israel, the Middle East, and war, skipping past the list of victims and the section about Dave Armstrong, until I got to the part about me. It wasn't long, mostly a photo diary, a collage of old headlines. But it was me. My life: ten years on four pages. The center montage featured close-ups of my hands before and after surgery. Some of them were pretty gruesome.

The caption read, "Janine endured multiple surgeries and years of painful rehab." At the time, the doctors in New York said that it was the most difficult hand surgery they'd performed to date.

I turned on the light to the brightest level, so I could compare the newest pictures to my palms, the scars that remained.

What it didn't say: My hands didn't just look different. They were different. My fingerprints changed. My nails didn't grow right. It took years of hard work to learn how to do even the simplest things. Even now, I had a hard time typing for a long time. Writing wasn't simple. And forget about playing an instrument. They considered their surgeries a huge success, but I still couldn't text anything longer than a couple of keys. I needed a stylus to get it right.

I turned back to the story.

The coverage surrounding Janine Collins' rescue rivals the biggest stories in history, including the death of Princess Di and even 9/11. For years, sympathetic strangers showered her with gifts of money, even though it was common knowledge that she would benefit from her parents' insurance and trust.

Blah, blah, blah. It was mostly recycled crap. The same questions. The same non-answers.

Who was Janine Collins today?

I looked at Dress-Form Annie. "What do you think?" I wasn't sure. I wondered what they thought.

At sixteen, Janine's an average American girl, and except for the scars on her hands, you'd never know she was the Soul Survivor.

True, but not earth-shattering. It's what came next that bothered me. Somehow, this writer found out I liked fashion and wanted to be a designer. That I did okay in school, but that I hadn't bothered to get my driver's license, which for some reason, the writer found weird. Also, I had a pretty ironic sense of humor. But that I held a grudge. She wrote, "Janine would do anything for her small circle of friends." There was a picture of me at last year's prom, right after I ripped the bottom off my dress so we could run through the cornfields. Another in my kitchen, after a night of cooking vegetarian crepes for a French assignment. And one at a football game, waving my hands in the air. That night was so funny. Miriam begged me to go to the game. She had a crush on the quarterback. We waited at the locker room for two hours, just so she could say hello.

Those pictures were private. They were taken by friends— friends who knew I never wanted them displayed in this magazine—friends who were loyal to me.

Friends like Miriam. And Abe. And Dan.

The article ended with a personal note by the writer, a woman who was in high school when the bombing took place.

I remember following Janine Collins' rescue, the joy I felt when someone walked out of that terrible bombing alive. I remember thinking that in some ways, she was lucky, but in other ways, her life was ruined, and that nothing for her would ever be the same. I was not alone in my fascination.

What is perhaps most interesting are the expectations and rumors surrounding this girl. There are a lot of people who believe this girl is a symbol for faith and healing. They admire her. But because of that, there are a lot more people who are angry with Janine Collins. I met many people who think she is wasting her second chance at a meaningful life. They think she was saved for a reason and should do something important. They don't understand why she isn't living her life more fully. Of course, there are also people who are angry because they are bored with her story—they will probably complain about this entire issue. They call her shallow. Famous for nothing. They would rather hear about brave people who have sacrificed their lives.

I had plenty of mail just like this. Plenty of advice. Things like "You should be more politically active." And "You have let people down." Lo told me to throw it all away—the people usually just needed an outlet. "Forget about them," she said. "They don't know you. They have no right telling you how to live your life. Their problems aren't your concern. They forget that you were just a little girl at the wrong place and time."

Already, this issue was on the grocery store shelves. Tomorrow, the phone would probably ring all day. Every year, people wanted to know what I was doing or thinking. If I were honest, I'd agree with everything she wrote.

I didn't have a cause I cared about. I stood for nothing. This woman wrote about her memories because there was nothing else to say about me.

Maybe I was wasting my life.

I turned off the lights, lay down in bed, and called Dan. "What do you think my parents would say about me?"

He didn't have much to say. "God, Janine. What's up with you? How am I supposed to know?" When I had no clue, he sounded impatient. "What do you want me to say?" All he wanted to talk about was the Phillies. And this show he watched late last night. He didn't even seem excited about my portfolio. Of course, at the moment, neither did I.

My parents were heroes, risk-takers. They had big ideas. I didn't. They wanted to change the world. Not me. They took me to Israel to tell the world a story.

I picked up the retrospective and hurled it across the room.

Look what that got them.

THiRTEEN

No surprise, I dreamed about my mother.

But it wasn't my usual dream. I was not under the rubble. I was not fighting for my life. She didn't save me. I didn't hear her telling me anything that anyone could reinterpret later.

Tonight Mom was working. She sat at her desk with her feet up, just like she did in the picture. Today she was wearing all white. There was an arrangement of white flowers on her desk—the epitome of elegance and reverence and good taste. She also chewed the end of a pencil.

"Mom." I felt a sharp, searing cramp in both wrists—but I didn't worry. She was here. In my room. The flowers smelled great. I didn't care that it was a dream.

I also didn't complain when she wagged her finger the way Lo did when she was annoyed. "One of your friends has loose lips. All that insider information? Those pictures? They were not public property."

"I don't want to talk about that." I wanted to talk to her. My mother. Here in my room. She looked so alive, so real, it was easy to forget that she was dead. "What are you doing here? Is there something you need to tell me about today?"

I waited for her to get up and kiss me or give me some maternal lesson, but she stayed at her desk and motioned to someone behind me. I could hardly stand it—I was sure it was my dad.

It wasn't.

Instead, out stepped the old lady reporter. In my dream she wore a red skirt. A red shirt. A red jacket. Even her eyes were red. "I guess you are supposed to be the devil," I said. My mother rolled her eyes.

Journalist as devil; mother as angel. I wasn't really all that creative.

Still, I tried to focus. "Why did you bring her?"

The old lady said, "Think of this as one of those old fairy tales you used to like so much. It shouldn't be too hard. You are the orphan princess." Now she smiled at my mother.

My mom begged me to forgive her. Then she said to the devil, "Just get it over with."

The devil sat on the edge of my bed. "In that last interview you did a few years back, you said you wanted pretty hands— that you hated your scars. That your hands were what made you miserable. That if it weren't for your hands, you could live a normal life."

All these things were true. These scars, those operations— they made people crazy. They meant things to people that they didn't mean to me.

She said, "So I have a special surprise for you. Look at them." She held out her hands for a big hug. "Don't hold back. Whenever you're ready, you can thank me."

For a second, I thought I had it all wrong. She wasn't the devil; she was my fairy godmother. I examined my hands, and I couldn't believe it—they were better than perfect. My skin looked pure white. The scars vanished. I started to say something to my mother, but when I looked up, she was gone.

Something was not right.

I asked, "What is happening?" I didn't want to complain, but my hands felt funny—sort of numb. And hard. My fingers were stiff—even worse than usual. When I got up to look for my mom, my beautiful hands would not move. They didn't bend. They couldn't do anything.

I asked, "What did you do to me? Where is my mom?"

The old lady acted like everything that was happening was no big deal. "Don't make a big stink. You hated your old hands, so the devil gave you a new pair."

That's when the dream turned manic.

My hands were made of wood. I tasted dust and rock. It was hard to breathe. I looked for my mom or Lo, but I was alone. My ears rang. I needed to get out. Emir appeared, strapped to a thousand tons of dynamite. I told him, "She cut off my hands."

He grabbed my wrists hard, and those perfect hands fell to the ground. The world exploded. All I had were stubs—ugly, shriveled stubs. It took Lo an hour to get me to stop screaming.

***

In the morning, my sheets were soaked and my hands were stiff, but they were mine. As I stared into my closet, looking for the right answer to the usual question (what should I wear), Lo asked if I remembered anything.

I did. The whole thing. "But I know it was just a dream."

"You're not upset?"

"I have a weird imagination."

I pulled out a short-sleeved sweater, and we walked down the stairs to the kitchen table. Sharon was cooking eggs. She had taken down Lo's favorite teapot—a cast iron pot with a lotus flower etched into the side. Lo had three shelves' worth of pots. There were pots that looked like ovens, pots that looked like carriages, and some that were just plain weird. My favorite was the pot that looked like a vintage radio. Sharon liked the yellow ceramic Coleman's Mustard pot. Although Lo couldn't remember why she started collecting teapots, they did brighten up the room.

When I was halfway through my omelet, Miriam walked in the side door. "The word is, he's doing just fine," she announced. Right behind her was Samantha Strahan. This was not completely unexpected—Samantha walked to school with us when she didn't have lacrosse practice or soccer practice or she wasn't the lead in the play—but all things considered, it wasn't a pleasant development.

Samantha was Miriam's outside-the-tripod friend, which meant I couldn't tell her to go. She was also a senior. Miriam once told me that she respected Samantha because she took her life seriously.

"As opposed to me?" I'd asked.

Since they were here with plenty of time to spare, Lo convinced them to sit down at the table and drink tea. "Did you hear about the tree?" Samantha always spoke with precise enunciation, like she was on stage and she had to project.

"Yes," I said, putting down the mugs a little too hard. "I was with Miriam when she found out." I wasn't jealous.

Well, only a little.

Their friendship was a temporary fascination, like a crush, only slightly weird, because Samantha was a girl (which made her harder to break up with). Every time I saw Samantha, I wanted to like her—I tried to like her—I was determined to at the very least admire her—but somehow, I always failed.

There were real, logical reasons for this besides jealousy: She talked nonstop. And she pronounced every syllable—even the ones that were supposed to be silent. She mostly dressed in that non-style also known as "granola," which was really not a good look on anyone.

She was everything that writers and readers wanted me to be—the president of four clubs, star of this year's musical, a pretty decent athlete, and according to her (not to brag) a lock for co-valedictorian. No matter what was going on, she was always extra positive, which shouldn't have bugged me, except when she was around, somehow, I always came off extra negative. She was already into her first choice (Brown) early decision.

In general, when someone seemed that perfect, they never were, but in this case, Miriam was completely snowed. She thought Samantha was officially one of the most amazing, smart, interesting, and humble people she had ever met and, worse than that, she really wanted us to be friends. She said that Samantha was nervous around me. That she thought I was the amazing one. That she would give anything to be as famous as me.

That got on my nerves most of all.

I finished eating while they sipped their drinks.

"I like your top," I told Samantha. I wasn't just trying

to be nice. She wore a short-sleeved sweater covered with embroidered eyeglasses. Since she normally looked so bland, I considered it my civic duty to give her positive reinforcement.

Miriam was wearing a semi-sheer blouse. Dry Clean Only. And trendy flowered jeans.

Naturally, Lo assumed I'd forgotten something. (I was pretty sure she thought Samantha was exceptional, too.) "Why are you dressed up? Is something special going on?"

Miriam almost spit her tea. "Are you kidding me?" she asked. "You don't know?"

Lo shrugged, and I said, "No. Should I?" I hoped she wasn't talking about Abe. It couldn't be the retrospective—she wouldn't dare—and although the tree and the farm were important to them, I was pretty sure even Samantha wasn't skilled enough to put together a protest that fast. Maybe she was getting a prize from the principal.

"It's all over Facebook," she said, rubbing her hands together. "Roxanne Wheeler is coming to school. She's doing a story about Abe."

FOURTEEN

My first instinct was to laugh. This had to be a joke.

Roxanne Wheeler may not have been prime time, but her biweekly column was syndicated in fifty-seven newspapers. Every once in a while she filled in on the Philadelphia news affiliate. When she first started working for the *Morning Call*, people dubbed her "the eyes and ears of the Lehigh Valley." Lately, her articles had been a little on the fluffy side, but she was still too big for a gossipy story and James Madison High School. No matter how hard it was to come up with new material, I couldn't imagine her stooping to this.

Lo called the principal to discuss security. After ten minutes of yes, no, and "I don't think that's smart," she told me to go upstairs and relax. "We think you should stay home. Don't be a fool, Janine. That woman is ambitious. Didn't yesterday teach you anything?"

In Roxanne's official bio, she claimed her idols were Katharine Graham, who oversaw the *Washington Post*'s coverage of Watergate, and Michael Kelly, who was one of the reporters who died in Iraq. He was also famous for being a fantastic human being and tenacious reporter, as well as the editor of a writer who made up all his articles.

Roxanne grew up reading the *New York Times*, the *Post*, and *The Atlantic*, but if you asked me, her style was definitely more *People*. She was quoted as saying, "I grew up believing you had to dig for the truth. That there was always a story inside the story."

Normally, I'd be happy to take the day off. Normally, I would acknowledge Roxanne's ambition and the interest people might have in this story. After yesterday, I should have demanded it. But not today. Today was the day I'd been working toward for the last six months. It was my official portfolio day—and I didn't want to postpone it. "If she shows—which I sincerely doubt—I'll just tell her *no thank you*."

Miriam looked half-confused, half-annoyed. "I don't believe it." Her voice cracked.

"Why not?" What else should I do? I had no intention of putting my life on hold.

"Well, that's great," Samantha said. "Good for you." I was pretty sure Miriam and Samantha were kicking each other under the table. They were excited—starstruck—imagining the possibilities, no matter how unrealistic they were.

Around here, Roxanne was practically a celebrity herself. Samantha said, "It's common knowledge she's still loyal to the area. That she keeps up with all the local news." She smiled at Miriam. "Plus Abe said she was really nice. He said she seemed like the kind of person who might help us."

Miriam looked a little smug. "Last night, they talked for over two hours."

Now I felt like I had to throw up. "Two hours? Are you sure?" All hopes of sounding cool about this just went out the window. If Abe had told her he believed I healed him, Roxanne was going to be relentless.

My mother would have been, too.

Miriam told me not to be mad at Abe. "He had no choice, J. Some guy shot the whole thing on his phone. Before he said anything, Roxanne knew what happened. What did you expect him to do?"

Two hours. "I don't know." Lie? Say nothing? Stand by your friend?

Samantha went to the bathroom to check her makeup. I asked Miriam, "What else does Roxanne know?"

We talked softly. "You mean about your mom's voice? Do I look like an idiot?" She swore she'd said nothing. "Don't worry. I didn't even tell Abe. I know what that would sound like."

"Good." I sighed with relief. She was a good friend. "Thanks."

"You're welcome." She turned the hamsa so the stone was right-side up as Samantha emerged. I had to hold back surprise. Her eye makeup and lipstick were now way too dark, which was close to inexcusable. Even if she read *Glamour* only once a year, she'd know that too much mascara made your lashes look like spiders; if you insisted on heavy eyes, you should really go with gloss.

I asked, "So. You think she's going to help you with the farm?"

Samantha looked depressed, excited, and clownish at once. It was so hard to take her seriously. "She's our only hope. Last night they removed one huge branch. No one knows if they can save it." She shook her head. "I think the town's just waiting for us all to go on break so they can kill the tree and sell the land."

I often believed in conspiracy theories too, but in this case it seemed far-fetched.

Miriam turned to Lo. "What would you do?" Samantha added, "We mean, from a legal standpoint. Has anyone been successful stopping something like this?"

Lo tapped her nails on the table. "I think a smart lawyer would probably have a good chance of blocking the sale. But if the tree is dead . . ."

"The tree can't be dead." Samantha's cheeks flushed. "We can't afford a lawyer," she said. "But even if we could, everyone I know thinks we should stick with the emotional story."

Lo didn't agree. "Well, then you'd better be prepared. If an expert determines that the tree is unsafe, you are out of luck."

Samantha turned to me. "That's why we were thinking . . . Janine . . . if we had to be a spokesman of sorts . . . someone famous . . . to raise awareness . . ."

Actually. We. Someone famous. A spokesman.

This was a thinly veiled hint—an emotional ambush. (People are always trying to get me to use the time I've been "given" for something important to them.)

Even though I had no intention of saying yes, I reminded myself that Samantha was Miriam's friend—and that meant no insults. "Are you asking me to talk to Roxanne for you?"

Samantha grabbed my hands and squeezed them tight in a forcefully earnest way that might have worked on stage, but at the table seemed like overkill. "Janine, we're not stupid. We know she wants to talk to you—not us. So . . ." She paused. "So . . . if you tell her that you care about the farm—if you tell her it's important to you—then I know she will help us. And of course, we'd be forever grateful."

I had to hand it to Samantha—she definitely did not lack guts. She had thought this through. I walked across the room and opened the freezer, mostly to buy time. "I wish I could, but . . ."

"What I'm envisioning is a huge protest—a big-time referendum. The key is doing something to get a lot of attention." She spoke quickly. "That's why you're so important." She smiled. I didn't. "Do you think Dan would like to come, too?"

I was pretty sure Dan thought the farm was okay—a harmless project—but including him in the plan did not make me want to do this more. It didn't make me like her more either.

I put three cubes in my glass, then poured the rest of my tea on top. "Miriam should have told you. I don't make any statements to the press. Really, I try my best to avoid all contact with the media. Even when the cause is important."

"I did tell her." Miriam crossed her hands over her chest. She was mad. Maybe hurt. She'd done a million things for me—put up with all my issues. "It's really important to me." As if I wasn't aware. "If you could just do this . . . this one time . . . for me . . ."

I sipped my drink. Slowly. Miriam was my best friend. She hadn't told anyone about hearing my mom's voice. No one was going to get bent out of shape because I wanted to save a tree.

It would be one statement. One phone call.

I knew what she was thinking: *I would do that for you.*

Samantha handed me a piece of paper. "Not to be pushy or anything, but a person like you could make all the difference.

Here are all our issues. We can talk more at lunch. If you're nervous, I'm willing to coach you."

Her handwriting was so tiny and perfect and even, it looked like she printed it off the computer.

"I'll think about it," I said. "*After* my meeting with Ms. Browning." That tree was not more important than my future—I was pretty sure Miriam could agree to that. And my future lay in the impeccably manicured hands of Sophia Louise Browning.

Before she decided to teach, Ms. Browning had worked for a bunch of designers, including Sonia Rykiel's daughter Nathalie, which was almost as cool as knowing the Madame of French couture herself. For the last five years, if she liked your work, you got into a design school. A *good* design school.

Miriam knew how much I wanted to go to Parsons. She also knew Ms. Browning didn't want me showing anyone anything until she gave me the go-ahead. She had high standards.

Samantha thought this was hilarious. "Are you serious?" she asked. "You're a lock for Parsons. Do you really think any school with an ounce of sense is going to reject the freaking *Soul Survivor*? You could buy your portfolio at Fashion Bug and they'd take you."

***

As we walked to school, she acted like the worst day of my life had handed me a multitude of perks and possibilities—a million great advantages. "Even though what happened to you is really sad, you have to admit, you have it made. You are famous. There's no way any school wouldn't want you. You can do and say whatever you want. People will always listen."

"And you think that's good?"

"I think it's great." Samantha told me I was lucky. "You're an icon. People know you by name. Any time you want, you can make your mark on the world." She talked with her hands. "If you see something you don't like—like losing the farm—you aren't stuck. You can say what you think. And people will listen. You know they will. You don't have to work to get attention."

Well, that last part was true.

Two blocks later, we saw the caution tape blocking the entrance to the farm. I almost smiled (out of spite) until I saw the tree. One branch lay on the ground. Another one stuck out at an odd angle. Men in hard hats walked around, taking pictures and measurements and shaking their heads. Anyone could see they didn't look optimistic.

Personally, I couldn't decide if the tree looked proud or stubborn—if it was just lopsided and sturdy or lopsided and vulnerable. This was the problem with physical deformities. It was impossible not to stare at the open wound, the splintered white middle, just like it was hard not to look at the scars on my hands. The missing branch changed the entire balance of the tree. Just like my hands—which were ugly but still (mostly) worked. The tree might be fine. Just less attractive. Or, as Lo would say, more interesting. "Different." That's how she described my hands when I felt sorry for myself.

Samantha rubbed her eyes—like we were supposed to believe she was near tears. "Now do you see why we need you?"

I just wasn't sure anyone would care. "I don't see how we're going to stop them. Especially if they cut down the tree."

Samantha believed in the power of people and the ballot. Before they could sell the land, the planning board would have to make an official statement. The board of supervisors would vote. And that would go on their public records. If they thought enough people were against the sale—if they thought people wouldn't vote for them in the next election—maybe they'd stop it.

She said, "People will listen to you. They'll pay attention."

It sounded like a long shot.

But the more they talked, the more excited they got. The tree was not dead. They were not about to chop it down. And if there was any chance it could be saved, there was no reason to sell this land. I thought: I liked happy endings, too, but the truth was the college had made a good offer. The tree looked bad. Maybe it was tired. Maybe it was sick. Maybe it didn't mind dying.

Maybe the new farm would be beautiful.

***

When we arrived at school, I looked for the cameras, for adults dressed up to look like students. I checked the flagpole, the picnic table, the path by the parking lot. I looked inside the gazebo, where the most popular girls in school usually hung out. There were a lot of people in nice clothes practicing their made-for-TV poses and statements, but there was no sign of Roxanne or, for that matter, any other reporter or photographer. Samantha looked disappointed. She would never specifically blame me, but she acted like it was the end of the world. Miriam said, "The one time we want the press to show up, they ignore us."

It was ironic. "Don't worry," I said. They always showed up when there was a story. That was the job.

My mother once wrote that the fun was in the chase, but she was the chaser. For the chasee, the rules are different. Waiting to be bombarded by reporters was torture. Actually, waiting for anything wasn't all that great. And I was pretty sure that chasing after me was a pretty sorry assignment.

The bell rang. I started for the door. If Roxanne Wheeler wanted to talk, I wished she would just show up. These questions weren't tough ones. Once she knew that, she could go back to Philadelphia and chase after some real story.

FIFTEEN

First hour, school resembled a hectic press conference.

"How is he?"

"What was it like?"

"When do you think they're going to release him?"

Abe was a good guy. Unlike me, he had lots of friends outside the tripod. These people might stand a little too close, but their questions weren't inappropriate. Miriam thought it was a lot of fun being the center of attention. She answered every single question. She said, "I feel like a movie star. Everyone wants to talk to me."

Second hour, Miriam was still smiling, but I was tired. The questions began to cross the line.

"Did you think he was dead?"

"Did you do CPR?"

"What was the first thing he said when he woke up?"

"I heard you were going to be on *Late Night* tonight."

I had a hard time keeping my temper and paranoia in check. "It was scary. No, I didn't have to. When he woke up, I was in the parking lot. Are you serious? I wish. I would kill to be on *Late Night*."

Dan looked like he wanted to hit someone. "You must be ready to scream. These people keep asking me to give you the retrospective to sign. It's really annoying."

"Tell me about it." I didn't care how selfish people found me, how much they thought the retrospective with my signature would be worth. Once you signed one, you had to sign them all. Once you gave in, you could never go back.

He walked me down the hall. "I don't know how you deal with it."

The cover of the retrospective was taped to my locker, complete with long curly-cue mustache. Dan let me know that some of Samantha's friends had accused me of orchestrating the entire thing. "I explained that you didn't, but they think you can't stand it when people talk about anyone but you." It wasn't a whole lot different from a cable-news cycle. From story to commentary to, hopefully, something new—right here at school.

By the time I got to the art room for my critique, I was wiped. My charming had completely run dry. I wished people would ask me questions with simple, straightforward answers, like what's your favorite color? What do you want to be when you grow up? Do you like cats or dogs?

Ms. Browning closed the door behind me. "How's Abe?" she asked, reaching out to hold my hands. "I've been so concerned."

I let her touch me. "Actually, he's doing really great. He's going to make a full recovery." A question with an answer. What a relief.

We sat in the center of the room, surrounded by empty easels and half-finished portraits. "That's great to hear. He's a lucky kid." Ms. Browning loved a kid with a great joie de vivre. "Do you want to table this for tomorrow?"

"No," I said. "Let's do this now. I lugged everything in. I can't wait to hear what you think." She was one of the few people I trusted; I could be completely honest with her.

I spread out my sketches on the tables and hung up the finished pieces on easels. I've had three years' worth of classes in this room, from general design to painting to jewelry to independent study. I knew what Ms. Browning liked; I knew what she hated.

"Let's see what you've got." She stopped at each sketch. She paused a few times. But mostly, she said nothing.

At least I thought I knew.

Then we examined my finished work. Three dresses. One pair of pants. A jacket. And a wool coat. She didn't ask about the brown dress, even though she knew I'd been trying to finish it.

"So?"

"So." She looked at me with the kind of earnestness that preceded bad news. "You've made a good start." My portfolio looked "fine." But there was no rush to show it off.

In the world of art, "fine" was a death sentence. Rushing off was what I thought we were after.

I started to gather up the sketches. "I'm disappointed. I thought you'd be more enthusiastic."

She stopped me, told me not to be hasty. "Maybe I'm being a bit harsh, but I think—if you really want to wow them— you have to show more. You just can't underestimate the competition for these slots." She showed me a few examples

95

of sketches that just missed the mark, as well as a few places where my sewing looked sloppy, where the lines didn't look right. "Your work is solid. When you take your time, you have good construction skills. But what I don't see here is anything innovative or different or . . ." she paused, "*authentic*. I don't see anything that I would definitely say comes from you." For about the fiftieth time, she gave me the "great artists" speech. She thought that the masters responded to the world they lived in, and there was no sense of my world in this work. "You have such a unique point of view. Give yourself time. Put more of yourself—your heart—your emotion—in this work. Challenge yourself to take some risks. Show me what you can do."

I thought I did all that. I said, "This is what I can do." And "I thought you said that visiting in the spring would be best."

She told me to pack everything up. "Why don't you take some time and come back when you have something new?" She walked me to the door. "Trust me, Janine. There is no rush showing this off."

***

At lunch, I replayed the whole thing with Dan. "She basically canned every single piece."

He put one hand on my thigh, well past the critical radius. I pushed it off.

He put it back on and squeezed a tiny bit too tight. "No need to be snippy." With his free hand, he motioned to a brown paper bag on his tray. When I opened the top, steam escaped. It smelled like french-fry oil. He smiled, so I could see his dimples. "I got these for you."

Tater tots. My favorite. Perfect for victories. Essential in defeat. Now I felt bad. I popped two in my mouth, but they were so hot I had to spit them onto the tray.

Dan slid his hand down to my knee. A safe place. "You can't tell me Ms. Browning didn't eat up that brown dress. That thing was a total *do*."

Out of the periphery of my eye, I watched Samantha and Miriam walk into the cafeteria. They stopped to talk to the local Young Life advisors, who always hung out at the cafeteria during lunch. They seemed nice enough, but naturally, I stayed as far away from them as I could. They made me really uncomfortable. Too smiley. Too friendly. Officially, they were educational assistants, but every Tuesday night they held a prayer meeting at their home.

Everyone was invited.

Maybe Miriam was just telling them to go visit Abe.

As Dan talked on and on about the amazing brown dress, they fluttered from table to table, handing out pieces of green paper that I was sure were flyers. Finally, I couldn't take it anymore. "It no longer exists," I said, looking away from them back to Dan. "I wrecked it."

He spit a big wad of tater tot debris across his tray. "Sorry."

"Ew."

He cleaned up the mess. "You did not."

I shrugged. "You were the one who told me that I could do better."

"But I didn't tell you to *destroy* it." He acted like it was the greatest thing I ever made. "Do you want that picture I took? I think I still have it. If you want to, you could remake it."

I didn't think Ms. Browning even paused at the sketch. "I think I'd rather make something else."

He pumped his fist like a jock. "Like the dress you dedicated to your mom?"

I dipped a carrot into ranch dressing and chomped down on the inside of my mouth. "Don't get too excited." I tasted blood. "It's just an idea. I don't know how I'm going to pull it off."

He said, "I know you'll figure it out."

I wasn't so confident. Making a dress to honor my parents would say something about me—something personal and private and scary. And right now, I wasn't sure how to do that.

All I knew was, I didn't want to talk about it in front of Samantha.

"I hope we're not interrupting," she said, snatching the tater tots right off my tray. She popped one in her mouth and sat down opposite Dan. I couldn't help noticing her lip color was now neutral.

Miriam sat down across from me. "What a day. I am so frustrated."

Three things happened (There was no need to ask. Samantha explained everything in excruciating detail even with her mouth full.)

One: The tree was officially, definitely still alive. I thought this was good news, but according to some botanist that Samantha had magically spoken to, it needed a lot of help, so it wasn't.

Two: Mounting a protest was not something even Samantha Strahan could plan in an hour. She needed a boost. Some momentum. If Roxanne was out of the picture, she asked me while winking at Dan, "Whom can we contact?" (Yes. She actually used the word *whom*.)

Three: The farm was still roped off, so they couldn't get in and do anything. "It's a conspiracy," she insisted in a very serious, dramatic voice, "to keep us away."

I said, "The tree *was* hit by lightning."

Miriam glared at me. "It doesn't really matter where we meet. We have to talk. In privacy. So, we're going to my house after school. Can you come?"

I looked at Dan. He looked at me. We didn't have plans. Neither of us was very good at coming up with a lie when we needed one.

He said, "We'll try."

"Excellent." Samantha took another tot. I ate two more carrots, then jogged back to the line to buy an extra-large bag of potato chips. And a chocolate bar. And one of those pre-made strawberry banana smoothies—the cafeteria ladies' favorite healthy choice. Of course, the seeds got stuck between my teeth.

I didn't want to go. It wasn't just Samantha and the way she picked her teeth when she thought no one was looking. I wasn't sure I agreed with them. I definitely didn't want to protest. I thought they should let the tree live or die and then go from there.

Miriam wouldn't understand that. "Don't you think we should go visit Abe?" I asked.

I was pretty sure there was nothing I could say that wouldn't annoy Miriam. "We're going to visit him." She pulled out her phone. "Why don't you learn to check your messages? He's been texting us every hour on the hour."

She handed me hers, so I could see what I'd missed. Big news! Able to walk across the room with one crutch. And Can you bring me some ice cream? And You are not going to believe who just visited me!

"So, who was it?" I asked, fingers crossed that it wasn't anyone bigger than Roxanne.

She couldn't remember the guy's name. "Some player from the Eagles. He gave Abe a photo and a signed football and tickets to a game." She rolled her eyes. "You would think it was the greatest thing that ever happened to him."

"It is pretty cool," Dan said. He liked the Eagles. And the Phillies. But not the 76ers. He explained this to me once, but now I couldn't remember why.

"Actually, it's totally not cool," Samantha said. "He didn't mention the farm. Not even once. Some friend he is! Doesn't he understand that his kind of fame is *always* short-lived?"

As she ranted about Abe, Roxanne, the board of supervisors, and the stupidity of people who were not her, I reached for my hamsa and wished for her to stop talking, so I could get out of this chair and out of this room. Dan squeezed my thigh. He was either thinking the same thing or he was just frisky.

When my phone vibrated, Samantha finally shut up. I looked at the number. "I don't know who this is," I said.

"It could be Roxanne," she said, practically jumping over the table.

I cursed my phone. The vibration mode was supposed to be silent, but it was loud enough to hear over the noise in the room. "I doubt it," I said. I picked up my backpack and got up to leave.

Miriam half-waved. "Don't forget about the meeting."

Samantha practically shouted, "Remember, we need you. Roxanne is our only hope. If you hear from her, don't forget . . ."

I walked to class, trying to convince myself that the worst was over. This story was dying—that was clear. Because if it had had legs, Roxanne and a whole bunch of other reporters would've shown up by now. Photographers would be peeking in the windows. My phone would be ringing off the hook—and it wouldn't be just Abe telling me to call him. One thing I was sure of: if nothing else happened, by the time Abe was released, no one would remember why he wasn't in school. There would be no new story. No rumors. No more questions. Tomorrow might be an ordinary day.

I sighed. It would be so nice to be completely anonymous.

As I got through my classes and nothing else happened, I relaxed. Maybe I'd worried for nothing. Maybe I wasn't that important after all.

SIXTEEN

At the end of the day, Dan met me at my locker. "Hey, J," he said, making a point to kiss me hard and long on the lips.

"Not in public, thanks." I pulled away. He laughed. This was just a location rejection. He knew I liked kissing him—I just wasn't into PDA. It was too messy. Too public. I never understood why anyone thought making out at your locker was a fun thing to do. I didn't even like holding hands.

It was the principle of the thing. Kissing was a private matter. But I also couldn't risk it. Stupider pictures of lesser-known people had found their way into magazines. There wasn't much about the press I could control, but this was easy. I didn't want to read about my love life in some rag.

Usually, Dan appreciated that.

Big picture, there was only one exception to the no PDA rule, and that was when someone else was publicly after your guy. Or if that same guy was acting suspicious or weird. Then, I agreed with *Glamour* readers, who in a nationwide poll suggested that the best way to find out if your boyfriend was about to break up with you (or lying about something big) was to engage in a little old-fashioned PDA.

The more public the better.

According to readers, it worked every time. A guy with a secret never kissed you in public.

When Dan draped his arm over my shoulder, I wondered if he'd heard about that theory, too. "Cut it out," I said as nicely as possible. "I'm distracted. It's been a crappy day. I need some space."

Now Dan dropped his shoulders and pouted, so that he looked simultaneously pathetic and cute. "Okay. I hear you. Let's get out of here. So we can be alone." But then he kissed my ear. He kissed it lightly so it tickled. That made me squirm.

I was still thinking about Ms. Browning's critique. "She didn't even like my sewing. She told me I have to work slower."

"You can do that." He picked up my backpack and flung it over his shoulder. "There's this really cool spot I want to show you. I think you'll like it." He smiled. "It's very romantic."

Now I understood. Unfortunately for him, I was not in the mood for that either. "Can you show me some other time?" I asked in my cutest I-still-like-you, I-just-don't-feel-like-being-serious voice. "I have a ton of sketching to do. I really should visit Abe. What do you think she meant by authentic?"

Normally, Dan liked talking about clothes. In terms of together time, we were pretty much on the same page. But today, he made a very cute pouty lip. "Can you relax and let me show you? I just want to talk for a few minutes. It won't take long." When I didn't say no (or yes), he held out his hand.

I initiated twenty questions. "Animal, mineral, vegetable? Is it bigger than a breadbox?" When I couldn't get him to tell me anything, I asked, "Did you sell me out to some magazine? Are you setting me up for an ambush?"

"God, are you paranoid."

"Not really." I was half-joking. If he watched any reality TV, he would keep his mouth shut. Most people would do anything for name recognition like mine.

"It's just that . . . well . . . you are so self-centered about it." He held the steering wheel with both hands. He drove past the deserted steel factory and a sign marked Dead End to the alleged cool spot, a gravel dead-end road overlooking the river.

I was not impressed.

I leaned as far away from him as I could. "Do you really think I should make the tribute dress? Or go back to the brown? What do you think she meant by authentic?" As I waited for him to answer, my phone vibrated. I pulled it out of my pocket, just to see who it was. Dan tickled my shoulder. "Don't pick it up. For one minute, I want you all to myself."

He never talked like this. "It's just Abe." I showed Dan the text: CALL ME NOW!!! I waited for him to laugh.

Dan had a personal policy against messages in all capital letters and he hated exclamation points. He said, "That guy has a thing for you." He sounded jealous.

"He's just bored." I hid my phone, so he couldn't see that Abe had left seven messages in the last eight minutes.

We were so out of sync.

Dan turned on the heated seats and the light radio station that perpetually played love songs by people who are now dead. He pointed out a tree that he thought was really beautiful— and almost as old as Miriam's tree. I counted six discarded tires on the opposite bank. He noticed baby ducks swimming in a row. I saw a garbage can overflowing with Happy Meals and beer cans.

He whispered, "The other night we came so close."

I looked away. There was no way I was doing it in this car.

"You know, I liked you for almost an entire year before I asked you out." He told me that even if I didn't save Abe's life, he thought I was pretty miraculous. Then he stroked my hair. "You're so pretty."

I shifted into the corner when he tried to kiss me. My phone buzzed. I didn't even flinch.

He pulled me closer and said everything he'd learned girls needed to hear. "What I wanted to tell you . . . I think we're really good together" and "I really care about you" and "You're really awesome."

Sad to say, he could have said anything—I couldn't concentrate. The car wasn't comfortable; I wasn't in the mood for some big conversation.

"You're not listening."

"Yes I am."

"No you're not."

My phone buzzed again. Nothing was ever mutual.

He held my hands. "I brought you here because I wanted to ask you something."

I lost my patience. I didn't know what he was about to say, but whatever it was, it wasn't working. I was tired. My phone buzzed again. I wanted to see who was calling. I wasn't going to lose it in a parking lot in the middle of the day.

I was pretty sure my body language was making that clear. But maybe it wasn't. I pulled my hands away. "I'm really not in the mood. Okay?"

He leaned away from me. Finally. "What are you talking about?" He looked clueless.

"I don't want to have sex with you here. I want to go back to work."

He slumped. Then glared. For a second, I wondered if I had it all wrong, if this was not about sex, if it was about something else altogether. So I said, "Isn't that where this was going?"

Dan stared out the front window, the way Lo did when she was completely irritated and needed to count to ten. "No. That is not what's going on."

Now I felt like an idiot. I asked him to face me. To tell me what he wanted to say.

"It's too late." He was hurt.

"No, it isn't," I said. "I'm listening. Now I'm listening. I'm really really listening."

He kept his eyes forward. Now he wasn't talking. He turned on the ignition and stepped on the gas. "Just forget I ever wanted to say anything. I'll take you home. So you can work. So you can worry about yourself."

He was hurt and mad. I still had no idea why.

If I weren't in such a morose mood, I'd tell him to stop. But since I was now feeling crappy and guilty, I said nothing. I let him drive. I turned on the all-talk station. (It was really hard sitting in a car in total silence.)

Crime and poverty were up. A well-known celebrity just adopted a baby from Haiti, and a bunch of people thought she did it just to keep her figure. The Pennsylvania teen had made it to the next round of some station's most-desperate-to-be-on-television/willing-to-make-an-ass-of-yourself competition. *Don't forget to vote, everyone. Charlene is counting on you!*

I tried to apologize. "I'm a jerk," I said. "You're right. I'm selfish." He didn't disagree. "Please tell me what you were going to say."

He drove in silence.

When we were two miles from my house, I swallowed every ounce of pride I had left. "Come on, Dan. I'm sorry. I mean it."

He might have softened up if my phone hadn't vibrated again. But it did. Twice. Dan said, "Tell Abe I said hi."

I opened my purse. It was Lo. "What's up?" I asked.

She sounded more upset than Dan. "Do you have plans? Can you go somewhere for a while?"

I looked at Dan. "Not really. I'm almost home. What's going on?"

Before she could explain, we pulled up to the house. There were at least thirty people hanging around. Some sat on the grass. Some stood. Others sat on the stone wall by the garage.

I didn't have to ask what the fuss is about.

Dave Armstrong was here. I would recognize his thick white hair anywhere. He stood on the driveway, his arms above his head, reaching up to the heavens.

He was waiting for me.

SEVENTEEN

He looked like an aging movie star.

His hair was short. His clothes were pressed. His cordovan shoes shone without looking cheap. He wore a dark navy suit, wine-colored tie, and kimono-cloth pocket square—a color palette Dan and I had admired in last month's issue of *GQ*. This was a guy who knew what looked good. He was comfortable in front of a camera.

For a second, Dan forgot that he hated me. He said, "Look at that suit. Brioni? Or maybe something Neapolitan. Look at the soft shoulder—"

I shook my head. "The man is a preacher. He's supposed to look pious."

Dan told me to lighten up. "And because he's religious, he's supposed to dress like a slob?"

I didn't really have a problem with Dave dressing well. In fact, if it were up to me, everyone in the universe would care more about his or her appearance. It was just that Dave's motives were so transparent. He was playing to the camera.

Even though he shook hands in a friendly way and talked to people and acted like this was all about faith, he never stopped smiling. He always stood with his better side to the camera.

"Hey, look who I see," Dan said pointing to a small crowd of people. "I thought he was supposed to be in the hospital."

It was Abe. "He shouldn't be here." I couldn't believe they let him out. He looked terrible.

His left leg was in a bright red and orange cast—the same colors as Dunkin' Donuts—and his left arm was bandaged up, too. You didn't need to be a doctor to see he was in a lot of pain. He didn't look stable.

I almost felt sorry for him, until I realized whom he was talking to. She was a woman in a gray skirt suit. She had long, dirty blonde hair tied back in a sleek ponytail. It was Roxanne Wheeler. She was here.

This was my nightmare. It was the worst thing that could possibly happen. (At the same time, I knew I shouldn't have been completely surprised.)

I took out my phone, and even though it was not easy to do, I texted Abe. "Look up." And also: "Don't say anything."

Twenty seconds later, we watched him pull out his phone, read my messages, and start hobbling toward us. It was painful to watch. His face was bruised under both eyes. He walked slowly.

"Would it kill you to help him?" I asked.

Dan didn't move. "Why don't you?" He half-laughed—it was a little bit catty. He knew I wouldn't. My lawn was a mob scene. Too many people. Way too many cameras. There was no way I was getting out of this car until all these people were gone—I didn't care how mad Dan was.

By the time Abe made it to the car, he was sweating like crazy. I opened the door. "Get in."

He was out of breath. "Give me a sec." He reminded us he had a fractured fibula, six broken ribs, seven bad contusions, and a dislocated elbow. He threw his crutches into the back seat, fell in, and moaned in pain.

He smelled sour—like old milk or a dirty sponge. Dan said, "You're not going to have a heart attack in my car, are you?"

At that moment, I wasn't sure which one of them made me madder. First, I told Dan to shut up. Then I turned to Abe. "I can't believe you sold me out. Don't think I don't know that you spent two hours with Roxanne Wheeler. But Dave. That was low."

He had the nerve to look offended. "I did not sell you out. I didn't tell her anything." He took a couple of deep breaths. "Check your phone. I must have called you a hundred times." He wiped his sweaty hands on his pants. "You should be thanking me. I came here to stop them."

He refused to say another word until I read or listened to every single message, until I felt like a total jerk, until it was clear that Roxanne camped out first, followed by Dave and the believers. Then, last, Abe.

His face looked feverish. "When you didn't call me back, what else was I supposed to do?"

I didn't feel the need to thank him. "So tell me everything. Where did all these people come from? Has Lo come outside? Have the police been here?" Her car was still here—so she should be, too.

Dan half-laughed again. "Sharon is going to have a conniption."

Abe said, "The people are from Dave's mission. They're actually nice." As for Lo, she hadn't shown her face—and he'd been here over an hour. I rolled my eyes. He winced in pain. "You know, J, you could act a little appreciative. I discharged myself against medical advice. Believe me—I'd rather be in bed."

I told him to elevate his leg. His toes looked swollen. Blue.

On the porch, Mrs. Demetrius started singing a song about the power and grace of God. Her red-and-orange dress flapped like a sail in the wind. A few people from the crowd joined in. Soon they were clapping and swaying. The cameramen loved it. They ran around getting close-ups of almost every person.

I didn't know what to do.

I couldn't stay here. I didn't want to open the door. I definitely did not want to face these people.

When the song ended, Dave turned up the volume and offered some gospel passage about the meaning of life. Every time he paused, someone shouted, "Amen." Or "Praise the Lord." A couple of shirtless guys ran in front of the cameras, hoping that this was live TV. One pulled down his pants.

Now I was scared. "Dan, I'm sorry. I mean it. I'm really, really sorry. Let's get out of here. I didn't know what I was saying."

"Yes you did. I get it." He opened his wallet and took out the picture of the two of us from one of those cramped photo booths and ripped it in four pieces.

We were breaking up.

He said, "Now get out of here. You shouldn't keep *your fans* waiting."

In the rearview mirror, I could see Abe cringe. Apparently, even with all his injuries, our awkwardness was what pained him.

Roxanne pointed her microphone toward the car and grabbed one of the cameramen. She strutted in her black patent-leather pumps without stumbling or getting those spiky heels caked with mud. I slumped in the seat when Roxanne rapped on the window. Her nails looked like daggers.

This was turning into a disaster. "Look, Dan. You have to believe me. I'm sorry. I mean it. Let's get out of here." Dan was a good guy. We liked the same things. He had my lip gloss, my denim jacket, and three library books that were due next week. We'd been dating too long to end like this. He knew I never cared or wanted anything to do with my *fans*.

Roxanne rapped on the window again. "Janine Collins? Can I ask you a few questions?"

The cameras rolled. I covered my face. Dan said, "No, J. I mean it. Get out of here. Now."

This couldn't be happening. I turned around to face Abe. "Can you get them to back off?"

Abe opened the door, said something to Roxanne and *thank God*, twenty seconds later, she motioned to her guys and walked back to the porch to talk to Armstrong. I got out of the car and faced the crowd. And just like the water in the Bible, the sea of people parted.

EIghTEEN

Up close, the believers looked like regular people.

The truth was a lot of them were. I recognized some of them: the lady from the library desk, the butcher Lo went to, the guy from the mini-mart who always gave me a mini peppermint patty—on the house. If I ran into any of them anywhere but here, I'd say hello.

I never pegged them for zealots. Maybe they were just here to get on TV.

"Hi Janine," my eighth-grade math teacher said. "We've been waiting for you."

Someone with a stump for an arm said, "*Humanity* has been waiting for you."

There was a guy without a leg, one with no legs at all, and a girl with massive scars on the entire left side of her face. There were six people with walkers, five more in wheelchairs. One of them looked like he was my age. I tried as hard as I could to focus on the door, the tree, the window—anything but his smiling, eager face—but it was hard not to stare back. The guy was looking at me. They were all looking at me. They wanted me to look at them. I could feel it.

They all wanted something from me that I couldn't give.

It didn't matter. Every step, their hands reached out to me; they touched me; they asked me, please, to touch them back. They told me their troubles. One man told me he was in severe pain. Someone else was sick. Pretty soon there were requests and cries and hands all over me—on my face, my clothes, my arms, shoulders and legs.

"Please don't touch me," I said. It was overwhelming, intense, scary. I wanted to scream for help. I wanted all of them to back off. "Please give me space."

I needed air.

Now.

The boy in the wheelchair—the one who smiled at me—he had a really cute dimple—rolled forward and shouted, "Back away." He also had big shoulders and arms. Nice hair, too. In a flirty sort of way, he balanced on his back tires. I felt sort of nasty even noticing. This wasn't a party. He wasn't here to ask me out. But if we had been at a party, I might have said yes. That's how cute he was.

A lady in a vintage preppy pink cardigan and kelly-green skirt stood next to him. "My son was not born in this chair. He shouldn't have to live the rest of his life this way." He looked a little embarrassed, the way I did when Lo offered her yoga wisdom to my friends.

I looked at him—not her. "You're right. He shouldn't. Nobody should."

It really was a shame. He had such a sweet smile. And really green eyes, too. The way he looked at me, I could almost shut out everyone else here. When he held out his hands, I forgot to pull mine back. Our fingers almost touched. "Will you bless me?" he asked, not moving his fingers. "Will you give me a chance to heal?"

I froze.

There were a hundred people and twenty cameras. They were all staring. It was absolutely silent.

I couldn't heal him.

But I couldn't move either.

Before I could figure out what to say, he lunged forward and grabbed my hands. He had a tight grip. A few people gasped.

I stumbled forward, and the hamsa dangled in the air between us. "I'm sorry you can't walk."

His hands were sweaty and hot. He didn't let go. "Just you watch," he said. "Someday, I'm going to. Someday, I'm going to be strong enough to get out of this chair." He sounded just like a wounded soldier or an athlete when they were getting carted off the field. Thumbs up. All optimism. He was the kind of guy who probably made others feel good about humanity.

He was also strong. I tried to pull away, but he would not let go. I couldn't move. I couldn't get away. This was making me really uncomfortable.

My hands were burning.

I should have worn something with pockets. I should *always* have pockets. I should make a mental note to never ever go outside again the rest of my life without pockets.

Even when he closed his eyes and started praying, I couldn't squirm away.

I looked for someone to help me, but every single one of them had their eyes shut. They were smiling, too, like it was a beautiful day and everything was possible. It made me feel left out. Even here, surrounded by people as unlucky as me, I was still alone. I was still the different one. I couldn't close my eyes without seeing the things I never wanted to see again.

He squeezed my hands one more time and asked *me* for strength. Then he let go. "Thank you," he said. His eyes were hopeful.

The whole thing made me feel terrible. This kid was probably no older than me. How did these people believe in a God that would do this to him? Why did he believe that the same God that made him paralyzed still cared? How could all these people continue to pray and hope and close their eyes and smile?

I turned away and started walking through the crowd, but now more hands smothered me. I opened my mouth to breathe or scream, but my throat was closing fast—my hands prickled, like when you slept the wrong way. I dropped to my knees. No one backed off. I was back in the synagogue, and the boy was covered in bombs. No one noticed that I couldn't move or get up—that I was dying here—right in front of all these people.

Except for Dave.

He heard me. He knew.

He told them to back off, and he pushed through the crowd. By the time he was standing over me, I was gasping for air; my hands burned. He picked me up and held me like he did ten years ago. He told the group in a very loud voice, "Janine Collins is here. Please greet her with love. And faith. And compassion. Welcome her. I know you are all anxious, but for now, let her relax. We want her to feel safe. We want her to come to us when she is ready, so that we can all pray together."

When he put me down, people surrounded me. They said, "Amen." Others rocked back and forth. One girl pointed at me. "Look at how the light reflects off of her." When I passed by, they all bowed their heads.

From the center of the crowd, Dave Armstrong exalted the power of God. "We are your servants," he shouted. "Deliver us!"

The front door flew open.

Lo stepped onto the porch. She pushed her way through the crowd and grabbed me hard by the arm. "Go inside," she told me, shoving me with enough force that I almost fell into a girl about my age. "Now," Lo said. She glared at Dave.

He embraced her like they were old friends. "Leora. I tried to call you, but . . . "

"Let go of me," she said.

As I pushed my way toward the house, past the girl and an old woman with two black teeth, Roxanne shoved her business card into my hand. "It's a pleasure to meet you. Abe told me so much about you. He's lucky you two are friends."

I said, "I'm not interested in making a statement."

She said, "That's your prerogative."

That was a lie. This wasn't my decision. I no longer had a choice. She was never going to let this drop. She had a story, maybe even a big one. My mother would have done exactly the same thing.

NINETEEN

Lo slammed the door. She drew the curtains. She yelled at Sharon to get away from the window. "Stop staring at them. That's just what they want."

Sharon didn't think it was safe to turn our backs. "Leora, please. Let me call the police. You really don't have any idea what these people might do."

Lo would not agree. "I don't want to make a scene." She dropped to the floor into *savasanah*, the corpse pose, as if that would make everyone disappear.

It was almost funny. I said, "Lo, get up. It's already a scene."

She didn't laugh. "The last thing we need," she said, still not moving, "is Roxanne Wheeler or anyone else telling the world that I had a bunch of God-fearing people hauled off and arrested. Trust me. Then we'll have a scene."

She closed her eyes while, outside, Dave began a call and response. To drown them out, I turned on the TV. Unfortunately, it was the worst hour on the schedule, the time when the stations resort to reruns of *Housewives*, game shows, or messed-up people telling their secrets to the world. Weekday afternoons were about full disclosure and airing your dirty laundry; there was no market for privacy.

On one show, a mom bragged that she gave her fourteen-year-old son condoms—so he would be prepared—and the entire audience applauded. They thought she was being smart. Proactive. On the next channel, a former child star sat on a red couch talking about the recent death of her sister. Breast cancer. The doctor said it was one of the number-one killers of women. Sharon tried to remember the woman's name but couldn't. "I remember that girl. She was always so cute. I saw her movies a hundred times." Now her mascara was too thick. Her skirt was way too short for the talk show camera angles, so as it rode up her thigh, she had to sit with her legs crossed and her arms glued to the bottom of her hem. I didn't understand why this woman had to share all these personal details about her family. She wasn't running an organization for better access to mammograms. She was just talking . . . to get on TV.

"The tragedy reinforced my belief in God," she said, smiling warmly at the strangers in the audience. Her voice definitely sounded coached. It was raspy and low, and she breathed deeply after all the important thoughts. "Her death made me realize that I cannot control everything around me. Thank God I have my faith. I do my best work when I take time to know God. Every night, I hear her talk to me. She is at peace." Then she mentioned her newest project. Wild applause and a short clip of the new show followed. Studio audiences loved it when people shared their private business with the world. They loved it even more when lemons became lemonade.

"Is it just me, or is the entire world talking about God?" Politicians. Actresses. Sports heroes. Former pilots. "Since when did religion become news?"

"It's always been this way," Lo said, "at least since 9/11." She rolled onto her stomach and pushed up into a cobra pose. After twenty seconds of deep breath, she sat back and rested on her knees. I flipped the channels, in search of anything inoffensive, entertaining, or objective. No sports. No talk shows. No self-improvement. Lo said, "If it upsets you, turn it off."

I settled on a rerun of *The Simpsons*. "It's not upsetting— I'm just sick of it. I don't get why people get so wrapped up in telling people what they believe—why anyone cares." Faith wasn't news. It was a personal topic. It should stay private, not public, and that actress should have stayed home and taken care of herself. She shouldn't want to risk being known as a person who used her sister's cancer to maker herself more famous.

I turned off the TV.

I wanted quiet. But I didn't get it.

Now there was nothing to drown out the Dave Show outside. He said into his microphone, "I'm here today to tell you: I don't believe in coincidences. Ten years ago, I was not just in the right place at the right time. God had a plan for me. And today, that continues. I knew it then, and I still know it now."

I stood at the window. He looked and sounded like one of those bad fortune-tellers that come every year to the annual fair. They ran their fingers over your palm and told you how successful you were going to be. As he talked, I tried to get Abe's attention. He was standing by himself—his parents were standing closer to Dave, where there was nothing to lean on.

Abe needed the rail, a step from the front porch. About four feet away. I took my chance.

I rapped on the window until Abe turned around. "Come in. Now. I'm not mad."

It was a lie, but I was worried. He looked sick, and when he came inside, I could see his toes were blue and swollen. I grabbed him by the good arm and helped him to the closest chair.

Lo grabbed a bag full of ice. "Put your leg up. Or do you want us to take you back to the hospital?"

He scooted his chair next to the window. "If you don't mind, I really want to hear what Emma has to say."

"Who's Emma?"

"This girl who belongs to Dave's congregation. She came with him to visit me." I pinched his arm on a purple spot, just to remind him how annoyed I still was. He didn't flinch. "You have to meet her. Everything she says makes sense."

I looked at the girl he was pointing to. She stood next to Dave and wore silly saggy pants, an oversized sweatshirt, and a big floral scarf tied around her head and chin. She looked like she came from another time. Or planet. "You're kidding me, right?"

He wasn't kidding. "Just wait. Her philosophy about faith is very challenging. As soon as Dave finishes up and the press leaves, she'll have something to say."

I was a skeptic. "She has a 'philosophy.' How impressive."

Abe did not appreciate my sarcasm. "Janine, before you make fun of her, you should try listening to what she has to say. Her story might change how you see things." He said, "In a lot of ways you are alike. She doesn't like publicity either. She says she doesn't want the story to ever be about her. She wants the cause to be the star."

I laughed. "I guess Dave's good with that."

It took a while, but after the crowd thinned out, Dave introduced her. He called her "his good luck charm" as well as "an angel sent from heaven."

I was a little disappointed (but not totally surprised) when she said absolutely nothing I hadn't heard a million times before. How God was with us when we needed help—that we needed to not be afraid to access our own spiritual strength. The whole thing was as rehearsed and fake as the talk shows on TV and even more woo-woo than Lo's yoga pals, but Abe was impressed. The believers totally bought it. They said "Amen" and "That's right." When she said that we all needed to accept the bad with the good, that faith and God were most important when we were suffering, that we should be humble and not conceited, Dave picked her off the ground and embraced her like she was God's gift to the religious universe.

"You think she's amazing?"

"Yes."

"No." I told Abe to close the window. I had never bought into the holy sufferer routine before, and I wasn't about to start now. "She'd be more convincing if she wore something that fit."

He never understood why clothes were so important to me. "Emma is modest. She doesn't care about clothes. She thinks that greatness is fostered from within."

This made me laugh. "That's so untrue. Just some people think that ugly clothes make them look smart. Or sincere. Look at Dave. He dresses for authority." I pointed to Abe's leg.

"Why did you go for the colorful cast? I'm sure you could have gotten a white one."

Abe ignored the dig. "Well, Emma is better than that. She cares about people. She doesn't run away from who she is. She doesn't need all the superficial things that most people"—he meant me— "seem to live for." Before I could ask him what that was supposed to mean, he pulled out his phone and typed.

I grabbed his phone and read the text. He was such a hypocrite. "Listening to gospel with Janine Collins. You're posting *that* to Facebook?"

He wasn't embarrassed. "If you haven't noticed, people follow me, J. A lot of people wait for my status reports."

I waited for him to laugh, but he wasn't joking. "Abe, you really should think about how much you want to share." Fame wasn't as great as he thought it was. Especially that kind of fame.

He should understand that.

He put down his phone. "Janine, you saved my life. You made a miracle." He got up and stood close—too close—like boyfriend close—like he-wanted-to-kiss-me close. I took a giant step back. "Why can't you accept it? I'm alive because of you." He turned back to his phone. He started to sing, then stopped. "It would be a crime to keep something like that a secret."

When his mother barged in the front door, I tried to talk some sense into her. But she had no time to sit down. "Come on, hon," she said to Abe. "*Your friend* just called. We have to go."

"Your friend?"

"She means Roxanne," he said, in a not-very-guilty way. "Janine—just try and see this from my point of view."

I prepared myself. If he told me that the world needed to know what I did, I was going to strangle him right here, right now. "I thought you already spent two hours with her."

He looked away. Now he was guilty. "I held out for a lot. I gave her a lot of conditions. For you."

I said, "Then what are you waiting for?"

"Janine is right," Mrs. Demetrius said. She didn't recognize sarcasm. "We better go. Roxanne is a very busy woman."

"Then go ahead." I paced back and forth. I didn't want to scream at him in front of his mother. "Tell your story. Make a ton of money. But when you're famous and no one will leave you alone and you hate it, don't say I didn't warn you."

When they were gone, I went to the kitchen and ate three brownies. Lo told me to slow down. "It would serve all these people right if they never got better." It was a terrible thought, but I understood. She was scared.

Outside, the believers began to leave. From the window, I watched the boy in the wheelchair. His mom helped him toward a car. Before he got into the car, he looked at me and waved.

My hands tingled. I was scared, too.

TWENTY

First I called Miriam, but she didn't answer. She was probably still saving the farm with Samantha. I hung up.

Five minutes later, I called again and this time, I left a message in my most casual voice. "Hi. It's me. Sorry I didn't make it, but I need to talk to you. You're not going to believe it, but Dave Armstrong was at my house. So was Roxanne. Abe's talking to her right now."

I could just imagine her sitting there with Samantha, listening to my message after having tried all day to figure out how to attract the very people I wanted to get rid of. I tried to sound neutral. "It was a madhouse. Call me when you can."

I stared at the phone and willed it to ring. Maybe she was busy. If she was screening calls, she'd listen and call me right back. I looked at my phone. "Ring now." I counted to ten. But it didn't work; she didn't call. Her phone was probably in her purse. She'd hear my message later. But just to make sure, I picked up the phone to see if it was working.

(It was.)

Lo said, "You know, if you didn't want Abe to make a statement, you should have said so."

I didn't want a lecture. I said, "He wouldn't have listened. He's got stars in his eyes." I asked her if she thought he was jealous of me—if all this time, he had wanted to be my friend just so he could get his name in the press—if perhaps, he saw this opportunity and took it.

"Janine. He got hit by a car." She encouraged me to refocus my energy. Nothing was going to improve if I sat around imagining the worst.

Sharon nudged her. "You're forgetting something."

Lo smiled. "Why don't you go upstairs?" she asked in a slightly coy voice. "Do something productive. Make yourself a dress."

"Not today." Neither one of them understood anything about the creative process. I couldn't just sit down and start sewing. Before I could make anything, I needed to sketch. And buy material and notions. I needed to be in the mood. (I wasn't. Not by a long shot.) "You really expect me to sew after everything that's happened?"

Lo reminded me that throughout history, life's distractions had inspired a lot of great art. "I think this would be a perfect time to start something ambitious."

That sounded a lot like Ms. Browning's advice. But still . . . I didn't know. I had no ideas, no vision, no motivation. "I don't have the right material." After the critique this afternoon, I doubted myself.

My fingers were stiff. I hadn't stretched them all day.

Lo told me to lift my arms and stretch my chest muscles to open up the heart chakra. When I just sat there, arms at my sides, she reminded me that I always felt better after I'd spent some time working. "Please, Janine. Take my advice. Play around. Experiment. You don't have to make anything. Just practice. You know that's how we improve. A little bit each day."

Yoga wisdom. Blah. "Nothing is going to make me feel better today." I considered telling her about the critique, but I didn't need any more pity. Not now. "Maybe I shouldn't bother applying to art school." I stepped back. That kind of talk always pushed her buttons. She hated quitters.

"Janine. Just go. Stop whining. Get over yourself. For once in your life, be humble. Do what I say. Get out of here and go make something. Don't set out for perfection. Just play."

I trudged up the stairs to my room and dragged my remnants basket out of the closet. There was some nice silk, but there wasn't enough to make more than a shirt. I found some corduroy and a long swatch of gold taffeta that some day was going to make a great dress for a wedding. I rummaged through a small bag of notions. I had sequins, black buttons, and a million zippers.

Lo was wrong. I was drawing a blank.

Completely uninspired.

I didn't want wool. Denim was too stiff. Usually, one of my personal sewing goals was making something great with material that didn't cost a lot, but today, I wished for something magnificent and expensive.

I wanted to play with something beautiful.

I didn't want anyone to say I got into school for being the Soul Survivor.

Lo called up the steps. "Did you find it?"

"Find what?"

"Look under your desk."

There was a package wrapped in silver paper with a card that said: "I remember how much you loved this cloth" followed by twenty x's and o's. I opened my door and yelled to Lo, "What did you buy?"

"It's not a hand," she said, laughing.

I almost cried when I ripped open the paper. The bolt of fabric was lush blue/purple and slightly distressed. I remembered this. There was no way you could forget fabric like this.

I caressed it. I rubbed it against my cheek. The cloth was silky and soft. Even better—it was just this side of unexpected. I spread it out over my bed. Then I grabbed my sketchbook. I closed my eyes and envisioned my mother.

This dress was going to be serious. It was going to make a statement. It was going to be exciting and different. If I could just get it together in time, Ms. B. wouldn't be able to do anything but change her mind and give me the thumbs-up— and every school I apply to will say yes.

I draped it across the dress form. I pulled it off and draped it again. It was never smart to jump in and start cutting. First you had to get to know your cloth. You had to see how it moved. You had to see how it sat on a body. You had to make sure that it could really truly become exactly what you wanted it to be. You had to see your creation before you made it.

After almost an hour, I was ready. I had a plan. My fingers were as limber as they were ever going to get.

I knew exactly what I wanted to do.

I transferred my vision to a pattern. When I was sure that it was right, I pinned. Then I sharpened my shears and began to cut. When I needed a break, I put on some loud music—a playlist meant to help me concentrate. The fabric was delicate. I had to cut slowly and carefully. A dress could be ruined with shoddy cutting.

Another hour later, I switched playlists and began to pin. Usually, this was the boring part. But today, I didn't mind.

There were some dresses that felt like work. Others felt like they were copies of other peoples' work. This felt original. This one practically made itself.

This was going to be beautiful.

I was going to get in to Parsons. And RISD. And FIT.

I imagined meeting the admissions director at Parsons. She'd look at my finished work and applaud, confiding in me that she had had low expectations for me—my celebrity and all—but that in person, my work was impressive and sophisticated—and I might as well pack my bags now. I could just hear her saying, "I can't wait to get to know more of the real you."

The authentic me, just like Ms. Browning wanted.

At least I hoped so.

I'd known Ms. Browning long enough to know that she'd want me to sit back and slow down. That the day of a bad critique was not the day to make a dream dress. But she was wrong. I was sure of it. I was sure there were plenty of people who hadn't taken all her advice and had still gotten into great schools and had great careers. Why did she think she knew everything? Just because she had experience didn't mean she was the only authority.

I was a designer. My work was good. This was the real me. I went to the closet, got out the iron and board, and set it up. I ironed some seams. Then I sewed them. On the dress form, the collar looked good. Two hours later, so did the bodice.

I had no doubts. Then I had a few doubts. Then I snagged a seam. I could hear her telling me, "This isn't authentic. Why do you think this dress has anything to do with your mother? What were you actually trying to say?"

I gripped the hamsa. Now I wasn't sure. Maybe I knew nothing. Maybe I had just wrecked this amazing fabric.

(Sometimes I hated my imagination.)

Heart. Soul. Mind. World. Protection. I started to wish, then I stopped. I could do this.

Maybe this didn't have to be so hard.

My grandparents waited a long time to give me this piece of her. It must mean something. That's why I had that dream. That's why I was hesitating now. It must mean that there was something else I needed to know now. About my mom.

It was a sign. A clear one.

I put down my work and found Lo. "I want to see it," I said.

She hated it when I talked out of context. "Want to see what?"

"The Book of Death." I sighed. "My mom's last journal." Now that I'd said it, I could hardly wait. I needed to read it. Before I could finish the dress, I needed to know what she wrote before she died.

Lo hesitated. "Today? Now? Haven't we had enough excitement already? Why don't you wait? We can read it next weekend. After all this nonsense is over."

"No," I said. "I need it now." When she started to argue, I told her it was mine. "You said I could have it whenever I wanted."

"It's in my closet. Top shelf." Before I turned away, she added, "If you change your mind, I can tell you what it says. Or we can read it together. You don't have to do this alone. Some of it will upset you."

I paused. "Of course it's going to upset me."

We stood eye to eye. She blinked first. "Make sure you read every word. All the way to the end."

I was pretty sure she was still talking when I went upstairs and found the book. I brought it to my bed and opened it to the first page. On the inside cover, it said, "You can't demolish the rules until you know them by heart."

I liked that. Already I felt my ideas coming into focus.

In the margins, unlike every other journal, there were no doodles.

TWENTY-ONE

The phone call came at 3:04 P.M.

The man on the line asked, "Is this Karen Friedman Collins?" He said he was calling from the network—the network also known as my fantasy workplace, the pinnacle of my profession. He said, "We were hoping to talk you into working for us as a correspondent."

My first thought: This must be a joke. Someone from the office was playing a mean trick on me.

My second thought: Answer! Say something!

I think I said, "I would welcome the chance to talk to you." I probably sounded like a frog. "Do you have a particular assignment in mind?"

"We do." Of course they did. "We think it would be right up your alley."

That could mean anything. Women's rights. Politics. A shady politician. The Middle East.

He said, "We loved what you had to say a few weeks ago about the peace process."

He said *love*.

About my work.

"Would next week work for you?" I asked.

He said, "How about something this week?"

This was big. "Absolutely," I said without hesitating or screaming or checking my calendar. When the network called, you didn't say no.

I didn't want to.

Before I could grab my laptop, he started rattling off specifics. It was a job that would take some travel and some sacrifice, but that if I was up for it, he thought I would be perfect.

Love. Perfect. Those were great words. I said, "Could you say that again so I can make a recording? For my husband?"

When he didn't laugh, I let it go. I said, "So tell me about it."

The basics were too good to be true:

Three weeks in the Middle East.

Four daily reports. By me.

Two interviews daily. With me.

He said I'd travel during the second or third week in April—that got my attention. I knew what this was about. The pundits were already squawking about an international visit to the region. Diplomatic meetings. Maybe even the president. "So, would you like to set up an appointment to talk?"

Sometimes it's good to play coy. Sometimes it works to play hard to get. Today, I didn't pretend to check my calendar. I didn't pretend to mull it over. I did not wait for him to change his mind.

I said, "Yes. I would never miss an opportunity like this."

I am sure he smiled. You could hear it in his breath. "That's wonderful, Karen. We were hoping you would say that."

I kept reading. I read about her telling my dad and picking out what she wanted to wear to her interview. I read about the day the job was officially hers and the research she had to do to get ready. Even though I knew the ending, I wanted to share her excitement. I wanted to feel her anticipation.

But after fifteen more pages of more of the same, I had to admit: I was bored and completely uninspired. I wanted a memory or a story. I wanted something new. I wanted to read about me and Dad and some things we did or funny things we said. I wanted to read about what kind of kid I was becoming— what I liked to do with her.

I wanted to read if going back to Israel meant reconciling with my grandparents. Maybe they had changed their minds. Maybe they were ready to accept all of us.

But there was nothing. Page after page, there were no funny stories, no sad ones. There were no stories period. It was like my father and I didn't even exist.

The dress seemed far, far away.

In this journal, she was excited about meetings and plans, assignments and new people and interviews that she needed to set up. Historically speaking, my mom was about to do something really exciting and meaningful. She was going to talk about important issues that just might change history. She was going to do her best to encourage the process toward peace.

I should have been proud. I shouldn't have expected every page of every journal to be about me. For a moment, I put the book down. Then I picked it back up and skimmed a few pages. I considered going back to an old journal. Maybe she wanted this book to be just for work.

Then I saw the letter, M.

M wants me to bow out.

Now I was interested. M was for Martin. My dad.

According to Mom, he thought that the assignment, as exciting as it seemed, was taking too much time. He said they didn't need the money and that there were plenty of qualified correspondents and that she was not the best for the job—not by a long shot. According to her, he said she was too opinionated, too biased, too connected. In large capital letters, she wrote that he was unfair, that she had worked hard for this big break, and that my dad—of all people—should understand that.

I'm not acting like I'm the most important person in the universe, but we had a deal. An agreement. When I am playing by the rules, I shouldn't have to listen to a complaining, thoughtless, insensitive husband.

I didn't remember reading about an agreement, and I was sure she'd never called him insensitive before. Only two things were clear: they were not happy. And I was still not on the page.

Today, when I got home, he told me that I was acting reckless. He said that I was too inexperienced, that they were using me like a pawn because of my father—maybe even at his bequest. He said he knew that they hired me because they knew I couldn't be objective. Wasn't that the problem with the television media today? According to M, the network had some top-secret agenda, as if that was so surprising, and that I was playing right into their hands. He said that I was a mother first, that I should think about what was best for my child. A mother first. Has he lost it? What does that even mean?

I wanted to say, "Stop fighting. You know what it means."
I wished I could ask, "Are you really fighting because of me? Do you really want to leave me?"

As I read and they fought, I didn't understand why my dad even wanted to go—or bring me. It was only a month-long assignment. Couldn't he see how out of sync they were becoming—that she had a dream? The dad of the other journals would have supported that. But in this book, every time she got excited, he said no.

I said, "You stay home for a while. You see how great it is. You see how many times you get asked to cover a good story when you have to manage your childcare."

Now I knew they were fighting about me.

Two entries and four pages later, even though I knew that the three of us went to Israel during the second week of April, I was actually surprised when we got on the plane together. We had five days before the meetings and reports began. I looked for the events that Lo told me happened, the days that matched the pictures: Drinking Coke. The first time we ate falafel. Building sandcastles on the beach in Haifa. But my mother wrote nothing about these events in her journal.

The whole thing was about syntax and scoops and some nice feedback she got from the network.

She did not call my grandparents. That surprised me.

I took out my pictures. I stared at our faces, our bodies, how we posed.

We were there. Together. She looked happy. So did he. But now I was sure they weren't.

I went back to the book.

Five days before she died, the whole page was filled with stars and smiley faces. Her first broadcast was set to tape and air after she attended a big meeting at a synagogue. I knew what meeting that was. It was the meeting that killed them. It was the meeting that made me famous.

He will not leave me alone.

First he said, "Let's give it one more try," right when I was in the middle of writing my first report.

Then he said, "Come on. You can wing it."

Then he said, "If you won't talk to me, I'm going to take Janine home."

I said, "That would be fine with me."

I had to be reading this wrong.

I read it again.

But the words didn't change.

I said, "That would be fine with me."

I took a deep breath. It wasn't like I thought they never disagreed. But it was never like this. They loved each other. They loved their work. They loved me. I knew they did. They didn't hate each other.

That wasn't possible.

I looked for the retraction. The remorse. An asterisk with a note explaining how embarrassed she was to have written such junk, even though she had no reason to believe anyone but her would ever read it.

Instead, I found their so-called agreement.

One more time, I reminded him that we had a deal.
Stay home five years.
Then do whatever I want.
That was the plan. It still is my plan.

She told him to go, get out, take the kid, too. Her words hurt; they stung. But he stayed. I didn't understand why. Why would my dad take this? My only explanation: he knew she didn't mean it. She must have been mad about something else.

She must have still loved me.

But then I turned to the page before the bombing, the day we went to the Dead Sea. The tone of her words seemed confident. Even the letters themselves were bigger.

These were her last words.

After we see L, I am going to tell him that my plans have changed. I am going to stay in the Middle East.

I am going to tell him to go home.

I can't leave this land. Not yet. It is too beautiful, too important. The people are so passionate.

I belong here. I always did. I just didn't know it until I came back.

I have so much more to do. I have a mission. I have to tell the world what is happening here. Americans need to see how the people of this region live. I need to be part of it—to help bring peace. I love the feel of the air and the energy of these people. I need to convince the world we have to embrace a solution. Without conversation, there will be no peace.

Peace is what matters.

Peace is what we need.

It's not going to be easy, but M and J will just have to understand.

Understand.

No, I didn't.

My first response: my mother's job was more important to her than her family.

I grabbed the Dead Sea photo. If I believed the journal, these smiles were faked. These people weren't having fun. They were lying to keep me happy—to create a picture that was wrong.

I went back to the book, turned the page over, and looked for something more. But there was nothing. Just the mission. Just the desire for work. And peace. It was so weird. She sounded like Dave. Like a fake, insincere preacher who was looking for cash. After that, the lines on the pages were empty. She was dead. I shook out the book. This was not the end of the story. It couldn't be.

She was my mother. She was the person who kept me alive. She was the person who gave me strength when I didn't think I could wait one more minute. She was the person who sacrificed herself for me.

All my life, I thought they were happy—the perfect couple. I trusted those pictures. I thought they told the truth. I thought she loved me.

This writing—it didn't even sound like her. I had to be reading it the wrong way. She walked away from Israel; this was a job—she didn't want this life. I thought she chose my dad and me. The three of us in one frame.

I read it again. I looked for clues, but there were none to find. The truth was plain. It was clear: her life was in the Middle East. She didn't want to be part of our family anymore. She didn't want to be just a mother. She didn't care about being a wife. She hoped we'd understand.

I understood.

I threw the photo on my bed.

I ripped off the hamsa and hurled it across the room.

I grabbed a pen and wrote on top of her words, "I hate you." It wasn't enough. I reached for a thick marker and scrubbed out every word, until the black seeped into the next page and the paper started to disintegrate. No one would ever read these words again. No one would ever be able to see that she didn't want her daughter.

TWENTY-TWO

The second she saw me, Lo jumped up out of her chair. "Are you okay? Do you have any questions?"

"No. I don't." I motioned to the TV. Roxanne Wheeler was sitting in the pretty blue-and-green studio of the Philadelphia news team from the ABC affiliate. "Turn up the sound."

She and the weatherman were talking about her upcoming special report in honor of Easter and Passover (and I guess all the other springtime religious holidays). She called it "The Power of Faith." She was sure the viewing audience would love it.

In that report, she was going to look at how faith has entered every corner of our world. Religion and faith in God had become a part of sports. At every awards ceremony, from the Grammies to the Oscars to the People's Choice, winners always thanked their Savior. I stared at her as she talked about how she knew she had to do this story after hearing that Dave Armstrong would be speaking in her hometown, Bethlehem, Pennsylvania. She talked about meeting him outside the home of Janine Collins, whom, of course, everyone remembered was the Soul Survivor, blah, blah, blah. She said, "I promise you. When you hear what these people have to say, you will change the way you think about prayer."

I turned the TV off, flung the remote across the room. Lo wanted to comfort me, but I pushed her away. "You could have just burned it."

I didn't want her to tell me it was going to be okay—that soon I was going to be fine. Because I wasn't. I would never accept this. Or understand it. "Why did you save it? Do you hate me that much?"

"Of course I don't." She rambled a bit about my mother's intentions, some conversation that she had with my parents at the Dead Sea right before they died. "I'm sorry," she said. "I couldn't destroy it. She *was* my sister. I didn't save it to hurt you."

"Well, you did. You all did." I walked out the door.

The sun was still up, but the air had begun to feel like night. It was cooler. At times, the wind gusted. I swung my arms and took very large steps, and waited to warm up. When my cell phone rang two, three, four times, I ignored it, kept moving.

There was nothing Lo could say.

I couldn't believe that for ten years, she hid this from me. She let me believe in a fantasy—a happy family—a mother who loved me. But that was a lie. My mother wanted to leave us. She didn't want to change the world as much as she wanted to be the person who told everyone else that the world was changing. She was no different and no better than Dave or Roxanne Wheeler or any of the other reporters who've plagued me over the years.

M and J will have to understand.

She was everything I hate.

I walked faster, down the main streets. The only thing still open was the coffee shop/used bookstore—the one Lo liked. On the door was a sign. It said DREAM in swirly blue letters with sparkles and stars. In smaller letters: Love. Peace. Hope. In smaller letters: If you can picture it, it can come true.

At least it was warm inside. I had enough money to get something to drink.

But the cappuccino machine had its own sign: out of order. The store was practically empty. A guy with a way-too-long beard sat on a table, talking to a woman wearing about fifty bangle bracelets. She looked old enough to be the guy's grandmother. "Can I help you?" she asked.

I turned away. Reflex. Even though I would bet a million dollars that she was the yoga lady. "I'm just looking," I said.

I scanned the shelves. Literature. Travel. History. Politics. I picked up an extremely fat book about Lyndon B. Johnson— which I had no interest in, but I felt like I had to look at something—when I saw a familiar girl standing underneath the word HEALTH.

It was Emma.

She didn't see me.

I watched her read. She turned the pages fast—with enthusiasm. A few times, she smiled and jotted something down in a notebook. But she didn't buy it. She put the book down, said thank you, and walked out the door.

I couldn't stop myself—I wanted to see what she was reading. I walked over to the table where she had been sitting. There was only one discarded book. It was fat and technical looking. I picked it up: *Current Medical Practice and Diagnosis.*

That was too funny. Little Miss Faith Healer was reading a book about medicine. Which meant she was sham. And a fraud. If she was reading a book like that, there was no way she believed any of that crap about trust and God and healing.

I wondered if Dave knew. Did he suspect that she didn't buy his "Pray for a cure" philosophy, or was he a fraud, too? His whole mission—maybe it was all an act. Maybe none of them believed a word they stood for.

It meant that she didn't believe in me. It was all a joke. I was a joke.

Not for long.

I bought the book. "Thank you," I said, and I meant it. I knew it was mean, but I couldn't wait to show this to Abe, to tell him that this is what Emma had been reading. His hero was a hypocrite. I couldn't wait to expose her. She wasn't going to make a fool out of me.

I walked faster, down the road, toward home. I passed the school and, of course, the farm. When I got there, I tried to see what Miriam saw.

I stepped over the drooping warning tape. I walked across the soft, tilled plots. Little signs with pictures of carrots and beets lay strewn on the ground. Twine that once divided land was now a scramble.

I stopped at the tree.

The trunk was huge. I had to tip my head back to see the place where the lightning hit it. From here, it looked clean and white. Maybe Samantha and Miriam would get what they wanted. It didn't look like the tree was going to fall down by itself.

It looked strong. But what did I know? It was also alone. There was nothing big enough to help stabilize it.

I sat with my back against the trunk and paged through the book, wondering what disease she had been studying. Then I called Dan. Even though I hated to admit being wrong, I knew I'd acted like a jerk. I needed to make it up to him. When his phone went straight to voicemail, I tried his home phone, too, but his mom said he was out. "Try his cell," she said. When I told her I already had, she said, "Funny. I guess I thought he was with you."

Next, I tried Miriam. This time, she picked up on the first ring. "Janine! It's you! I'm so glad you called back." I could tell she was flying high on the power of grassroots organization.

I sighed with relief. She wasn't mad. "Oh my God," she said, "the meeting was amazing. A ton of people showed up. Not just kids either. I am so excited."

I said, "That's so great. I should have been there."

She told me not to worry at all. She knew I was thinking about her. I could hear Samantha talking to her in the background. She yelled, "We missed you," but I was sure she really only missed the people she thought I could bring.

I told Miriam everything: how I fought with Dan, touched a guy in a wheelchair, and that I read the Book of Death.

That got her attention. She had never understood why I wouldn't read it. "What did it say?"

"My parents were splitting up."

"Oh." She said she was sorry, that that must have been a hard thing to read, but before I could tell her more, she changed the subject to Roxanne and Dave. "I can't believe they were at your house. Did you tell them . . ."

"No. Are you serious? I stood my ground and said no comment. Talk to your friend Abe, though. He and his mom left my house to meet her." I hated that after all the years we've been friends, she still didn't realize how hard this was for me.

I must have been on speaker, because I could hear Samantha groan. "Listen," she said, her voice getting louder, "we were thinking . . . if you call Roxanne and tell her to meet you tomorrow . . . or maybe even the next day . . . we'll have plenty of time to set up everything." She sounded confident, like this plan was a done deal.

(Like we were friends.)

I said nothing.

She kept talking. "Miriam told me you don't like attention, but this really isn't about you." She begged me to help—which just made me feel more stubborn. "If you did us this favor, we would be so grateful. We would owe you big time."

I wasn't an expert, but for being hit by lightning, this tree still seemed pretty stable. The trunk looked sturdy. It was only missing one big branch. I said, "This tree can live without one branch. I think it's going to be fine. You won't need me."

Miriam came back to the phone. She said, "Please Janine. Just tell her about us. See if she'll write one story. That's all we need."

We went back and forth. Between "please" and dead air. Between "I can't risk it," and "Just this once. Use your fame for something good."

She was not going to let me say no. "Okay."

"Really?"

"Yes. Really."

Miriam yelled, "She'll do it!" She said "thank you" about

twelve times. "This means so much to me." She held the "so" just the way she did when we were young.

I pictured her sitting on my bed. I could hear her voice.

"He is soooooooooo cute."

"That game was sooooooo unfair."

For a moment, I was sort of happy. Excited. "What are you doing? Maybe should we all go out? Get a smoothie?"

She wished we could, but "We have to get ready." She squealed again. "This is so amazing."

That was three amazings. Two giggles. And one ugly truth: The only reason I was doing this was because I was jealous. I was jealous they were laughing. I was jealous they were becoming friends. I was so jealous I'd do what they wanted me to do, even if it was against everything I stood for.

TWENTY-THREE

When I woke up the next morning, Lo sat on the edge of my bed. She held the hamsa in her open palm. "I would really like you to put it back on."

I jumped out of bed and tripped over *Current Medical Diagnosis*. "Did I oversleep? Is there a crowd outside?" I stood at the window seat and made sure no one was outside waiting for me.

My room was bright. Lo had removed the shade screen from the skylight. I smelled coffee. Next to my sewing machine sat my favorite mug.

"No. Not yet." She paused. "I just wanted to . . . I don't know . . . I wanted to offer a truce. And talk."

When I told her that I didn't want to talk about the Book or wear the hamsa or forgive my dead mother, she lightened her voice. "Well, we at least need to discuss our schedule for next week." When I didn't look excited, she said, "Your college tour. Am I missing something?"

(Last night, she and Sharon probably took bets about whether I'd made appointments with schools. They probably determined that a week of tours and brochures and shopping would be the antidote to all this attention.)

"I don't want to go until I have a portfolio in hand." When Lo looked confused, I told her the bad news. "Ms. Browning wants me to go back to the drawing board." I got back into bed and faced the wall. "She says my work looks inauthentic."

Lo tried to hug me. "Did she really say *inauthentic*? I think your work is great. Maybe she's not as smart as you think she is." She got up from the bed and picked up the half-finished dress. "This is gorgeous. I say let's throw caution to the wind and see if we can't crash their open houses."

Ms. Browning was opinionated for a reason. She was not the enemy. Dave was. My mother was. Lo didn't know that FIT and Parsons don't make last-minute appointments.

Looking at the dress, I got it. Nothing I made was original. Even this dress—I was pretty sure I could find a Vogue pattern for something just like it in five minutes. It didn't look anything like me. Anyone could have made it. "She thinks I should plan to wait until this summer. Or fall." I looked away. "And I agree." This dress was supposed to be a tribute, but now that was the last thing I wanted to make. "It doesn't matter anyway, because I'm not going to finish it."

Lo picked some lint off her skirt—a too-long, overpleated number that I'd begged her to donate to Goodwill at least a hundred times. She walked across the room, folded two shirts, and lined up the three bottles of perfume. Then she shook out the dress-in-progress and laid it across the bottom of my bed. "Just tell me you're not giving up because you're feeling sorry for yourself. Or trying to hurt me. Because that won't get you anywhere. You'll only hurt yourself."

"It's just a dress."

Lo looked irritated. "I want to talk about your mother."

"Well, I don't."

She didn't defend herself. She didn't beg for my forgiveness. She didn't even bother pretending that all this talking about process was anything more than an icebreaker. "Janine, look at me."

I looked at my basket of remnants, my bookcase, and the pile of dirty clothes at the foot of my bed.

"Janine?"

I looked at some dried flowers, still hanging upside down, next to the skylight.

She stood over me and waited for me to look at her. Then she actually compared what I was going through to a really hard yoga pose that it took her two years to accomplish. "You have to dig in your heels and . . . "

"This is not about effort." I tried very hard not to freak out or laugh. "Yesterday, I wanted to read the Book because this dress was going to be a tribute to my mom. I wanted to feel close to her." It was so ironic. "I thought her last words would inspire me."

"I wish you had told me." Lo put the hamsa on my bedside table, sat back down, and took each of my hands, one at a time, into hers. She pressed into the scars, and when they felt a little warmer, she pulled on each of my fingers, one at a time. She loosened each joint without cracking them, so that if I held them very still, there was no pain whatsoever.

I didn't move. I imagined normal, ordinary, scar-free hands. No reporters. No Book of Death. Living, breathing parents.

This wasn't Lo's fault. I knew it. Still, I had to blame someone, and she was the only one here. I said, "I can't help thinking you wanted to hurt me. That maybe you even resented that you got stuck raising me." I said what I'd never been willing to say out loud before. "That this wasn't your choice either."

Lo brought my hands to her lips. "You know that that is not true or fair. I have always been honest with you. I wanted this life. At the time, I almost felt guilty—I wanted it so bad."

"So you could get away from your parents?"

She sighed, like this was a conversation she never wanted to have. "So I could get away from everything. Including my parents." Lo stroked my hair. "Maybe I was wrong to keep the Book, but I thought it was important that you have the chance to read your mother's last written words. I knew it would hurt, but I trusted you wouldn't ask for it until you were ready."

That made no sense. "Trusted what?"

She scratched her head. "Fate? Destiny? I'm sorry your mother wasn't a perfect person. I'm sorry she wrote those hurtful things. But she was also a hero. A champion. She had a mission, and you can't resent her for that." She took the Book from me and put on her "I'm here for you" smile. "Over break, let's go somewhere fun, eat some good food. Shop till we drop. In not too long, you'll be gone—off to school. We should seize the moment. Have a little adventure."

Frankly, I was tired of excitement. "I just want to forget everything about her. I never want to think about her again."

Lo's lips turned flat. Her skin drained of color. She got up and walked to my stairs. In a flat tone she said, "Go get ready for school. I'm happy to talk, but don't ever say that to me again. Your mother was my sister. She loved you, and I loved her. Now she's dead, and we won't get anywhere trashing her memory."

When I went downstairs, she was gone.

TWENTY-FOUR

I walked to school alone. I was a girl with no boyfriend, and my friends weren't answering their phones. So I walked past the church and the tree alone, and the whole time, my phone buzzed. Unknown name and number, every time. I turned it off. At the light across the street from the school, a policeman directed traffic. "I have a nephew who's been dealing with Lyme disease." I grimaced and tried to avoid eye contact. One of these days, I really should try to get a license. "You want me to escort you to the door?" he asked.

"No thanks," I said. "I can handle them."

"Are you sure?"

I reminded myself he meant well. "I'm sure." He held up his hands so it was clear to cross the street.

So far, the scene didn't look too bad. There were the usual groups of students hanging around. In between, I noticed five or six unfamiliar adults. That wasn't a lot. I'd dealt with worse.

When they saw me, they simultaneously began to walk toward me.

"What was it like?"

"How did it feel?"

"Now do you think your hands are holy?"

Their questions were pretty standard.

"No comment," I said. I kept walking toward the door, my hand shielding my face. They followed at a safe distance—they wouldn't do anything stupid on school grounds. All around me, other students turned and watched. They posed. A lot of them looked like they had dressed up, hoping to get the attention of a camera.

Any one of them would love to answer questions about Abe. They all knew him—or at least knew something about him.

I was ten steps from the front door when a short guy with scruffy facial hair and a plaid, wrinkled shirt and scuffed shoes bumped into me, knocking my backpack off my shoulder. "Sorry," he said, reaching down to help me, as if the collision was an accident and he was some klutzy substitute teacher and not a reporter.

I said, "It's okay. They're just books."

He stood between me and the door. "What do you think about the power of faith? Have you spoken to Dave Armstrong?" When I just shook my head—these questions were possibly the most obvious ones I'd ever been asked—a crowd formed around us.

I looked around. Where was the principal? How about a teacher? The closest familiar face was a girl from my English class. I couldn't remember her name. She asked, "Do you deny that Abe Demetrius recovered? How can you turn your back on other people who might need your help?"

A week ago, she had ranted about double standards—that women weren't recognized professionally as often as men. I thought she seemed okay, even though she was a bit uptight. Now she was shouting. "If you can heal people, don't you want to share your gift with the world? Don't you have to? With all these witnesses, isn't there anything you want to say?"

We stared at each other as the cameras flashed. "I honestly don't know," I said, not because I didn't, but because right now, I was a bit embarrassed, a bit ashamed. I understood responsibility—I was human—but I also had to contend with reality.

This is what no one understood.

Unlike her, if I gave up my seat on a bus, someone might take my picture. If I worked in a soup kitchen for the holiday, someone always found out and wrote a story about my desire to feed the hungry. If I cheated on a test or wore a fur coat or supported the wrong cause, even better. Someone got himself a headline.

Think that wasn't so bad?

Just the price of being famous?

Ask a movie star or even a mayor or any semifamous person—especially after their pictures are splashed across some seedy headline—how they feel about their "fifteen minutes," and they'll tell you: being famous (even for a little while) was not fun. When you were famous, you always had to consider how your actions would play to the press. You had to be careful and think about the downside of every word you said. Even if what you wanted was the right thing to do, there was always a negative. I hated it. I thought it was annoying. I never wanted to read about myself. "Of course I understand responsibility."

The girl said, "Then make a statement. Tell us everything that happened." She waved her fist in the air in a very forceful, confident way. (Of course, she could also be exploiting her own fifteen minutes.)

I was considering the personal damage I'd have to absorb if I punched her in the nose when I heard someone shouting my name. Across the street, Samantha and Miriam stood and waved. The second the policeman stopped the traffic, they sprinted toward me. Samantha stepped into the small crowd. "Of course Janine is delighted to know that Abe has recovered. She is also very concerned about other very important issues in the local community."

She'd clearly practiced her opening line.

Too bad Miriam was a terrible actress. This was supposed to look spontaneous, but when she raised her hand like a schoolgirl, the first reporter smirked. "Important issues? Can you explain? Are you speaking about the community farm that the town is planning to sell to the college?"

One reporter walked away.

The rest looked at me. I was the target. They would stay until I left.

So I stayed. As Samantha talked about how the farm was close to my heart, how even though it made good economic sense to move it, it also had an emotional value, I listened. I watched the reporters stop writing and zone out. I watched them look at their phones. I watched them look at me, waiting for me to do something.

I didn't.

I stood there and nodded until the bell for school rang and Mrs. Hollingsworth, the secretary to the principal, an old lady with a very tight bun, walked out into the front lawn to escort me inside. "Go home," she told the posse. She had no patience for grandstanding. It worked. They walked away. No one wanted to be scolded by a woman who looked like a grandma.

I had never been so happy to see Mrs. Hollingsworth. "Thank you," I said. If she had been a little shorter and more cuddly, I would have hugged her.

She wasn't the touchy type. She looked straight ahead and said, "Follow me." When we were alone in her office, she apologized for what she called *the ruckus*. "I don't understand your world one bit." She explained that "in her day," this never would have happened. People respected each other's privacy. She thought it was a pity—a crying shame—that she wasn't permitted to control everything that happened outside the school.

Because inside, it was another story. For today, the principal had posted extra security at every door, but if anyone snuck through, I should let her know immediately. She said, "Although I am confident your classmates will be nothing less than respectful, I also sent the entire faculty a memo." She reminded me, "You should feel safe here. No one is allowed to talk about things like religion. This is a school. There's no mixing church and state."

It was a minor miracle I didn't scream. My peers did not understand. I felt threatened now. Religion was everywhere. No one could escape it.

It was the reason there was war.

It was why my parents were dead.

The separation of church and state was a joke.

Just last year, after some kid told his friend he was going

to hell because he didn't believe in Jesus, the school held a symposium to officially talk about all the different religions. They invited a whole panel of believers. At the end of the row was a rabbi.

He said, "The land of Israel is sacred." He said, "We are more than a faith—we are a community, a chosen people." He called the Torah "a mine, waiting to be excavated." He said Jews believed that you had to work to understand new ideas—that you had to release your old opinions to gain new ones. He called us "witnesses" because we see and hear. Then he challenged us to think.

Miriam thought it was cool—for religion.

When I asked Lo about it, she was just relieved no one dissed gay marriage. Yes, she still "felt" Jewish, but that didn't mean she wanted to go to services. Faith was a good thing, but religion . . . it didn't matter which one . . . she didn't like the politics.

I asked, "Is that because my grandparents were religious?" I was sure this was why.

She said, "No. Not particularly." Then she talked in big generalizations. "After everything that happened, I became cynical. And more private. I'm glad the rabbi was nice, but I have no interest or need to start praying in public."

Behind her desk, Mrs. Hollingsworth folded her hands. Her nails were painted pale pink. On her desk she had a picture of a whole herd of grandchildren smiling in matching white button-downs. Across the top it said, "We love you, Grammy!" Next to that was a tiny green nest holding chocolate Easter eggs. And a half-green, half-red apple. She said, "Time to go. You don't want to be late."

"Thanks," I said. "I'll let you know how it goes." There was no point telling her I wasn't optimistic, that my peers were almost as bad as everyone else.

Or maybe worse.

First period, three people insisted I was appearing on Letterman, Conan, and the *Daily Show* respectively. This was not the first time people told me this. The difference is, the first time, I thought it was funny. Now not so much.

Second period, it got worse. Some guy who had never said two words to me asked me to go to the prom. When I said no—I didn't even know him—he said, "Do you already have a date? Or is it because you are dropping out of school to star in a movie?"

Someone else heard I was doing a nude photo spread. And people in the hall started calling me "Healer Girl." And the captain of the football team slid onto his knees and crossed himself at my feet.

A few people laughed. If it weren't happening to me, I might think it was funny, too.

What wasn't funny: Miriam and Samantha. They wouldn't stop pestering me about Roxanne. Every time I turned around, one of them asked, "Have you called her yet?"

"I will," I promised. But I didn't. And so they kept asking. Every hour. At the same time, I hoped that Miriam would change her mind and tell me not to bother. She knew how much I didn't want to make this call.

"Not to be critical," Samantha says, "but if I were you, I'd be thanking us. I mean—you could do a lot of things with your fame. You know, like stop AIDS. Or end hunger."

Yeah. My responsibility. A lot of people said things like that.

They thought being famous was easy/fun/exciting/meaningful. I just couldn't believe that someone as smart as Samantha really believed that my kind of fame could do anything.

Miriam could see I was about to blow. "J, you told me I could count on you. And now I am."

I took out my phone and her business card. Tricking Roxanne into covering their story was not a good idea. I knew that. This whole thing gave me a sick feeling. But I wasn't going to be able to get out of it either.

She answered on the first ring. "Janine. I was just thinking about you."

As we suspected, she was more than happy to meet me. "At the protest," I said a few times, so Samantha and Miriam could hear that I was doing what they wanted. "That is where I'll be after school."

Finally, they smiled. Miriam said, "Thank you!" Samantha said, "We have so much work to do! See you at lunch!"

***

I spent lunch hiding in the last stall in the girls' bathroom. Right now, all I wanted to do was be alone. I didn't want to talk about me or the farm or Roxanne or Abe. I didn't care that Dan was avoiding me or that all of my teachers were looking at me funny.

Instead, I sat on the edge of the toilet. I read the graffiti that covered the walls and the stall door, realizing it was a kind of high-school news report.

Some of it was etched into the metal. "Ian loves Carol." "Marci is a slut." I knew a girl named Marci, but the message might be an old one. "For a good time, call 867-5309." This was the kind of fame most people had to deal with. It was the kind of notoriety people joked about in their yearbooks. At reunions.

In big block letters, someone had written, *High school proves THERE IS NO GOD.* I wonder who wrote that. We could be friends.

The door creaked open. I put my feet up on the toilet until the person was gone. A minute later, the bell rang. When I opened the door, the first things I saw were the signs pasted to the mirror.

SAT PREP COURSE. GET YOUR SCORES UP.

AUDITIONS FOR THE TEMPEST! Must be able to rehearse four nights a week.

SAVE OUR COMMUNITY FARM! PROTEST TONIGHT!

Everyone else had it so easy. They tried out for the play. They took the SATs and applied to college and got to introduce themselves without any preconceived notions. Whether they had been sluts or a good time or in love, they got to live their lives the way they wanted to . . . without the cameras. They never had to wonder what people had heard about them.

***

At the end of the day, I saw Miriam. "Are you coming?" she asked.

"Absolutely," I said. She was so confident, she'd told everyone she saw that it was going to be *huge*. They should come camera ready, wink, wink, nod nod.

She said, "You are so awesome."

I hated that word. "Fingers crossed. See you in a bit." I told her I wanted to change my clothes, but that was a lie. What I really needed was a little more alone time, so I could be mentally prepared to face Roxanne.

I walked out the door. There were no photographers. No reporters. For a moment, I almost felt safe. I almost thought I could walk home, just like everyone else.

And then I saw them. "Janine. Over here." Standing on the corner were Dave and Emma. He was wearing a perfectly tailored overcoat. It was definitely cashmere, just the right choice for those in-between temperature days when it's not cold enough for your Paddington-inspired wool coat, but too chilly to wear a leather jacket. "We need to talk to you," he said, waving me over. "Something important has happened."

Emma, of course, looked over- and underdressed at the same time. She wore a ski jacket and a headscarf—the kind people wore if they needed to wash their hair or if they were bald. And sunglasses. Like she was a movie star who didn't want to be recognized. When I was close enough to make eye contact, she took them off. She was shivering.

"Haven't you ruined my life enough for one week?"

Without warning, he pulled me into his arms and lifted me into the air. He spun me around and around and around. Emma seemed antsy. She told him to put me down. "You're going to make her dizzy."

He would not stop smiling. "You did it," he said. "Your hands, your hands, your beautiful holy hands!"

"Did what?" I asked.

Emma had very wide, dark eyes. Her skin was pure white. She looked around to make sure no one was listening. "Brian," she whispered. "The boy in the wheelchair."

"What about him?"

"After he left your house, he began to get feeling back in his legs." He picked me up and spun me again. "Janine, he's healed. He's not paralyzed. Because of you, he can walk."

TWENTY-FIVE

"He can walk? That guy in the wheelchair?"

"Yes." Dave said. "Well, right now he still needs a walker. But he says he can feel himself getting stronger every minute."

"Don't say it's a coincidence," Emma said. Again, she looked around, like this was national security. "I looked it up in three medical dictionaries, and they all agreed. Spinal-cord paralysis is not reversible."

I was sure my cheeks turned bright red. "That's great."

Emma led me to a small maroon car. "Before you held his hands, he was looking at life in a chair. Now he is getting ready to walk down the street."

They were not joking. Dave pointed his key at the car and clicked the door open. "We'd like to take you to see him," he said. "What do you say?"

I didn't move.

"Say yes," Emma said, getting into the passenger seat. "He wants to thank you. He is so grateful for everything you've done."

This had to be a trick. "Who else knows?" I peered around the back of the car, just to make sure we were really alone.

"No one," Dave promised. "Trust me. We've been very careful. There will be no coverage." He opened the passenger door. "When something like this happens, we control how the word gets out."

"That's funny." He didn't sound so pious now.

He looked at me like he knew something I didn't. "Janine, in this world . . . where there are so many people in desperate need . . ."

"Don't preach to me about this world." I'd had my share of revelations. "I already know—you can control very little." You can prove even less. This guy might be willing to thank me privately today, but tomorrow, no doubt, I was going to see him on TV grabbing his fifteen minutes of fame. "You can swear all you want that you won't tell, but we all know that if this kid wants to, he can sell his story and there's nothing we can do about it."

Still, I got into the car.

Yesterday, he'd been the good-looking paralyzed guy. Now he could walk.

I was curious.

Dave's backseat was full of boxes of shiny brochures. *Find the healing power that is within you! Trust in the Lord!* His mission's logo included two imperfect hands. They were posed to welcome me.

Of course, the hands were scarred—jagged crosses over each palm. The fingers veered off to the sides. I didn't have to ask whose hands they were supposed to resemble.

"When Brian's mother first called," Dave said, starting the

car, "I was sure she was exaggerating. Or hysterical. Honestly, I thought the stress might finally have gotten to her. She's been alone for a very long time."

Emma said, "We doubted her. But then we watched him stand up. We filmed him taking his first steps."

Dave drove a little faster, away from my neighborhood and into Bethlehem. "It was all very exciting. We've been waiting a very long time for an event like this."

Emma opened her window a crack, which created a vibration in the car, a thump, thump, thumping of airflow. She said, "He described it like hitting a wave. First he could feel his feet. Then his legs. He thought he was going crazy. Six hours later, he could wiggle his toes. Then he tried to straighten his knee. Then he called for his mom and right in front of her, stood up out of the chair."

"Incredible." I bet someone was already writing a script to turn his story into a ripped-from-the-headlines movie, the kind that play back-to-back late on Sunday nights.

Dave said, "Brian has always been a true believer. When we were still at your house, Emma swore she saw the light of God in that boy's eyes."

I closed mine. Even though Brian's were cute, I didn't like thinking about eyes. Eyes reminded me of Emir and death and pain. Just the word triggered the memory. If there really was a God, Dave would stop talking about eyes. This light would stay green and we'd drive right past the white church. No stopping. No memories. No questions about Abe.

Naturally, the light turned yellow. Instead of speeding through, Dave took his time. A family walked right over the spot where Abe lay dying. I asked Emma to roll up the window.

She looked at the intersection with interest. "Is that where the miracle happened?" (She might have been sweet and amazing, but she was also very predictable.)

"It was an accident, not a miracle." This was the longest light in the town. "His doctors believe in medicine. I'm sure there is another reason for Brian's recovery." The light needed to turn green.

"I don't agree," Emma said. "Traditional medicine does not always have an answer. Sometimes, people have to look at alternatives. Sometimes," she said, smiling at Dave, "they need to open up their mind to see the answers."

Turn green. Turn green. "That's easy to say, impossible to prove."

"No one is doubting the validity of science," Dave said. "But my feeling is this: when science doesn't work, it doesn't mean you're out of options. That's all." Emma told me about a lady who had some undiagnosed fatigue disease. "Drugs didn't work, neither did therapy. Once she put her faith in God, she began to grow stronger."

On "stronger," the light finally changed. Dave made a quick left, then another right. This was not the way to the hospital. I asked, "Where are we going?"

Dave smiled into the rearview mirror. "To the hotel. The college rented me an executive suite. Part of the perks of being a scholar-in-residence."

I looked at Emma. "What about you?"

"A few of us from the mission came along. I'm staying in the hotel too. So are Brian and his mom."

That sounded wrong. "Wait a minute. Your parents let you do this? What about school?"

"My parents support my beliefs," Emma said. "I already have a GED. What's so strange about that?"

What was so strange was everything. She was a girl—she looked no more than fourteen, but must be at least seventeen—and she was following this man, a preacher, instead of going to school, making friends, hanging out with guys. She was strange because she didn't seem to have a bad thing to say about anything. She wore ridiculously ugly clothes that didn't look new or even vaguely appropriate. For a moment, I wondered if she had done something terrible—if maybe she was hiding from the cops. Or if Dave had kidnapped her—you heard about things like that—men brainwashing girls and holding them captive for years.

I just said it. "You two aren't . . . you know . . . ," I stumbled.

They both laughed. Dave said, "Janine. Don't be ridiculous. Emma is like a daughter to me. She's also a huge part of the mission."

I stared at my hands. The air had made my knuckles look a little bit purple. "Could you turn up the heat? My hands are cold."

Emma told me not to be embarrassed. "Last year, I probably would've thought the same thing." She turned around and faced me. "Before I met Dave, I was cynical. But he changed my life. His words made so much sense. Bad things do happen. But if we have faith in God, we can help ourselves." She blasted the heat, but the creases in my hands still looked discolored. "Miracles happen, too. They happen every single day. Successful people rarely get there by traveling in a straight line."

Four turns later, Dave drove onto the main street toward the Hotel Bethlehem. The hotel was the tallest building on the block.

Dave parked the car in the garage. We walked up the stairs, past the man in the big black coat and tall hat, into the lobby. "This is nice," I said. Lo and Sharon sometimes came here for Girls' Night Out, but I hadn't been here since Miriam's bat mitzvah reception. At the party, Miriam's mom had joked about the paranormal activity that was part of the history of the hotel. Apparently, some guests had sworn ghosts had woken them up or appeared in their mirrors. Dave hadn't seen anything like that. "It's really very nice. Much nicer than the last place we traveled to."

We sat down in the lobby. "Brian and his mom will be here any second."

I stared at the elevators until the door opened and out stepped a woman in a dress she was ten years too old for. The hem was too short, the neckline too low. She was trying too hard—the fabric looked way too shiny.

She looked dressed for a party.

She held the elevator door with an outstretched arm. "They're here, Brian."

He took one step. Then another. Until he stood next to her. Yesterday, he had popped a wheelie. Today, he walked out of the elevator on his skinny, shaky, bare legs and pumped his fists.

TWENTY-SIX

He could walk.
He could really, actually, all-by-himself walk.

For the second time in one week, I wondered if I was losing my mind. I questioned who I was. For the first time, I couldn't come up with a logical explanation.

***

When we held hands, he was in a wheelchair. Paralyzed. Now he was standing.

This was not happening.

***

I did not do this.

I couldn't do this. No human could.

It defied explanation.

He walked right up to me. He said, "I don't know how to thank you."

He was grateful.

He was humble.

Face to face, he was also very very very very good-looking. When we hugged, his knees started to buckle. "Whoa," I said, laughing, holding him up until he had his balance.

Dave invited us to go upstairs and sit down. He pressed the elevator button.

Brian would not let go of my hand. "Don't take this personally," he told Dave, "but I am never sitting down again." He pointed to the outdoor patio and asked me to join him there. Then he said to the others, "Could you guys leave me and Janine alone for just a few minutes?"

Even though I wished with all my might for them to stay, they all took the elevator up. That left me and Brian and some marble stairs. We took them slowly. "I want to thank you," he said, three or four times. It was a little bit awkward—being alone with Brian. Even though he was cute, he couldn't have had a lot of experience dating.

I kept it casual. I said, "I'm just so happy for you." And "It's so great that you can walk."

Brian looked at me like I was a supermodel. "Say that again."

I laughed. His walk looked a little wobbly and weak, but he seemed to be getting stronger every second. "I'm happy for you. It's so great that you can walk." When he smiled, I caught a glimpse of that dimple, the cute one. He was even better-looking than Dan.

"It's all thanks to your hands, and of course," he said, half-bending one knee for one second, "God's grace."

God's grace. My hands. I sat down at the table and frowned. That was just what I didn't want him to say. He reached under the table and held my hands. This was not where I wanted this to go, but that dimple. That smile. I shifted the conversation. "Your doctors must have been excited."

He winked, like we had a secret. "More like they didn't believe me." His hands felt sweaty. "Ever since I got sick, they told me there was nothing they could do. No cure. No possibility." A waiter brought us some sodas, and for a few minutes we sipped in silence. "They told me it would be in my best interests to adjust to being in a wheelchair for life."

Doctors had told me I'd have to adjust. They sat next to me and said I'd have to get used to having stiff fingers and tired hands. They joked about how I'd just have to find nice boys to open jars for me. They said, "That's not so bad, right? You're a pretty girl. Play the damsel in distress."

That made me mad, too. But now I said, "They meant well. They don't know what it's like."

Brian was still complaining about the doctors when Dave returned. He wanted us to come up to his suite. "You really can't fault your doctors," he said in the elevator. "Adjustment can be a very sacred step. They are not the only ones who believe that acceptance is the true path to happiness."

Acceptance was important—I'd learned that, too. I asked, "How did you get hurt in the first place?"

Now that he could stand, I had to look up to him. His shoulders were broad—probably from pushing that chair. When he flexed his elbow, I saw a prominent vein the length of his biceps. "I got this disease. It attacked my nerves. One day I was fine, the next my legs felt funny. Pretty soon, I couldn't walk."

Dave said, "There are a lot of diseases that cannot be cured. Science isn't God."

Brian seemed to like that logic. "For a long time, I blamed God. It was a terrible time." The elevator stopped, and this time, Brian almost fell into me. "I'm not used to that," he said.

"It's okay." I had to admit: seeing him move was both thrilling and contagious. When he walked, I thought he looked like a baby deer.

Vulnerable.

Innocent.

Dave told Brian, "Just take your time. You don't want to wear yourself out." He opened his suite door. "Don't you think we should give thanks?" We walked into his room. There was a kitchenette. TV and couch. A table next to the window. In the next room, I guessed, I'd find a bathroom and a bed. Brian's mom and Emma sat at the table. Even though it was a little cramped, we all sat down. Dave asked us join hands and close our eyes and pray together.

Holding Brian's hand was hard enough, but there was no way I could close my eyes. Every time I did, I got a headache; I got scared. It was hard to balance. Worse, if I kept them closed long enough, I knew what would happen. I'd go back to that day. I'd see the boy named Emir. He'd step into the aisle. And then I'd see his eyes. Then the walls would come down. I couldn't risk it. I opened my eyes.

Emma's face was so pale, so pretty. Dave's lips were permanently shaped into a smile. Brian squeezed my hand.

There was that dimple. They all looked happy. Content. Grateful.

I wanted to feel that, too—without any resentment or fear or anger at all.

"Dear God," Emma said, "thank you so much for bringing Janine to Brian. For giving her the strength to help and heal him. Dear God, whatever you ask, we are your servants. We will do whatever you need us to do. Let us pray silently."

Their heads tipped back to face the sky. Even though their eyes were still closed, they looked like they saw something— something perfectly beautiful. They looked happy. They looked like they were strong.

I stared out the window. I saw people walking down the street. A store was having a sale. In the sky, I saw a cloud shaped like a horse's head. Then a flutter caught my eye—it was a dragonfly on the balcony railing. Dave said, "This world is a miraculous place. We are all God's grateful children." The sun dipped behind the biggest cloud. It looked like an elephant, like a cloud I saw a long time ago.

I was four or five—a little girl with loose wavy hair and chubby, happy, unscarred hands. My dad was there, too. I saw him. He wore jeans and a loose shirt, untucked. He had big worker hands, and he leaned against the tree with his legs crossed. I almost shouted—I never had a memory come to me before—not like this—not so fast and sudden.

I didn't move. I never wanted this memory to end.

We sat under a tree, and I was drawing. He hummed while he worked on his laptop. In my memory, he tickled me. "What do you see up there, Binky?"

I pointed to one particular cloud. "Elephant baby holds balloon." I heard myself burst into laughter.

I never remembered my dad before the explosion. Now I could see him and hear him. I couldn't wait to tell Lo. The moment was a perfectly nice memory. No fear. No death. Just me and my dad. I had a nickname. Binky. I wanted to get up and cheer.

As Dave continued to pray, I searched for more memories. More calm. I wanted that hope. I wanted it so bad. I looked at their faces and the clouds and a thousand what-ifs raced across my brain.

What if I did heal Abe and Brian? What if I could help other people? What if all this was real? What if Emma was right—what if miracles did happen? I looked down at my hands and stared at my scars. When people saw them, when they touched them, they always called them a sign of my strength. They looked at my scars and told me that I should thank God every day. That I should feel grateful.

Emma opened her eyes and looked at me. I waited for her to say something—to tell Dave I wasn't closing my eyes and praying—but she didn't. She didn't give me away when she saw my open eyes staring back.

I mouthed, "I just remembered something."

She smiled and nodded. Put a finger to her lips. Under the table, we reached for each other. Her hand was bony, but warm. As Dave continued to pray, I thought about the clouds. I didn't know what she was thinking, but the way she was smiling, I was pretty sure it wasn't a prayer.

This was our secret.

TWENTY-SEVEN

When I got home, no one was around. I opened the refrigerator door and grabbed everything that looked good. I ate an entire half-gallon of rocky road frozen yogurt. Leftover salad. Three slices of turkey on one piece of bread.

Brian walked.

The whole thing was crazy. It didn't make sense. There was no reason why the feeling and strength in his legs returned. No reason that didn't involve some sort of faith. And miracles.

And me.

I ran upstairs and looked at the half-finished dress. I needed something to do—something to calm myself down—but I had no idea what to do with it. I didn't know how to make it authentic. I didn't know how I was going to figure out what I wanted to say now that I knew my mother didn't want me, now that it seemed my hands might have just healed two people.

She said, "You have a holy soul."

This couldn't be what she meant.

I was halfway through a slab of cheese and some crackers

when Lo walked in the door with Abe and a whole lot of pissed-off body language. "Hey," I said, ignoring the slamming door and hands over her chest, his disappointed posture. "Sit down. I have so much to tell you. You aren't going to believe what happened."

"That's funny," Lo said, although she wasn't laughing. Abe limped to the kitchen table. His hair was sweaty. His face looked flushed. He looked mad, too, although neither of them was willing to say why.

"Did something happen?" The usual scenarios flashed across my mind. Another bombing. Another article. Had I healed someone else?

Lo tapped her finger on the table. "No. Nothing much." She wouldn't sit down. "Did you forget something? Something you were supposed to do?"

"I don't think so."

Lo looked at Abe. Abe looked at Lo. I shrugged my shoulders. "I really don't know what you're talking about." I tried not to smile, but it was tough. I was too happy. "If you're not going to tell me, can I tell you what happened to me?" I put some water on the stove and took out three teacups. And some sugar.

"Sit down," Lo said. She didn't want tea. She didn't want me to say another word. "Janine, this isn't a game. Did you arrange for Roxanne Wheeler to come to Miriam's protest?"

The protest. Crap. "I'm such an idiot. I completely forgot."

Lo stomped past me and took the kettle off the stove.

"I told you she spaced," Abe said. He shook his head. "Whatever you were doing, it had better be good, because we were all freaking out when you didn't show up. Miriam was sure something terrible had happened to you." Abe could be so dramatic. "The thing was a total debacle. Roxanne couldn't believe she brought out her crew for nothing. She really does not like being stood up."

I smirked—couldn't help it. All things being equal, this served Roxanne (and Miriam and Samantha) right. I said to Lo, "This is not my fault. I was trying to do Miriam a favor. I thought you would be proud—I put her needs ahead of mine."

Lo—of course—was not proud. She was furious. "Miriam had me calling all over town. Why have a cell phone if you don't keep it on?"

"It was on." I pulled out my phone—just to prove to her that I was not as irresponsible as she thought I was—and of course, the thing needed to be charged. "Look. I'm sorry I said anything. They wouldn't leave me alone until I called Roxanne and told her I'd be there." I wanted to tell her about Brian. "Trust me—I didn't mean to blow her off. I was going to go. But then I got distracted."

"You got *distracted*." Lo poured herself a drink that wasn't tea. "And what if you hadn't been? What were you going to do then?"

Abe said, "If I were you, I'd call Miriam right now. You should listen to your messages. And come up with a better word than 'distracted.' That is, if she'll talk to you."

I plugged in the phone. Crap. I had twelve messages. Message #1 was short: Miriam sounded excited. "Hey J. Where are you?" By Message #8, her voice was shrill. By Message #12, she sounded like she'd been crying or shouting or both: "Where were you? What happened? How could you just ditch me? The protest was a total disaster. When you didn't show up, people left. They called me a fraud. Roxanne didn't take a single note. No pictures either. She accused Samantha of stealing your phone and pretending to be you. She called her *in over her head*. And *a poser*." At this point, Samantha said something not so nice about me and our friendship. "You should know Roxanne told Samantha to grow up. She told her she had better things to do than write about a bunch of spoiled, entitled kids and a stupid old tree."

That wasn't nice.

I called her cell, but no surprise, Miriam didn't answer. I tried her house. Her mom told me to give her a little more time. "I'm sure you can understand. She's very upset."

Abe took her side. "So where were you anyway?"

I turned to Lo. "Before you start screaming at me, let me tell you, I didn't do any of this on purpose. My plan was to go to the protest, even though I didn't want to be in the same room as Roxanne." I looked at my scars, and I wasn't imagining it—they looked like they were fading. "But when I left school, I ran into Dave. He took me to his hotel. That boy in the wheelchair? He can walk. I went to see him, and it's incredible."

Abe looked confused. "The young guy? The one who held your hand?"

Lo picked up the empty teacup and slammed it on the counter. She told Abe to get into the car. "I'm taking you home now." To me, she said, "You went to his hotel?" I looked at the cup. It was chipped. She said, "I'm going to try and calm down. I don't want to fight anymore."

I went up to my room and lay on my bed. I refused to feel guilty. I should have been honest—really, I should never have agreed to call Roxanne—but now that it was over, I didn't feel all that bad about letting Miriam down. The truth was, she and Samantha used me. They talked about doing the right thing, but it was easy for them—no one knew who they were—their cause was so not complicated. They didn't consider my feelings at all. They should have asked Roxanne directly instead of trying to trick her into talking to them.

I reached down under my bed and picked up the retrospective and reread the article. Then I looked at the pictures. They were not public property. This reporter got them from someone—someone who had access to my personal property—someone who knew me pretty well.

I thought about it. I considered every ex-boyfriend, every girl who'd ever looked at me the wrong way.

Dan?

No. It couldn't be him.

The more I thought about it, the more I was sure it had to be Samantha who leaked them. She probably stole those pictures from Miriam. All this time, she didn't want to be my friend. She was just looking for ways to make me look like a fool.

I looked at the half-finished dress hanging from my closet door. Ms. Browning said I needed to respond to my world. I think she meant that day. The day I became the Soul Survivor, the day my parents died.

Could I put what I was feeling into this dress? Could I reference my story and create something authentic?

I looked at the lines and the fabric. I picked up a swatch of extra material and rubbed it against my cheek. Then I looked at my hands. I really looked at every line and every scar and every angle. I forced myself to be completely honest.

I listened for Lo to come home, to hear her familiar stomp around the house. I waited for her to come upstairs, but she didn't. She stayed away.

1:00 A.M. 2:00 A.M. Still no Lo. No phone message. She probably went to Sharon's. I stared up at the skylight. It was impossible to sleep.

When it was early morning, I got up and picked up the phone and called Israel. My grandmother answered on the second ring.

"Shalom, Janine."

Even though I almost never called, she knew who I was. Even though she knew it was still dark here, she didn't sound surprised to hear from me. At first, I didn't know what to say. It was awkward. She told me my grandfather wasn't near the phone, that he was already out . . . working. "I put those boxes in the mail," she said. "I hope they'll help you get to know your mother a little better."

"What do you remember about her?" I asked.

My grandmother probably had a hundred answers to this question. "She was always full of energy. She always wanted to be the best, no matter what she did."

That didn't mean much. "No," I said. "What was she really like? What made you mad? Did she make you laugh?" I didn't want to hear sound bites. I wanted the truth. Details. Stories. "Tell me one thing she did that no one else knows about."

I listened to her breathing.

There were miles between us.

"Of course, she made us all those things," my grandmother began. "She was our daughter. We loved her very much. She always had to be the center of attention." Then she began to laugh. "Once she signed up to play piano for a talent show. But she didn't know how to play. When I asked her what she thought she was going to do, she just shrugged. It didn't matter." Now she sighed. "Even when she was very young, she was determined to be famous."

Blah. I had hoped she'd wanted more. But when I thought about it, I couldn't say I didn't want to be successful, too. It was natural. We all wanted to do things that would leave a legacy— to be remembered for. No one dreamed of leaving this world in total anonymity. The problem for me: anonymity wasn't possible. Publicity was a hassle, and it wasn't even reliable. The picture they'd drawn of me wasn't right. I didn't want to be the Soul Survivor. I wanted to do something. I wanted to be known for something other than *that day.*

I didn't want anything that came out of *that day.*

My grandmother said, "I'm sure you know that we didn't always understand or agree with her, but we were always proud of her accomplishments—especially when she decided to return."

That was so sad and ironic. "Do you think she knew that?"

"Yes. In my heart, I know she did." My grandmother said she believed that, even though she also accepted that she would never really be sure. "We were devastated when she died. We wish we could have had even one more chance to see her, one chance to make things right. That's one reason we want you to visit. And why we gave you the hamsa."

***

After we hung up, I could finally sleep.

I didn't dream. When I woke up, I didn't even peek in Lo's room. I didn't want to tell her I called Israel. I didn't put on the hamsa. The only thing I wanted to do was get to Bethlehem. Forget school. I called a cab. When I told him where I wanted to go, he stepped on the gas a little too hard. "Aren't you that girl, the one they were talking about on TV?"

I wished I could drive. Or had sunglasses. Or had changed my hair. I considered telling him to pull over and let me out. But I needed to see Dave. I tried not to sound like nails on a chalkboard. "Yes I am. And I'll say a prayer for you if you don't tell anyone. Just take me to the Hotel B. As fast as possible."

The rest of the trip, he didn't say another word. I tried not to think too much about what I was doing. I knew I had to see Dave and Brian and Emma, but I had no clue how all this fit together.

There was something I was missing. I was sure of it.

Lo would probably be angry, but Dave wouldn't. He would say, "You have to trust your gut." And then he'd clasp his hands together and thank the Lord. "This is the meaning of faith."

TWENTY-EIGHT

When she opened the door to Dave's suite, Emma said, "I knew it was you."

I said, "You look great." I meant it. Her hair was blown out loose, and it framed her face. For the first time, she looked older. Her makeup was impressive, too. Her eyes totally popped. Good girl—she'd kept her lips a shiny neutral.

From the door, I saw at least five other people. Three at the round table—now moved back to this side of the room; two more at a low coffee table. Classical music played in the background.

Emma could tell I was hesitating. "Come in. Don't worry. Nobody here is going to mob you. We have too much to do."

A man in the corner said, "As you go, preach this message: 'The kingdom of heaven is near.' Heal the sick, raise the dead, and cleanse those who have leprosy, drive out demons. Freely you have received, freely give."

"Matthew," Emma said. When I looked confused, she shrugged. "From the Bible." She told me that the man had just found out that he had more time to live than the doctors had originally given him. "It's a very liberating thing," she said. "To have no more doubts. He feels the power of God. He prayed for these results for a very long time."

I had doubts. The man should be thanking his doctor.

And yet, I wanted to know how you could trust in something that you couldn't see. So I walked over the threshold into the room. I reminded myself there was something here I needed. I had to find it.

No buts.

***

I met a guy whose daughter was shot in a school and a woman with four kids with AIDS. Both of them were stuffing envelopes—invitations to hear Dave speak. An older man sat down next to me and showed me a flyer he was making on the computer. He told me that, three years ago, he had dedicated his life to Dave's mission and he'd never regretted it. "When my strength was gone, God gave me strength." He said that my story helped him find a reason to get up in the morning. "Listening to Dave makes me want to be a better person."

"Why did you join?" I asked Emma.

She'd had a good friend with cancer. A sad story. Diagnosed at ten, the treatments never worked completely. Her friend suffered for a long time—her illness ate her alive. "I was so angry and resentful. I blamed God. My mother took me to hear Dave speak. He made me think. He questioned what I was doing on this planet—if I was doing anything to make it better. I thought about my friend. And that was that."

She looked at my hands. It made me uncomfortable.

"Sometimes I still get mad. I want answers. Guarantees. But then something good happens. Like coming here. Meeting you. Brian."

Now the room seemed too small. I said, "I think what you're saying is interesting, but I don't believe in God."

This made her look sad. "I think you're just angry." She stood up next to a picture of the manmade Star of Bethlehem, shining brightly. "When I found God, we found peace. And strength. Her illness gave her things that she would never have had otherwise."

I'd never met anyone this naïve. "The point is, it wasn't fair. None of it is. Your friend. Me. My parents."

"I disagree. I think we should look at it another way. You lived, Janine. Your parents died—and that is terrible—but you lived." She stared at my hands. "Why can't you be grateful? What's the point of being so bitter?"

I pushed my hands in her face. If she wanted to see them, she should take a really close look.

She did. Without embarrassment. "Your palms look like a map." She wasn't the first to say that. "But if you look carefully, they also look like flower petals. They are blessed." She smiled. "Really, they're quite beautiful."

Dresses made of flowing silk were beautiful. Tailored pants and jackets with sharp edges and angles were beautiful. "No. They're ugly." I yanked them out of her grasp. "At least give me that."

She half-laughed. "So they're beautiful and ugly. You may not like them, but I do. They're interesting. They catch your eye and make you think. The way your fingers splay—they look like they're grabbing something."

"I hate my fingers. They ache all the time."

"You shouldn't hate them. They're powerful. Your hands have done great things." When I told her she was making assumptions, she said, "Beautiful things are nice to look at, but it's the imperfections in life that people remember. It's how you deal with tough things that shows who you are." The other people in the room turned and agreed. The man with the dead daughter said, "I like ugly. Always did. Ugly makes me stop and linger. Usually when you see something that isn't perfect, there's a good story behind it."

Now I had to laugh. These people were so honest. I'd never met anyone who could resist staring at a fake leg, a scar, or even a mole, but most people weren't brave enough to admit it.

Emma said, "Your hands make me think. Your hands attract other hands."

That stopped me. "Say that again?"

"Your hands. They attract other hands. At the same time, they have power. They're your story. They . . . "

"Be quiet, please." I closed my eyes and saw an image of a dress. "Do you have some extra paper?" I needed to sketch before I forgot it.

First, I just made shapes. Then I thought about perspective, about what people found beautiful. And what turned people off. I thought about my hands and how maybe Emma was right about one thing. Maybe my hands did both.

Emma looked at the sketch. "Wow. That's cool."

It wasn't finished. Just a start. "I need to work on it." I didn't want to tell her how excited I was.

But she could tell. "Will they be real hands, or hands like

the one on your necklace?" When I said, "Real," she noticed I wasn't wearing the hamsa. "Why aren't you wearing it?" She added, "It was so pretty."

I closed the notebook and inched closer to the door. "I'm never wearing it again."

She invited me to come with her to her room down the hall. "Tell me what's wrong. Don't deny it—the second I mentioned the hamsa, you looked different. I can tell you're upset about something. Why did you come? What do you want? You're acting strange."

I said, "I don't want to talk about it."

"Why not?"

"Because I don't." This was the kind of thing I would normally share with Miriam. Or maybe Abe, if he was in a serious mood, if he could keep himself from singing.

Emma pressed me for an answer. "When something is bothering me, I always feel better getting it off my chest."

I shouldn't trust her. But I did. I told her everything.

"All this time, I believed my parents were happy—that they were heroes. I thought we were a happy family. But I was wrong. In the journal, the only thing she dreamed of was fame and power—and leaving us. That's what she wanted. To be famous."

I waited for Emma to empathize the way Miriam would, but her face showed only minimal sympathy. "So . . . you feel sorry for yourself."

I felt my cheeks turning red. "Yes. No. *I don't know.* Maybe." I looked on her bedside table. There was a picture of her with two smiling adults. You could tell they were her parents because they pushed their heads next to her and smiled so wide their eyes disappeared. I said, "You look like your mom."

She said, "But I'm a lot more like my dad."

I used to believe I was exactly like my mom, but now I wasn't sure. I didn't know who I was like. "How would you feel if everything you thought you knew about your parents was wrong? If you spent your whole life believing one story, only to find out that it was made up for your benefit?"

"You think you're the first person to find out something not-so-great about your family?" She took the picture of her family and put it facedown on the bed. "You're upset because your mom was passionate about her work—that she had an ego. Because she wanted some time away from you and your dad. You had this big romantic notion about what her life was like, and now that's all messed up. You feel hurt because they fought over what was best for you. Because your aunt didn't tell you the truth."

"You make it sound trite."

"No, you do." She shook her head. "Janine, if they didn't love you, it wouldn't have been a hard decision for any of them. If their choices had been easy, she probably wouldn't have needed to write it out."

This was not what I wanted to hear. "You can say that, but you weren't lied to. Your parents support your decisions. Your parents are alive." I sighed. "All these years, I thought we had this magic bond—because I heard her voice—because she loved me that much. I thought that was what made me special. Now I know she just wanted to get away from me. I'm so mad I could scream."

"So scream." I looked up, and Dave was standing in the doorway. "Scream. Get mad. Have a good cry." He walked into

189

the middle of the room and stood next to me in front of the vanity mirror.

He was tall. His blazer took up most of the reflection. I wanted to get to the door. "You act like this is no big deal."

"That's not true." He did not move. "I just wish you'd stop punishing yourself. Instead, think about what your parents wanted for you. Think about your own goals. Look at your hands and into your heart and speak to God. Be humble and face your fears with the strength God gave you."

That was funny. My mother was all about facing your fears. Her mottos were: Be brave. Be strong. Go out and get what you want. Lo, on the other hand, wanted me to be more humble. She thought humility was the big ticket to success.

Putting them together didn't make sense. To face your fears, you couldn't be humble. When you were humble, like Emma, you stayed in the shadows. God had nothing to do with this.

I tried to inch toward the door, but he was in my way. "I don't want to be brave or humble. I don't believe I was chosen for anything. I think people just say things like that to explain why life sucks."

Dave took a deep breath. He sat down so we could see each other eye to eye. Sitting that close to him, I was afraid. I wanted to get out of here. He talked in quiet, wispy breaths that floated away almost the second he said them. "Think about the odds. In that small building, where everyone else died, you lived." His voice got even quieter. "You lived that day for a reason. You know it's true. Of all the people in that place, God saved *you*. God chose you. Only you. There has to be a reason."

Emma told him to stop lecturing. "Dave, she's not ready."

This was feeling very intense. I said, "It isn't fair. I don't want any of this." The expectations people had for me—I didn't want them.

Dave didn't care about other peoples' expectations. He said that fairness had nothing to do with it. "Now that we *know* you can heal the sick, you can't walk away. You must face your destiny. You must help those who need you. We believe in you. We always have."

"Shut up!" I pushed Dave as hard as I could. He had said too much—gone too far. "This is not my destiny." I pounded on his chest, but he didn't budge. "You have what you wanted. A ministry. A book. Fame." When he wouldn't let me walk out the door, I said, "Why can't you leave me alone?"

He looked at me with fatherly eyes and arms open wide. "Because we need you. Because we care about you. Because you need us. Even if nothing miraculous happens again, we want to get to know you. No matter what happens next, I will always be there for you."

That's what he said when he pulled me out of the rubble.

"Even if I do nothing?"

"Even then."

I fell in and held him tight.

He said, "Don't cry," and of course, I didn't. But it felt good—hugging him. No matter how mad I was, he was the man who found me. He saved me. I didn't remember my parents, but I knew him. I didn't want to be mad at him. I was grateful to him. Maybe even in a humble way.

What had happened ten years ago had been the greatest

gifts I ever got. He cradled my hands as the paramedics took me to the hospital. He told me over and over again that everything was going to be okay. And it was. I lived. I would never understand why.

Now he rubbed my back. "I'm sorry, Janine. Forgive me. I had no right to ask you to do anything. You don't have to be anyone. You are our family. Just the way you are. You are safe here with us."

TWENTY-NINE

For a moment, I felt safe. I relaxed. I didn't think. I let him tell me about family and home and God, and I didn't get anxious. I trusted him. I didn't look for reporters or cameras.

That was not smart.

"Do you promise me this isn't about publicity? When he flinched, I paused. "Why did you take the job here?" I stood back and looked him straight in the eyes. "You know, I've never believed in coincidences either."

Dave Armstrong had this way of looking guilty and innocent at the same time. "No, it wasn't a coincidence. I wanted to come here, during this year, during this time. I had a hunch that something amazing might happen if I did—there was something magical about this date. So I contacted the college. I arranged for my own funding. I wanted to see what would happen."

He planned this. But that didn't make sense. "But you couldn't have predicted what would happen with Abe. Or Brian."

"I don't have to predict," he said. "I trust."

I nodded. Trust. It wasn't something I was feeling at the moment. "Or maybe donations were down? Maybe you felt like your star was fading?"

He blushed. I was right. Dave Armstrong needed publicity. He was afraid of no longer being in the news. He liked being well-known.

Guilty.

He ran his fingers through his hair. "Before I met you, I had a great life. A happy life. Although I have to admit, I was a bit of a blowhard." He smiled. Innocent. "I made a good salary and had many friends. If I wasn't the most influential scholar in the world, I was at least satisfied with my situation."

Emma said, "And then fate brought you to Jerusalem."

He continued, "I went there to find a new angle for a book I'd been wrestling with. I tried to get into that synagogue, but they closed the door in my face. It turned out to be the most profound rejection of my life. I was close enough to feel the bomb. Surrounded by death, I heard God's voice, and then I heard yours. I changed. And I did good work. I helped people. Tell me you can appreciate that much. Tell me you understand why I had to come here—why I had to get myself back in the public eye."

I understood, even though I hated it. "Unfortunately, this isn't the life I want."

He held me by the shoulders. "Unfortunately, I can't leave you out of it. Your story is my story. When I decided to come here, I prayed that you would talk to me." He looked up at the ceiling fan. "And you did."

It was just too convenient. "Let's just say—for argument's sake—that I did heal Abe and Brian. What if it never happens again?"

Emma said, "Hope is never cruel. Hope is how we get through the day."

Dave looked at her the way I imagined a father would. Then he turned back to me. "It's true. It's nothing you should be afraid of."

I wasn't afraid. "You're making me sound selfish. Like I'm holding something back, when you're the one using me."

Emma said, "But look what you did."

"No," I said. "I'm telling you. I didn't *do* anything. I didn't save anyone."

Dave told me that miracles never seem logical or believable. "What happened to you when you touched Abe and Brian? Think hard. Did you feel a light? A sense of destiny?"

I couldn't tell him. "I wouldn't call it a light. Or destiny. More like fear." I told them about the chase and the church and the sound Abe made when the car hit him. "I thought Abe was dead. I thought I had killed him."

Emma said, "You must have been terrified. That sounds like the worst nightmare."

Every time I had doubts about Dave, Emma said something that made it sound like I could trust them. "I was out of my mind. We had just left the cemetery. It felt like my entire life was surrounded by death." It might have been the most stupid thing I'd ever done, but in that moment, I decided to trust them, to tell them the whole story. "So I held his hands."

"Nothing else?"

I hesitated.

Emma looked at me. "What happened?"

I shook my head. "It was nothing. Just scary. Just like the synagogue."

Dave nodded. "You heard her, didn't you? Just like before." He pressed me until I admitted it.

"Yes. I heard my mother's voice. But it wasn't anything like the first time. This time, I was hallucinating. She was dead." When he looked confused, I said, "This time, it was more like hearing a recording. The same words. The same sounds." I faced the flat-screen TV. Now that I'd told them, I felt so much better. "Lo thinks it's my PTSD."

Emma thought that was shortsighted. "Or it was an angel."

I cringed. Dave wrote something in a notebook. "Did you hear her again when you held hands with Brian?"

"No. That's the thing. I didn't." When Emma looked disappointed, I said, "But I didn't know Brian." There were so many people. I'd just wanted to get inside the house. "I was angry—not scared. Maybe I missed something."

Dave said, "You miss your mother."

"Of course I do." I got up. I needed some space. I walked to the window, opened the sliding glass door, and stepped out onto the balcony. I didn't want to tell him any more.

He followed me. Pointed to the Moravian Church. "You know, the founder of the Moravians was burned for his heresies. Because he believed."

I looked back at the room and Emma. There was no way out of this conversation.

It was so ironic. If he had saved my mother, neither one of us would be where we were right now. I might not have ever met Abe. Maybe we would have moved to New York. It wouldn't be odd to hear her voice. Dave might have gone back to being a professor.

I said, "She should have lived."

He agreed. "I wish she had. In her own way, she might have changed the world. She was a brave woman. She had a compelling voice. If you think about it, we wanted the same things."

"No. I don't think you understand what I'm saying. What I mean: she was alive. Don't you remember? I told you to find her. I told you that she talked to me."

THIRTY

I never believed in conspiracies, but I often wondered if on that day, he had realized what was happening—what he was setting in motion. I knew it was a cynical way to think, but the facts spoke for themselves. In saving me and only me, he helped create a perfect headline and story: One survivor. An American. A child. In a land that people were willing to die for. He said, "Are you saying..." Then he paused. He leaned against the railing. The sun was bright behind him. "It's been a long time since we've been by ourselves. Now that we are, is there something you want to ask me?"

I had always wondered if that was why they stopped looking. Did she die? Or did they realize that they had their story—and it was a good one. Did they know my story would become a source of hope in a time when that kind of thing was in really short supply? "Is that why you didn't go back?" I asked. "You understood politics. You knew what was unfolding. Did you believe that one survivor was better than two?"

For a moment, I thought he might cry. But then he put his

hands on my shoulders and kissed the top of my head. I leaned toward the door; he wouldn't let me go. "To live all these years with these fears. I'm so sorry. No wonder you've only begun to realize faith." As the wind picked up, he embraced me. "Janine, I'm absolutely positive your mother was already dead when you heard her voice. If there had been any chance of finding her— or anyone else—alive, we would have gotten them. I never would have left her to die."

I wasn't so sure. "But my mother was with me right up to the end, I know she was. I heard her." It had always been the one thing I was sure of. "She risked her life to save mine. I needed her. I still do."

"Of course you do," he said. He told me to think back. I laughed—like I hadn't done that every day of my life. "Maybe if you can accept your mother's death, you'll be able to move forward."

I didn't see how this would help. It had been ten years. We couldn't change what had happened. But still, I was willing. I followed him back into the room so I could lie back on the couch and close my eyes to search my shattered memory. "I remember holding my dad's hand." If it got too tough, I'd make my move for the door.

"Good."

Then only flashes. "But that is all."

He talked to me in a low voice. His hands were smooth. He touched my scars the way I touched expensive silk. "Go back to that day. Where was your mother? Do you see her?"

The last therapist hypnotized me. He took me into a tunnel and then out into the light of the synagogue. It terrified me, and I didn't want to go back. When it came to the explosion, I didn't want to remember any more than I do.

Emma said, "When I want to remember something difficult, I try to remember something peaceful. I start with something I am sure of."

I wondered if she would still say this if she had fears to face. "But I have nothing."

Emma knew this wasn't true. I had the memory of my father and the clouds. Our secret. I waited for her to tell Dave, but she didn't. All she said was, "Go there, Janine. Clouds. Trees."

It took me a while to focus, but eventually, I found what I was looking for—the hotel room—the one in Israel. I knew it was ours, because I had pictures of this room. Two beds. One desk. The walls were stark white, except for a dark red stripe around the top of the wall.

"Are you there?" Emma asked.

"I am. I'm there. I can see the room." I could remember my father standing at the sink; he was shaving. On the day he died, he probably let me smooth the shaving cream over his chin and cheeks. Lo told me he did that a lot. She said that the day at the Dead Sea, he'd told her that we had lots of little traditions: we stood at the sink together—every morning. Every night, he kissed me goodnight, as if I was a sleeping fairy-tale princess. On the weekend, he would drive me all the way to New York City to eat cheesecake.

Emma asked, "Are you okay? What else can you remember?"

I said, "I'm not sure." The hotel room was one thing, but the synagogue . . . I didn't want to go there. Even if I remembered everything, it proved nothing. It changed nothing.

They were dead.

I was here.

Dave pushed me. "This will help you, Janine. Close your eyes and hold my hand. Pretend we are your parents."

I did it. Just to show him how wrong he was. I hoped for a flash, a glance, a hint—anything that felt normal. I wanted to know that my mother had been there. I wanted to believe that she hadn't already deserted me.

My left hand felt right. I remembered my father sitting there, holding my hand, patting my hand. She should have been on my right. But that hand was empty. No matter how hard Emma squeezed my hand now, in my memory, the hand sat on my lap.

The next thing I knew, I could see the boy. I saw him walk in. I saw him stop in the aisle. When I was a little girl, I couldn't know that there were people who were willing to die for a cause. Now I knew. I saw him look right at me. I saw the deadness in his eyes. He didn't care that I was a child. He didn't care that he was about to die. That, if everything went the way he envisioned, we all would.

And then I felt the blast.

I screamed like I was there. I tasted dust and fell to the ground. I begged for help, but today, my mom said nothing. My hands clenched into fists and burned like fire. It felt just like it did ten years ago, except now, when I screamed, when Dave held my hands, he saw no blood.

My hands were fine.

I did not hear my mother.

She said nothing. She didn't stay with me. She probably wasn't anywhere near me. It made sense. If she'd been working, she would have been sitting somewhere else—to concentrate.

Dave was telling the truth. I couldn't have heard her, even if she'd still been alive.

I breathed like I'd been running. "Now what do I do?"

***

So I remembered—so what? Nothing was different. My hands were the same. The reporter from the retrospective would continue to believe I was wasting my life.

Dave said, "Do you believe in coincidences?"

I shook my head. "No. Not really."

"Well, neither do I."

I sighed. I knew where this was going. "You think God brought us together."

"Twice." He reached for my hands. "The first time, you needed me. Now, I need you." Now he stared at my palms. "When I see your scars, I see the map of God."

I still didn't know what he expected me to do. Ten years ago, I imagined my mother's voice. Did I think I heard an angel? Or was I just doing what I had to do to stay alive?

I turned to Emma. "What do you see?"

She said, "I see hands that make things. I also see hands that are in pain." She smoothed out her ugly dress. "I see hands that could help people, if you would only believe in yourself."

Dave said, "I believe."

Emma stood very still. "I do, too."

Something big had changed. "Can you take me home?" I asked him. "I have something I need to do."

THIRTY-ONE

When people talked about being born again, they talked about epiphany—or seeing the light. Faith came upon them instantaneously. That's what Dave said I gave him.

A purpose.

A mission.

Hope.

When Dave made me face the truth, that didn't happen. I never felt a purpose, not even close. Dave and Emma were a long way from convincing me that I could help others. But I did feel something. It wasn't joy. It wasn't peace. It wasn't magic—it couldn't be magic—but in a way, it was just as powerful. It was an image I'd carried for ten years. Ugliness and beauty, all at once.

You could call it love.

Or strength.

Or confidence.

Whatever it was, I was willing. I was willing to hear more. I wanted to look for more. I was willing to look at everything in a very different way. For the first time, I was willing to ask "What if?"

When I left Dave, I left with ideas.

THIRTY-TWO

This time when I got home, I wasn't hungry. I wasn't in the mood to talk. This time, I couldn't wait to start drawing.

I had no doubts.

In my head, I saw designs that I knew were authentically me. I saw an entire collection of clothes that reflected my view of the world as well as the world's view of me.

It might be the most superficial example of enlightenment ever realized, but this was who I was. No apologies necessary. Fashion was the way I expressed myself.

And now I had faith.

"Is anyone home?" I grabbed my sketchpad. My hands felt electric. My ideas couldn't wait. Once I got them, I'd start sewing. I would work really hard, and finally, the world would see what I wanted my life to mean. As I drew, my ideas became clearer. I knew there was no way it wouldn't blow Ms. Browning away. This portfolio was going to make her jaw drop. She was going to have no problem recommending me for Parsons. This portfolio made a statement. It said, "Here I am." It said, "I am going to be big."

My own hypocrisy made me laugh. Up until this moment, I hated fame—the very thought of it made me ill. But now I knew that wasn't exactly true. I wouldn't mind being famous, if it was on my terms. If I was being honest, I'd admit I wanted to be seen for the work I did, not just the story.

I kept drawing. I wanted to write my own story.

Two hours later, my fingers were numb. I heard Lo's keys in the door.

"You look different," Lo said when she came to my room. "What happened?" I jumped off the floor and hugged her and then I hugged Sharon.

"I'm inspired. I feel like I was hit by lightning." I told them everything. About Brian. And Emma. And my memory. And that I was sorry. "I'm sorry I called Roxanne. I'm sorry I didn't tell you I was going to Dave's. I'm sorry I didn't tell you everything the second it happened." Then I went back to my sketchpad. I pushed it into her hands. "Look."

Sharon said, "Wow." I'd sketched three very interesting shirts, a jacket with pants, and four very different dresses. The last one—the one that Emma had inspired—was amazing, if I said so myself. The lines were classic, but the detailing made it anything but.

"I'm going to make it now," I said. "With the material you bought." I was determined to show Ms. Browning something before Easter break.

Maybe we could still go look at colleges. At least one.

I ran upstairs, got the half-finished dress, spread it out on the floor, and dismantled as much of it as I could. It took a long time. Fine-point scissors were not my favorite tool.

Lo was confused. "What happened?"

I kept working. "Today I realized I'm never going to be great at anything until I face my fears."

"Your fears?" Lo asked. She sounded skeptical.

"Yes. Just like my mother said. I'm going to be brave. I'm going to make something that says something big about me."

I felt a little bit like a genius.

I took the biggest pieces of fabric and began to pin it to the interfacing. I had to work slowly and carefully—I didn't want to snag anything. Reworking fabric was tricky business.

When the pins were in place, I took the time to iron out any new wrinkles. Then I walked upstairs to the machine.

Dress-Form Annie's lipstick had smeared, like she'd just gotten home from a great night out. She looked happy, but a little bit wild, which is how I felt, too, as I began to cut and sew. First, I made cap sleeves. Then a slightly deeper V at the neck. I added boning to give the bodice a defined structure and shape.

It looked good. Better than good.

Next came the skirt. I used every ounce of fabric to create volume. Then I pulled out an old crinoline I'd found at a secondhand store a few months ago. At the time, I'd thought it might look cool under a formal dress. But now I knew why I'd been drawn to it.

I put the dress on Annie and stood back. It was getting there. It just needed some detailing. The authentic touch.

I searched my basket of remnants for interesting swatches. The fabrics were all different. Some were smooth and silky— they made my palms tingle. Others were coarse. They reminded me of my scars.

My hands.

They had changed my life.

I traced my hands onto a piece of cardstock and cut them out.

I was inspired.

***

"What if I cover this dress with hands?" When Lo looked confused, I ran upstairs for the dress, the swatches, and Annie. "What if I make a dress that says *I am more than my hands*?"

"You're kidding, right?" Lo warned me that a dress covered in hands might attract the wrong kind of attention. "Just relax for now. We can talk about it over break. Maybe we can take a trip . . . get some inspiration?" She thought a dress with hands would attract the kind of attention I tried to avoid. She thought I was acting a bit manic—even for me.

That was okay. I expected her to doubt me. That's what often happened when a real artist tried something new. "I'm tired of fighting it. I'm already exposed. No matter what I make or do or say, before I walk in the door of any college and program, they'll already know who I am." I traced my hand onto a coarse piece of denim, cut it out, and slapped it against the dress form. "I'm tired of waiting. They'll have an opinion about me, good or bad. They'll want to see my hands."

Lo and Sharon didn't disagree. They couldn't. They knew I'd lost my chance to make a true first impression a long time ago.

This was a chance I had to take.

What could be more authentically me than a dress covered in hands?

I gave the cardboard hands to Sharon. "Trace as many as you can onto these fabrics." Then I sharpened my best shears and handed them to Lo. "You get to cut."

Cutting hands out of silk was not a very easy task. I told Lo not to worry if she made a mistake. I joked, "Remember, they don't have to be perfect."

After we had a nice-sized pile, I began to tack them by hand to the dress. I confessed that I did not go to school. They confessed that they covered for me. "We hoped you were with Miriam," Sharon said. "But when we called looking for you, she sounded pretty upset."

I put down my needle and thread. "I tried to call her, but she doesn't want to hear my side of the story."

Lo clenched the scissors. She stopped cutting. "She's your best friend. She is suffering . . . in part, because of you. What you did . . . it was very thoughtless."

"You always take her side. If she'd just call me back, she'd understand why I didn't go to the protest." I went on, "Why is it all on me? Why aren't you calling her out for using me to attract attention?"

"Because she wanted to make our world better—that was all." Lo's face was long. "Her request had nothing to do with celebrity. She's been your loyal friend for a very long time, and when she needed you, you ditched her."

I said nothing. Lo was right. I broke my promise. I let Miriam down. "If you'll help me now, I'll corner her tomorrow and apologize first thing."

She said, "You'll be humble?"

Humble was not what I was thinking, but I would have agreed to anything. "Yes," I said, mostly to get her off my back.

"I'll be humble," I said, even though I was feeling exactly the opposite. I was going to show the world that I was ready for the big time.

I was going to show the world who I really was.

They traced and cut. I finished reshaping the dress, and when that was done, I picked up a pile and start tacking the hands to the skirt. Every time I touched them, the fabric frayed. I liked it. "Don't bother trimming the threads. I like them like that. It makes them look creepy and imperfect." Almost like trees. "It makes you want to look."

We worked until all our hands cramped, a few minutes before Roxanne's first installment of "The Power of Faith."

"Should we?" Sharon asked.

The dress already looked awesome. I had no use for humility; there was nothing Roxanne could say that would surprise or hurt me. "I don't see why not."

I turned it on. Roxanne thanked the regular anchors. Her bright red power suit showed a tad too much cleavage. But her hair was perfection—very Jackie O. Her pumps were kick-ass. She stood in front of a desk, and behind her was an extra-large computer screen. On cue, the camera panned back so we could focus less on her lipstick and more on the screen. She told us that what we were about to see would inspire or aggravate. It was a perfect story for the Easter/Passover season. A story about faith and miracles.

Then she looked straight into the camera. "Faith challenges everyone," she said. Big long pause.

Sharon laughed. "You think?"

Another camera shift. Roxanne turned her head so she was facing to the side, but looking forward. "It is the topic of our generation, the center of war and politics and everyday life."

Lo said, "I can't disagree with that."

I continued to tack down hands until the dress weighed a ton. The whole time, I half-listened as Roxanne talked about how faith had permeated our culture. One football player regularly thanked God for helping him succeed. A straight-A student prayed before every test, even though her parents told her that God was too busy for such little things. She showed us a picture of an Iranian girl who risked her life by expressing her views on a blog.

Roxanne promised that her first guest would change the way we thought about prayer. (The whole time, the phone rang. It started, it stopped, then it started again. We ignored it.) I expected her to interview a minister. That would make sense. Or maybe an interfaith panel. People liked seeing some diversity on specials like this.

Instead, when she was done with her intro, she queued up a homemade film.

I dropped my needle. It was Brian in his wheelchair. At Dave's house. First he sat in the chair and attempted to navigate a block of sidewalk. Then he worked out in rehab. Then he punched a wall. Over that image, Roxanne said, "There is nothing I can say to prepare you for what you are about to see."

Lo asked, "Is that?"

"Just watch."

The movie ended. Brian emerged in his chair—in the studio. Then without warning, he stood up and walked. He pumped his fist and jumped up and down, just to show off. Lo said, "She's right. I don't believe it." Sharon asked, "How long was he paralyzed?"

"Two years," Brian told Roxanne. "I spent two years in a wheelchair." He tried to describe the moments he knew he was sick as well as the moment my hands began to work their magic.

Roxanne's eyes looked really surprised and beautiful. That gray shadow on the lid smudged into the crease for depth did great things for her. She asked her questions with increased earnestness: "What was it like being in a wheelchair?"

"Terrible."

"What was the activity you missed most?"

"Lacrosse. With my dad."

"What do you want to do first?"

"First, I want to thank Janine Collins and Pastor David Armstrong." Roxanne showed some footage of me holding Brian's hand in front of my house, then the group of us praying at the hotel. The picture was fuzzy, our faces not too clear. The angle was bad. Lots of shadows. But it still looked like praying. Brian said, "When Janine Collins prayed with me, God heard my prayer. Either that, or she healed me."

Lo picked the phone off the hook and slammed it down. "What are we going to do?" She asked me one more time if I really thought this was the right time to make a dress all about hands.

I said, "It's not like I'm going to wear it." When Lo protested that I was tempting schools to only see me as the Soul Survivor—the very thing I swore I didn't want—I told her that I was actually glad Brian went to Roxanne. So what if everyone knew? This was good news. It was exciting. And what could we do? It was his story. "Now you know why I'm so inspired."

By the next commercial break, I'd sewn on enough of the hands to know that this dress was going to be a masterpiece.

My phone vibrated. I hoped it was Miriam. It felt weird not to talk to her. I realized I never finished anything without her input.

But it wasn't her number. "Hello?"

"Hi Janine. It's Emma." She sounded like she'd been crying. "You have to trust me—we didn't want Brian to go on TV."

I said, "I trust you" and "It's not your fault" about a hundred times before she calmed down. I didn't know why she was so surprised.

"Dave should have prepared you. Stories like this . . . they don't stay secrets for long. They never do."

When she was finally quiet, I told her to meet me after school. "Wait until you see the dress I'm making," I said. "I couldn't have made it without you."

A moment later, Dave got on and thanked me for not being angry. "She's a special girl, Janine. Like I said, she changed me."

I joked, "I thought I changed you."

***

At the end of the hour, Roxanne returned to thank Brian. She looked straight into the camera and told the world that this story was getting bigger every day. *Stay tuned!* Across the bottom of the picture, a news report ticked by. A female suicide bomber just blew up a bank in Gaza. Thirty-two dead. Twenty wounded.

I stayed up most of the night finishing the dress.

THIRTY-THREE

I knew I was asking a lot of Ms. Browning, but I couldn't wait. "Can you give me five minutes? I need to see what you think."

Her tote bag was packed. "How about one?" She looked at the clock. She probably had plans.

Well, this wouldn't take long.

I handed her my portfolio. "I worked on this all night long." When she opened it, I said, "The first few pieces are there to make you laugh."

She turned to the first pages, a series of T-shirts branding funny sayings. "Over the years, I've wondered if you would ever make a statement about your . . . um . . . your . . ."

"Celebrity. My reputation. You can say it."

Each one had a different saying on the front.

It doesn't matter what you're famous for, as long as you're famous.
Don't stop looking at me.
I'm ready for my close-up.
15 minutes is never enough.
Every day, we all smile for a camera.

She stopped turning pages and put her hand to her mouth. "Aren't they funny?" I said. "My plan is to paint them by hand, so each one will be unique—but still commercial."

"They're certainly timely," she said, nodding slowly—which was very disappointing. I still couldn't see if she was smiling, if she thought they set the right tone, or if they were awful and off-putting.

She turned to the next section, the suits and dresses. "Now this is good. These lines are really fresh. What kind of textiles are you envisioning?"

I tried to relax. "Light wool, of course." She smiled. Ms. Browning loved light wool. I pointed to my favorite jacket and skirt ensemble. "I was wondering if you thought I should treat it with some diluted permanent white glue," I said. "To stiffen it up."

"I don't know. Maybe. Maybe not," she said, turning the page to the first of the dresses. Now she looked almost happy. "Make this one. Absolutely." She tapped the page with her pencil eraser. "The T-shirts are one thing. They're cute. But this . . . they will want to see if you can pull off these micropleats."

I agreed, even though I was sure I wouldn't have to make anything more. I pushed her forward to the end of the portfolio and the last dress. "So?" I asked. "Do you love it?"

She shrugged. "Talk to me about these squiggly lines. Is it your intention to distort the silhouette?"

"Not exactly." I was nearly giddy. "Here. I'll show you." When she looked a little impatient, I said, "I've got it right here."

First, I locked the door. Then I made her turn around while I slipped off my T-shirt and put on the dress. After some maneuvering, I managed to get the buttons fastened and the skirt fluffed just enough. I gave it a quick twirl to let the threads fly. "Okay. You can turn around."

Ms. Browning stood back. She looked at me from all angles without making a gesture or smile. That was intentional. At the start of every semester, she told this story about how once, after a student presented an important piece of work, her smile disappeared and that wasn't fair.

But the payoff should come now. It had been long enough. She should be smiling and complimenting the dress, the detailing, the originality, telling me I'm the next Alexander McQueen. I gave a quick twirl, so she could see the movement in the hands.

"Slow down," she said. She looked at the dress up close. Then she asked me a string of questions that were supposed to make me think:

"What inspired this treatment?"

"What are you trying to say?"

"Do you like it? Who would wear this, besides you?"

I did not freak out. This was her gig. "Obviously, I wanted to make a statement about my hands and the fact that whenever people see me, all they see are my hands. I wanted to merge my feelings about beauty and what people think is beautiful with the ugliness I see in my story and my hands."

"So . . . you made a dress about your hands?"

I thought about that for a moment. "Not really. More a statement about the way the world has always looked at me . . . and my ugly hands." I wanted her to smile, to acknowledge how fabulous this was. "Like the T-shirts. It's about how the media has hounded me."

She told me to sit down.

"This is cute, Janine," she said, "and in a week or two or three, it could be profound. But today it also looks rushed. It's too literal. I think you've crossed the line to self-indulgent."

Ms. Browning put a lot of importance on the ability to accept constructive criticism, but she was wrong. This was well-conceived—and inspired. If she looked again, she'd see I didn't need to take my time. I had already done everything she told me to do. I asked her to look it over one more time. "I totally respect your opinion, but I think it's profound *now*. Did you *not* see the news? I had a really crazy experience, and this is what came from it. I think it's honest. And funny."

She bristled. "Janine. Listen to me. It's too literal. I think you don't need real hands. What you need is texture. And more movement. And shape and volume." She took another sip of soda. "I think you made this to get me off your back. So you could go interview for school while your story was in the news." She pointed out some construction flaws. She didn't like the fraying at the hands. She thought the whole concept was way too obvious.

I said, "But . . . "

Now she looked tired. "Janine, please. If you still have appointments, cancel them. You have the beginning of something, and I just wish you'd show me some patience. A little humility for the process. Take some time to let this concept develop. Push yourself. Embrace your—"

"Stop." If she said "face your fears," I'd scream. This was what I did.

This was the best I could do.

I asked, "Is this your way of telling me I'm no good?"

Now she looked exhausted. "No, Janine. It's not. All I'm saying is, go home and play with these themes. Make the suit—the sketch is gorgeous—and at least one of the shirts. Refine your lines. You've got some great ideas, and these sketches are a perfect starting place. But if you want to impress Parsons, you really need to slow down. Trust me on this. Your impatience shows and gives you away. This is college—your future. It's not a TV show."

Outside, the bell rang. Someone knocked on her door. Loud. She said, "Maybe you're right. Maybe your name will get you in the door. Maybe you think this is just a formality. But if I were in your shoes, I wouldn't be so smug. In the art world, you have to pay your dues. You have to earn it." Outside, the knocking continued. I heard someone yell my name. As she walked to the door, Ms. B. said, "I thought that was what you wanted. I thought that after everything you've been through, you'd appreciate that."

THIRTY-FOUR

Ms. Browning walked across the floor to the door.

"Can you wait?" I asked. As I walked toward her, the hands on my dress fluttered. "Just answer a few more questions?"

"I don't think that would be helpful."

"But I need to understand. I was so sure you would love this." I felt stupid standing here in my hands, and at the same time, I couldn't believe she wasn't falling over herself.

I had thought for once in my life, I was going to get what I wanted. But I failed.

She opened the door.

It was Abe—just the person I didn't want to see. "What are you doing here?" I asked him. Why did the worst moments of my life always have an audience?

He didn't even look at my dress. "Janine! Put some shoes on. We have to go."

"Where?" I looked at my clothes crumpled up on the desk. "Can you at least give me five minutes?"

"No." With his crutch, he swiped them to the ground.

"You don't have time. They're cutting down the tree. Miriam is freaking out." He turned around and started limping out the door. "She needs you."

***

It no longer mattered if she was mad at me. Miriam had been my best friend since second grade—my first day in a real school. Since the teacher told her to show me around. Since she didn't stare at my hands. Since she said, "Everyone has something they don't like."

At the flagpole, Abe finally noticed my dress. "Nice look." He was breathing heavy. "Is that supposed to be a nightgown?" He checked his watch. "Maybe you should change."

"Keep moving. I'm okay." I could be humiliated for her. "Just tell me what happened."

On the way there, I heard the details a good friend would already know. After the protest, the board of supervisors held a bunch of unannounced meetings and determined that the tree was a safety hazard. It was too close to some power lines. Too expensive to stabilize. A disaster waiting to happen. Just what Lo had predicted. I said, "I'm confused. I thought there was time. I thought they were going to bring in a scientist."

Abe needed to stop. His armpits hurt. His ankle throbbed— he was putting too much weight on his foot. "Just don't tell her it's all for the best." He grimaced in pain. "She's really sensitive. She knows you couldn't care less about the farm."

If my cheeks weren't red, they should have been. "Fine. I don't care. Not really. I don't understand why she thinks it's so bad if they put the farm in another place."

"It's the principle of the thing." He looked at me like I was an idiot. "I shouldn't have to tell you that people all over the world fight over land."

Fine. Good point. If he wanted me to feel even more stupid than I already did, he succeeded. "But it's still just a farm. It's not . . ." We walked in silence. No singing. Not even a sad line. It felt weird.

I asked him if he saw "The Power of Faith." "So is tonight your big debut? Are you going to tell the world what happened?"

I thought that would cheer him up, but it didn't. Still no singing. "She taped our interview, but she told me she'd give me a heads-up if she was going to use it. And since she hasn't, my guess is I've been scrapped." About this, he didn't look at all upset. "I know you won't believe me, but to be honest, I don't really care. I had some fun. I made a lot of new friends. I met Emma." He paused for a second to readjust his crutch. "But some things are more important." He meant Miriam. "I don't really believe you healed me."

That surprised me. "You don't?"

"No, I don't." Now he walked even slower. "My mother doesn't either. After all the excitement had ended, we talked to my priest and he says I should thank God—not you. He says I should consider myself lucky and blessed that God was watching me, but he was pretty sure you had nothing to do with that." As we got closer to the farm, he reminded me that Miriam didn't know I was coming—that I might (for once) try a softer approach. "And can you do me a favor? Can you not make this day about you?" When I started to argue, he said, "The tripod isn't a triangle with you on the top and me and Miriam on the bottom."

"I'm sorry. I mean it." I promised to try hard to make it up to both of them. "I owe you so much. You were right about Emma. I'm glad I gave her a chance. She is definitely amazing."

For a moment, Abe looked impressed. "That's really good, J. Really good."

I started to tell him about the hotel and how she helped me remember my dad and the bombing, but then I stopped. Too self-centered. Not what he needed to hear. "She has a lot of heart. You know, she changed Dave's life."

He laughed. "I told you she was awesome. The way she looks death in the face. I'm really glad you got to talk to her." Up ahead we could see the farm—or rather—what used to be the farm. Now it looked like a construction zone. Men wearing long sleeves and big chaps over their pants stood by. They carried equipment—slings and saws. Others stood ready to help out. There was a big orange-and-black truck parked in the middle of the farm, and heavy rubber blankets lay draped over the nearby power lines.

"Why the blankets?" I asked.

"Live wires," Abe said. "Can't turn off the power to the nursing home."

Felling a tree was a dangerous activity. Men in hard hats and bright orange vests kept the crowd at a safe distance.

The tree had already lost a lot of its smaller branches. It looked sad. A cable hung from the biggest branch. One man, standing at the top of the truck's arm, pruned some more small branches. The workers stood back as they hit the ground.

It was very quiet. No protests. Just a few directions to look here or stand there. The people just watched.

Abe said, "When Emma told me her story, I couldn't

believe it. I knew the two of you would be good for each other. I just hoped you would give her a chance and listen."

At first, I had no clue what he was talking about. But then I remembered—her friend with cancer. I got it.

I finally got it.

Emma was there for her friend. She didn't think about herself. To make things better, I had to do that, too. I just had to figure out how.

THIRTY-FIVE

The biggest group of observers stood clustered together in the grass in front of the nursing home. A huge sign was posted on the lawn near the intersection: "Save Our Farm. Build a Healthier Community."

Others stood around in the street, a safe distance from the action. These people didn't seem sad. They were mostly just gawkers or opportunists with their own agendas. Some filmed the events on their phones. Some held smaller signs, all for their own personal causes.

"End corporate welfare!"

"End all War"

"Separate Church and State"

"Bring back *Freaks and Geeks*."

"I have that show on DVD," Abe said. He waved to a couple of kids. One was from the school newspaper. Last year, he'd begged me to do an interview. "The saddest part is, nobody else cares."

I had to agree. In terms of demonstrations, it was a pretty pitiful event.

Even from far away, I could see Miriam and Samantha standing with the group on the grass. She was wearing jeans with a short-sleeved pink sweater—a piece I'd begged her to buy. Most of the others were sitting on the grass. "Should we go over there?" I asked.

"I wouldn't," Abe said.

I didn't want to upset Miriam, but I needed to talk to her. I yelled, "Miriam!" I waved my arms over my head. It's not that I thought she'd be happy to see me. I just wanted her to know I was here.

That couldn't be wrong.

But maybe it was, because when she looked at me waving my arms and screaming her name, she didn't wave. In fact, she turned around and hugged Samantha.

"That wasn't nice."

Abe wasn't all that sympathetic. "Just give it a rest."

He didn't have to remind me: True forgiveness took a long time. I knew I had to be patient and humble—those were just two things I clearly wasn't.

Especially when Samantha was involved.

As the workers systematically removed branch after branch, Samantha walked over. "Not satisfied with the coverage you've been getting? Do you really need to make a scene here, too?" She yelled at the kid with the camera. "Hey you. Janine Collins is here. In *costume*. Film *her*."

She had such a big mouth. A bunch of people put down their signs, turned, and walked toward me. They looked a little bit like sheep. Or zombies.

It was just what she wanted. An audience.

She grabbed the hem of my skirt. "Wow. This is impressive.

What's it supposed to be?" A few people laughed. Others left Miriam's circle to see what was happening. "Joan of Arc or a Thanksgiving Day float? Is this what you were making when you said you would help us save our farm?"

There were so many things I could say, but they wouldn't accomplish anything. I wanted to stand with Miriam. I wanted to console her when the tree finally came down.

"This is your fault," she barreled on. (Her staccato pronunciation was very effective over the noise.) "If you had helped us, this might not be happening." She looked at the crowd around us and said, "For those of you who don't know her, this is Janine Collins, the famous *Soul Survivor*. Maybe you've heard of her? She said she was going to help us, but she never did."

The crowd grew bigger. Closer. Angrier.

I wanted to run, get out of here—I wasn't helping Miriam. I didn't want to fight with Samantha. I wanted to go home. "I'm sorry about your tree," I said, looking for a way out.

She didn't. She swiped at my dress and balled some of the hands up in her fist. She pulled so hard a couple of them tore off. "People like you . . . you're so disgusting. You always have to be the star."

"That's not true. I'd give anything to be anonymous."

She laughed. "Then why are you here? In that?" I heard more laughter. Saw a few mean-spirited gestures. She tore off another hand and stomped on it like it was a cigarette butt.

Abe finally spoke up. "Samantha, that's not fair." Which was not an effective statement. None of this was fair.

But I got it—they had to blame someone. And that someone was going to be me.

Before I could walk away, something cold and wet hit my back and dripped down the skirt. I was afraid to look. Abe said, "I think you should get out of here."

Samantha added, "I guess you underestimated how many people care about this place."

This was weirder than my wooden hands dream. I accepted that I was a bad friend. I didn't blame Miriam for not coming over here to hear my apology. But how many of these people cared about this farm? How many of them were just here because the cameras were, because the story was, because there was nothing else to do? I was not the only villain.

From off to one side, someone hurled dirt at my dress. Then some leaves that had grown wet and cold sitting in the gutter. From the back of the group, Dan stepped forward. He was wearing my favorite shirt—a pink button-down. Guys think pink is a girly color, but pretty much universally it does great things for their eyes. I wondered if he was going to help me out, but he stood back. He said, "Don't expect anyone here to feel sorry for you."

Now I was scared.

I looked around for a friendly face. For sympathy. For help.

Emma would tell me that she experienced faith when times were at their worst. She would tell me that it wasn't always important to be the one in front of the camera, that sometimes the person behind the curtain could get her way, too. If she were here, I knew she'd tell me that God showed Himself to her when she needed Him most.

Well, I needed help now.

Maybe she had something, because just when I was sure they were going to pelt me with dirt, the crew fired up the chainsaws even louder. Everyone turned around to watch. This was the moment they had dreaded. They stood still as stone, and watched the men take the tree's remaining limbs.

A few people cried.

Miriam stayed as far away from me as possible.

When the great arm of the tree hit the ground, smaller branches scattered. It was like that old story, *The Giving Tree*. Tons of people sent that book to me when I was in the hospital, which sort of shocked me. It might have been a famous book, but it was also pretty morbid.

In the book, the kid basically killed the tree. First he took the branches and the shade. Then he took the trunk. When the tree was no more than a stump, the boy came back as an old man and took the only thing the tree had left to give—a seat. The first time Dave read it to me, I thought the old man was scary. Lo called it a representation of a vicious one-sided relationship, disguised as a book.

I would bet that Miriam thought I was that boy, but that wasn't who I wanted to be. I wanted to be like Emma: humble. I knew that was the only way to make things better was to help my friend.

I tried to convince her how sorry I was. "I wish you could have saved it."

No reply.

"I didn't want to desert you. Can we go somewhere and talk?" I took her hand. "I know I've been selfish. I never meant to treat you this way. I had a lot on my mind. Can you just let me explain?"

Unlike Miriam, Samantha was no good at the silent treatment. "Let me guess. Your problems are bigger than ours?" She told me that Miriam wanted nothing to do with me. "Go find your followers, your believers. Let them take care of you for a while."

When I started to walk away, Miriam finally stepped away from Samantha, but it wasn't to apologize. "You know, some girl was here. She seemed sort of desperate to find you—she said that something terrible had happened. I told her not to care so much, that you disappoint people all the time."

Emma.

"Will you come with me?" I asked. "We can go to Dave's. You need to meet her and hear what she has to say. And then we can talk. You can let me apologize."

She turned back. Now the tree was just one tall trunk. The crew helped one of the men stand up close to the highest third of the trunk. From here, it looked like he was hugging the tree. The men on the ground told us that the trunk was too big to take in one piece. They had to dissect it.

Miriam said, "It won't be long now."

Moments later, the worker turned on his chainsaw and began to remove the top of the trunk. Miriam looked at me like it was all my fault. "You don't get it, do you?" she shouted over the noise. "I needed you. I needed your help. I needed you to be there for me the way I've been there for you."

I could have said, "I didn't mean to blow you off" or "I feel really bad about the tree" or "I'd do everything differently, if I could," but none of that would be true.

We both knew that.

I waited for the crew to dismantle the top third of the trunk. "I was selfish," I said. "I know it. But I want to make it up to you. I want to rebuild the tripod. Come with me. I think you'll really like Emma."

"No." The crew lowered the man to the next section of the trunk. At the same time, farther away, others loaded pieces of branch and trunk into a machine that turned everything to mulch.

THIRTY-SIX

Alone, I ran.

I swung my arms and pressed through my feet. I ran as fast as I could. I had that feeling in my gut.

Something was wrong.

When I got to Dave's hotel room, I was covered in sweat. I banged on the door. "Where is she? What happened?"

He told me to come inside. "You need to see something now." He turned on the TV, and we sat down on the couch. "At first, I thought she was joking. But before she left, I watched it. She invited us to make a statement."

"Who?" I asked.

"Roxanne." He struggled with the remote control.

I shook my head. "I'm not making any statements."

He cursed a few times before a fuzzy image of a house appeared on the screen. "Just wait. You might change your mind."

It was a fuzzy shot of a white house with black shutters, probably taken from the other side of a fence. There was a red car in the driveway and a picnic table on a brick patio. I was about to ask if he queued up the wrong disc when Brian walked into the middle of the yard and said, "Hey, Mom. Come on out and watch this." Then he dropped to the ground and counted out twenty-five push-ups.

The whole thing seemed a little weird. Whoever took this was hiding, but the film wasn't anything special.

"I don't get it," I said.

His mother walked outside and said, "Show me." She wore cute yoga pants, a down vest, and a T-shirt from Dave's mission. The camera caught some random patches of snow as Brian performed more push-ups and sit-ups. Then the phone rang. Brian's mom walked inside.

I was bored.

Dave wasn't. "Watch now. This is the killer."

When she returned, she had the wheelchair. "Hurry up. He's on his way." Brian jumped up, sat down, and popped a wheelie. He cried about being paralyzed, about how much he missed his legs and being able to run and jump and go to a regular school.

It was confusing until I looked at the date. "I don't believe it. That liar."

The video was from two months ago—when Brian was supposedly paralyzed—when his mother was already following Dave and praying for a miracle. I said, "They made the whole thing up."

"It gets worse." First, Brian pretended he was walking for the first time. Then, his mother coached Brian on how to look weak. She said, "Do it again. Praise God. Tell the world that you were healed by prayer." Then they burst into laughter. She might as well have said, "Let's take that idiot for everything he's got."

"Turn it off. What are you going to do?"

He paused the show and dialed Roxanne on speakerphone. She picked up immediately and thanked him for calling so quickly. She said, "I'm interviewing Ted—Brian's dad—tonight." She chuckled, then got serious. "As you might imagine, he has a lot to get off his chest." Roxanne explained that this was no longer about faith. She shrugged it off. "We canned the whole thing." Now the segment was about what people were willing to do to be famous. She told us that Ted had blackmailed his wife with this tape, but after she filed for divorce, he wanted more. When that didn't happen, he called Roxanne. She said, "I had a hunch your story was going to lead to something big, but this . . . " She laughed. "This is big."

Dave said, "She told me she was an abused woman."

Roxanne asked if he would put that on the record. She said, "I found some old footage of her from one of those early wives' reality shows. She spent most of her time on camera screaming at the other women—calling them whores and liars and drunks—making fun of them behind their backs. I called the show's producer, and he said that the woman tried to sue him when he didn't extend her contract."

Dave googled her while Roxanne talked. I stared over his shoulder at the iPad resting in his lap. There she was—a housewife looking for fame. The mother of one son—a perfectly healthy young man.

I asked, "What about the doctors? Didn't you say you met them? Let's talk to them. If they were fooled, then you won't look so gullible."

Roxanne said not to bother. "When I looked them up, I couldn't find them. Their credentials were fake." She sighed. "*I* should have checked. An oversight I'm sure to hear about."

Dave watched the video a few more times. I couldn't— it was torture. The worst moment: when Brian stumbled on purpose, and the two of them anticipated Dave's reactions.

"He'll praise God."

"He'll thank the Lord."

Brian picked up a Coke bottle and held it like a microphone. "I'd like to thank my mother for believing in me all this time." Then he burst into laughter.

A week ago, I wouldn't have been shocked. But now I felt sad, guilty, mad. For a moment there, I had thought maybe . . . what if . . .

For a moment there, I'd almost believed.

Dave sat down. Suddenly he looked older, a little weak, his hair not so shiny. "Usually I can tell when someone is taking me for a ride, but she was so convincing."

"You mean you had a thing for her," I said.

He didn't deny it. "She told me she believed in miracles and healing. She said she believed in me. When she first encouraged me to reach out to you, it seemed spontaneous. She didn't push. I didn't think twice. The timing was perfect. She knew my position—she'd watched me on TV long enough to see I would buy her story. In this world, we need faith. We need hope. Without it . . ."

I stared at my hands, my ugly, deformed, useless hands. "She fed you what you wanted to hear."

Dave walked to the window. He paged through his Bible and recited a few quotes, none of which made sense to me.

I said, "It's just a story."

He didn't argue. "That's not the only problem." He didn't need to explain. "Roxanne is ambitious. She could keep digging."

Now I really was impatient—he was acting like a baby. I asked, "What would she find? Did you coerce them to do this?"

"No. Of course not. Janine—you know me."

"Actually," I said, "I *knew* you." This was my reality now. I didn't know my mother, and I didn't really know him. "I knew you once. But not so much now."

At "not so much now," Emma walked in. She said, "Janine, did Miriam tell you I was looking for you? I wanted to surprise you—to see what you made." She was the first person to notice I was covered in dirt. "It looks like you fell in a puddle."

Dave told me to leave. He needed to talk to Emma. "Alone."

I got up, but Emma asked me to sit back down. "I saw what they were doing to that tree."

Dave urged me not to say anything, but I didn't see the point of waiting. She was my friend. I wanted to tell her. "He wants to talk to you because we just found out that Brian was faking. He could always walk. His recovery was staged. Tonight Roxanne is going to interview his dad." I rolled my eyes. "No doubt, the story will go national."

I waited for Emma to offer the bright side—that all this wasn't really that bad—that he obviously wasn't a real believer and miracles could still happen. I expected her to tell me that faith and community were what was important—that every day she found a new reason to believe in God.

At the very least, I expected her to laugh it off.

But she didn't. Not even close.

Instead, she turned stiff, like a statue. She looked at Dave. "All this time, Brian could walk?"

He turned on the footage. "Yes."

"He was never paralyzed?"

Dave flicked on the tape. Onscreen Brian jumped up and made a double biceps pose.

I said, "It's not the end of the world. Maybe you don't know how this works. At worst, Brian will be big news for a couple of days. Then something else will happen, and everyone will forget. I've seen this happen a million times. It's big news for a week. Then no one will care."

Emma asked, "Are there pictures of me?" That was an odd question. When Dave said he couldn't be sure, she picked up a glass bowl. It caught the light, creating a beautiful rainbow of color across the wall. But she wasn't looking at the beauty. When I looked at her eyes, I saw Emir, the boy with the bomb. I saw his eyes in hers.

Threatening but still.

Calm and determined.

Willing to die.

That day, I looked up at him and he looked down at me. I was just a little girl—I didn't understand what it meant to be afraid for your life—but even so, I sensed something was wrong. I could not have known that something terrible was about to happen—it was so far outside my knowledge or experience. That day, I said nothing. In that moment, what could I have known to say?

But now I knew—I knew what eyes like Emma's meant. And this time, I wasn't going to stay silent. "Emma, what is wrong with you?"

It was too little, too late. She hurled the bowl hard, and when it hit the wall, it shattered in all directions. I felt shards of glass hit my face, my hands, my legs. Without explanation, Emma turned around and ran upstairs in tears.

"Let her go," Dave said.

I dropped to my knees and started picking up the glass, one sharp piece at a time.

THIRTY-SEVEN

Dave looked very uncomfortable. "I should have told you right away."

"Told me what?"

He told me to sit down. "Emma first joined the mission six months ago. She had just found out that her leukemia had returned after a year in remission. The prognosis was not good."

My mind reeled. "What do you mean, not good?"

He didn't say. "After many weeks of prayer and discussion with me and some very good doctors, she decided that she didn't want to undergo any more treatments. Instead, she put her trust in God and faith."

Now I was on overload. "What does that mean? Are you helping her die?"

"No," Dave said. "On the contrary, I believe I'm helping her live. I'm helping her free herself from the torture of treatment. And every day, she seems more alive. More committed. She grows stronger, she looks healthier. She says she's never felt better in her life."

There were so many things wrong with this. "You're encouraging this?" To me, it sounded more like suicide.

He grabbed me by the arm and forced me to sit down. "She thought you might see it that way. But no matter how you feel about faith, it's a viable choice. It is her choice. She decided to live the life she was given with dignity, and we have to respect that."

This would be fine for an old person, but we were talking about Emma. She was seventeen. She had her whole life in front of her. "What about her parents? Don't tell me they gave her the green light to kill herself, too." Then I figured it out. "Did you come here so that I could make her better? When were you going to tell me that? How long were you going to wait?"

He didn't answer my questions directly. "When I was invited to come here, of course—the first thing I thought of was that I wanted you to meet her. And not just because I thought you might help her. I thought you'd be good for each other. And then we got the news about Abe. And we began to wonder. And hope. I was sure that providence had brought her to you. And then more miracles happened. You started to trust me. Brian walked. You came here on your own."

I couldn't understand how he could play games with Emma's life. "And what were you going to do when I couldn't make her better?"

He shook his head. "That was never a consideration. She believes that God has a plan. She isn't looking for guarantees."

"And now?"

He grabbed his Bible and said nothing for a long time. "I think this is a test. Brian and his mother are God's way of testing me. If I can stay strong, she will be fine. She will get better. We just have to stay strong."

If there were another glass bowl, I would throw it at him. He was acting like me, believing that this was about him as much as it was about her. "Dave, you have to make Emma go to a doctor."

He went to the door and opened it. "Go home, Janine. That is not going to happen. Emma will not go back to the hospital. She wants no more painful treatments." He told me that, now that I knew, I had to be discreet. "You can't tell anyone what you know. She's in hiding, Janine. She didn't run away from her parents just to go back into that hell."

THIRTY-EIGHT

People said, what comes around goes around.

They didn't know what they were talking about.

***

Instead of taking the elevator downstairs, I went to her room. Emma was sitting in bed. I realized that in one way, I was as guilty as Dave. I saw only what I wanted to see.

Now it was so obvious.

Her arms were thin. Her knees stuck out. She was dying. It probably took every ounce of energy just to get through the day.

"I feel stupid," we said at exactly the same time, but neither of us smiled. This wasn't funny. Not for her, not for me. I would never understand anyone being willing to die without a fight.

She stared straight ahead. "Your hair falls out. You puke all day. You can't get out of bed—even to go to the bathroom. I'm not going to be a martyr."

It sounded terrible. "But lots of people get better. There's a girl from my school who—"

"And just as many don't." She showed me a picture of herself before chemo. She was chubby. Healthy. Smiling. "My strain of leukemia is particularly—how do they put it—aggressive. Best-case scenario was pretty much off the table."

She was not going to convince me that what she was doing was the right way to go about things. "What about your parents?"

She looked sad. "I miss them, but if I go home, they will make me go back to the hospital. They located a match."

"For what?"

"Bone marrow."

I begged her to reconsider. I'd seen the PSAs about bone marrow transplants. They saved lives. They worked real miracles. "Don't you miss your friends? Don't you want to live?"

Her posture stiffened. "Yes, I want to live, but no, I do not miss being the spunky sick girl that people have to visit to feel less guilty about their own good luck. I don't want to risk spending the rest of my life in a bed. If I can just stay with Dave until I'm eighteen—then I can go home. My parents won't be able to force me to do anything."

I looked at the picture next to her bed. A smiling threesome, not that different from mine. But these parents were alive. They loved her. They wanted her to live. Her mother should not have to read a Book of Death to know how her daughter was feeling at the end of her life.

I held up my hands and let her see every line, every scar, ever disfigurement. I said, "Do you still believe I can help you? Do you want to try?"

At first, she didn't move. She didn't have to tell me—she was scared. She wanted me to try. She still wanted to believe. She put her hands on mine, and we closed our eyes. This time, I knew what to do. I pictured her getting stronger. I asked God—whoever he or she or it was—to pay attention.

I prayed. I spoke directly to God. If there were any justice at all in this world, she would get better. This girl deserved to be healthy. She was good. She helped other people. "Make her better. Let her live." I scrunched my eyes tight. And then I listened. I waited. I wanted to hear my mother's voice. I knew—if there were any hope of this working—that that was what had to happen. I had to feel the way I felt when Abe began to breathe. I tried to conjure up optimism and hope.

But nothing happened.

I squeezed her hands tighter, but all I could think of was that line from the Kaddish, the prayer for the dead, the line that made me so mad.

He who makes peace in his high holy places, may he bring peace upon us, and upon all Israel; and say Amen.

I prayed desperately. "Help her. Now. Come down off your high holy place and help her. Mom, talk to me. I know you weren't perfect, but I need you. Don't abandon me again. I need one little miracle. I need to hear the words. I don't want Emma to die."

No voice spoke. My mouth was dry like dust. When I opened my eyes, my mother was not here; Emma's eyes were not closed. She said, "You can't fix me." I was pretty sure she'd been looking at me almost the whole time.

I grabbed her hands. "Let me try again."

She told me to leave. "If you care about me, walk away.

Live. Next time you go to a party, go for me. Next time you kiss someone, kiss him for me. You complained how people look at you? When people find out I have leukemia, they treat me the way you are looking at me right now. Like fine china or a contagious disease or a ticking clock about to stop. They think they can tell you exactly what you should do. The reason I left home isn't because I want to die. It's because I want to live. On my terms. I want to live a normal life. For once, I want to be just like everyone else."

THIRTY-NINE

I wanted to heal her.

I wanted to touch her hands and make her better.

I didn't know what I was thinking.

I called Miriam and told her what happened. I begged her to pick me up—there was no one else I could talk to.

***

We sat in the car outside the hotel. "She's dying," I said. "How did I miss that?"

Miriam tapped the steering wheel. She fiddled with the defrost and air conditioning so that the front window wouldn't fog up. I said, "The worst part is, she's dying and she expects everyone to sit back and watch."

"It's definitely tragic," Miriam said, but she didn't think there was anything I could do. "It's her life. This is what she wants." Only Emma had the right to say what she was willing and not willing to do.

That stunk.

No one should be allowed to give up like that. Because no one could know when it would end.

Miriam was pretty sure I didn't know all the facts. "If the treatments make her sick . . . if they're really that bad . . . if it doesn't work on her cancer . . ."

"That's a crock." I knew what it felt like to be left behind—to have so many questions—and I didn't wish that on her parents. I also knew what it was like to be in the hospital—how scary it was. All those numbers. All those decisions. The doctors weren't allowed to tell you that a treatment is 100 percent effective. They were taught to give you odds. But there was always a chance.

Always.

Miriam's phone jingled like a xylophone. I said, "She's just being stubborn. If she can get a transplant, she should take it."

She stared at her phone. When it jingled again, I said, "You can get it, I don't care. I just want you to know I didn't mean to blow off the protest."

The next time it rang, she picked it up. Her voice immediately sounded happier. She said yes and no a few times, then she laughed. When she hung up, she changed back to serious. She asked the million-dollar question. "If chemo is that bad—if you knew you were ultimately going to die no matter what you did—shouldn't you have the right to live the way you want to?"

I wasn't sure. Maybe yes. Maybe no. Maybe I just wanted Miriam to be on my side. Maybe I wanted her to come over to my house, sit in my window seat, and worry about whether any animals were tested making her nail polish. "I think you have a responsibility to live. I don't think anyone should be willing to give up and die." When she looked unconvinced, I said, "The only thing she can be sure of is that she'll die if she does nothing. She doesn't know what will happen if she takes the treatment." I looked out the window. I didn't like talking ethics. I was uncomfortable talking about choosing death.

But Miriam would not let up. "I know you really care about her, but this isn't your problem. It isn't about you."

She didn't understand. "But I can do something. I can tell her family where she is."

"And what do you think will happen then?" Miriam asked. "You'll be the hero? She'll thank you forever? I'll forgive you? Roxanne will tell the world that you are the greatest person in the world—that the disappointed people can rally around you after all?"

She knew me too well.

When I started to argue, Miriam told me she was done. "Do what you want." She drove in silence until we arrived at my house. "But if I were you, I'd talk it out with Lo. Remember: Emma is your friend. She trusted you. That has to mean something too."

***

I said goodnight. It meant a lot. That was the problem.

At 11:12, I watched Roxanne interview Ted. I watched the footage I'd already seen, and I listened as Ted informed the world of everything I already knew: Brian and his mother fooled Dave and me. Brian's mom wanted to be famous. Brian hoped that he would be, too. I cringed when Ted said, "I don't know how the kid sat in that chair as long as he did."

The second the show went to commercial; the phone began to ring. Lo said, "You don't have to get it," but I disagreed. I needed to do something different.

I said that I never was and never would be a healer. I said that I accepted responsibility for people believing I could help them. I apologized to everyone I could think of for things I did and did not do. I was so contrite, I probably sounded pathetic.

(Or humble, as Lo would say.)

By 2:30 A.M., Lo took out a big amber bottle and poured herself a nip. The house was quiet. I made ten official statements, all the same. Lo thought I was very brave. She made me hot chocolate.

I wondered what my mother would say.

When Lo was too tired to talk anymore, I went upstairs to my room. I put the hamsa around my neck and read the journals. My mother was passionate. She had principles. I may have hated some of them, but she did what she felt she had to do, every step of the way. She listened to her gut.

I needed to listen to my gut. I needed to do the right thing for Emma.

***

When the sun began to rise, I opened my eyes and dialed the number, and I wasn't surprised when she picked up on the first ring. There were a few things I wanted to say to Roxanne Wheeler, but at this hour I had to keep it brief, simple, and direct.

This was for Emma.

"She has cancer. She is hiding from her parents."

Roxanne took down every detail. She asked a lot of questions. How old is she? What kind of cancer? Do you know what her parents do? How long has it been since she ran off?

I didn't know much.

"Just promise me," I told her. No press. No pictures.

"What's in it for me?" Roxanne asked.

I offered myself. After Emma was reunited with her parents, I promised to sit down for an interview—that exclusive she wanted. I promised to tell her everything I knew—about the bombing, about Dave, about what it was like to be the Soul Survivor, to be famous for being found.

I picked up the Book of Death. I was going to do this, because I still wanted to believe in happy endings. This story could not end in death. More than anything, I didn't want Emma's mom to look for answers in a book.

I wanted to do for her what she did for others.

Roxanne reviewed the details one more time. She thanked me for trusting her, which I found extremely funny. Emma trusted me, but I didn't expect she would understand.

It might still be an act of selfishness. Miriam might be right—maybe I could never redeem myself or my mother.

But Emma would live. That justified everything.

FORTY

On the bright side, my dress and I made the front page of the local section of the morning paper.

All the fingers blew toward the left. The skirt billowed. Lo asked me if I wanted to save the picture—for my portfolio. The caption said, "Historic Tree Removed. New Municipal Building Planned."

I sat at the kitchen table, and Lo reached for a pink teapot commemorating the Queen of England's jubilee. On its side was written in loopy, dainty script: "Where there is tea, there is hope."

"I thought this would be appropriate," she said.

She didn't know Emma was dying. (For a moment, I wondered what pot she'd pull out if she knew I'd called Roxanne.)

I sipped my tea while Lo made breakfast, humming a little bit like Abe. In general, I was pretty confident I had done the right thing. Now I just wanted something to happen. So far this morning, my phone had been silent. No news about Emma. Nothing from Abe. Nothing from Miriam.

Lo made French toast. Usually, she saved that for a special occasion. "You and Miriam will get beyond this. Just be patient. Be calm and compassionate."

I hated being patient. Compassion was something you had for lost kittens. "So, you don't think I'm the worst person in the world? You're not going to tell me I deserved all this?" I didn't just mean Miriam. I meant all of it.

She sat down opposite me, her hands on her mug. After ten years, she still wore her long hair pulled back. She still liked those long, flowy dresses that hide your figure. They never really looked good—but women wore them to be comfortable.

Her face looked older, but she was still the one who'd walked into my hospital room, determined to make me smile. "None of this is your fault. You got trapped in a game." She put her hands under the table. She seemed very ill at ease. "Dave never should have dragged you into his mess."

I agreed, but I also recognized that if he'd left me alone, I wouldn't have met Emma. She would be dying right now. "It wasn't all bad. Some of it was almost . . ." I paused. I looked away. "Nice."

Lo agreed almost solemnly. "It must have been exciting to think you could help those people, to think you could actually heal them, that your parents had died for a reason." She paused. "How *did* you feel? What was that like?"

At first, it was just my eyes. They itched. Then my lip quivered. I stood up out of my chair, walked around the table, and stood in front of Lo. "It felt good," I said.

It was hard to admit. But it was true. It felt good to think I could help people, that my parents hadn't died for nothing.

She stood up, too, and held my hand, and we left the kitchen to sit down on the couch. I leaned into her, and she sighed and opened up her arms. I put my head on the soft place above her breast and below her neck. My head fit perfectly there. It always had.

I stared out the window to the empty front lawn. "They believed in me. They thought I was special." I swallowed hard. I couldn't look at Lo. "They liked me. They trusted me to help them."

I rubbed my eyes and reached for a tissue. I needed to blow my nose. To my surprise, my face felt wet.

Lo smiled. "Janine. You're crying."

At first, it wasn't much. But once it started, I couldn't stop. I cried the way a person who has been saving all her tears for ten years should cry. Tears turned into sobs, and my whole body shook. I laughed and cried some more, and it felt good. And honest. Lo said nothing more until her shirt was cold and damp and covered in snot, and I was quiet. "I don't think I have to tell you that there are many ways to do good work, no magic required."

"I wanted to heal them," I said. "I did. It felt so exciting to think that maybe my hands were powerful. That maybe a boy could learn to walk because of me, that maybe Abe had . . ." Out loud, it sounded so stupid, but the truth remained: for those few hours when I thought I had healed Abe and Brian, when I sat in that prayer circle, when I made the clothes and remembered my dad, I was willing.

I believed, too.

I squeezed her arm. "Now I know I'm not special. My hands really are just ugly hands. My dresses are just okay. Maybe I really do need to face my fear—that all these terrible things happened to me because . . ." I didn't want to say it. "My own mother didn't love me."

Lo shook her head. "Now, that is not true. Not remotely." She said, "Your parents loved you."

I wasn't so sure. "Then why did my mother want to leave us? And don't tell me it's complicated."

Lo reached for the Book of Death, but then she stopped. I waited for her to grab a picture of my parents, but she didn't move. "First, let me tell you a story."

I didn't need a story—especially one with some moral. I looked away, out the window, to the empty lawn and the quiet street.

"To make money for food, a father and his daughter performed in a carnival. The father held a pole, and the daughter stood on top of that pole. It was a trick that demanded a great deal of concentration."

Lo and her yoga stories. They always started this way.

"Most people assumed that to make their trick work, they had to look out for each other, but the father explained that they didn't. The father's first responsibility was to himself."

"That seems odd," I interrupted. "What about the golden rule? You know, do unto others?"

Lo smiled—obviously she was the one who taught me that. "The man worried about his strength, his posture, and holding the pole as perfectly as he could. The daughter concentrated on her job, her strength, stepping steadily on her father's knee, then chest, then shoulders. They each stayed safe because they each had a separate responsibility."

She opened the Book of Death to a page right before the end.

We have to make an effort.
We have to listen to our hearts.
We cannot miss the opportunity to do something spectacular.

It made sense. I understood. I wanted to make spectacular clothes.

Lo said, "Your mother thought that if she didn't take that incredible and important work opportunity in the Middle East, she couldn't be the best mother to you. I know this hurts to hear, but she couldn't be whole unless she took care of herself first. She had to do it, Janine, but I'm sure she would have come home in the end. I promise you. I knew my sister almost as well as I know myself. She loved you."

I listened. I thought about it.

I wanted to believe her. I wanted to believe my mother loved me.

But no matter how much I twisted her words, it didn't ring true.

I said, "I think, more than anything, my mother wanted to be a famous reporter." She was seduced by a big job with a lot of exciting perks. She chose that over me and my dad. This wasn't about responsibility. This wasn't sacrificing something important to do the right thing. It wasn't even about being whole or doing the right thing or love or even coming back. "My mother left us. She was selfish."

And I had been acting just like her.

I told Lo everything. I told her that Emma was dying and that she ran away from home because she wanted to be left alone to make her own decisions about life and death. "I called Roxanne. I thought I could save her. I told her everything I knew about Emma, so she could find her parents and get Emma help. But now, I'm not so sure I did the right thing—not for her. I think I took everything she wanted away from her. And the worst part is, Emma doesn't know anything. They could be on their way."

Lo grabbed her purse and bolted for the car. "If they get to her first, they'll treat her against her will. There won't be anything we can do."

All the way there, I called the hotel, but Dave's line was busy. Lo kept her eyes on the road. "We may be too late."

I begged her to drive faster. "I don't know if I can stop it, but I need to explain."

FORTY-ONE

There were two police cars in front of the Hotel Bethlehem. There was also a news van. Roxanne stood outside the entrance talking into the camera, describing what happened inside, just moments before.

Already, there were gawkers.

Click, click, click, click, click.

"Dave Armstrong, pastor and well-known speaker, has been hiding an underage cancer patient against the instructions of her parents. After receiving an anonymous tip, we called the police and found her here. Her parents have been frantically searching for her for months."

I thought I'd said no press. I thought we had a deal.

As Roxanne continued to tell the story of finding Emma's parents and telling them she knew where their daughter was, Dave walked out in handcuffs, flanked by police. One of them told him to walk as quickly as he could to the patrol car. The other hid his face with a pillowcase.

Just behind them, two officers walked with a woman and a man and Emma.

This wasn't what I thought it would look like.

I thought they would embrace her. I thought she would be relieved. The ending was supposed to be a happy one: parents and daughter reunited, daughter healed to live a long life, to tell the world how it was wrong to hide from your family and even more wrong to give up on life.

I wanted to tell her how important she was to me—how all I wanted to do was heal her—it was the perfect happily ever after.

But this wasn't a story. It was my world. The camera was rolling.

Click, click, click.

Roxanne, of course, reported my arrival. "Janine," someone shouted. "What do you know about this girl?"

I knew I only had a moment. I grabbed Emma and pulled her back into the hotel lobby. Her eyes were cold. She stood on the marble stairs so we could see eye to eye. "Why?"

"Because it was the only way I could help you. But trust me, I didn't . . ."

"You didn't what? Think about what would happen to me? Think about what I wanted?"

I begged her to forgive me. "I did this because you helped me. Because I want you to get better." I told her that sometimes, the ends justified the means; sometimes someone had to take responsibility and do what needed to be done. Even though this was a big mess—and I knew I should've done it differently—running away had been wrong. Giving up had to be wrong. I said, "You need treatment. There isn't anyone here—including you—who believes you can get better any other way."

I gave her the hamsa. "Take this," I said. "So you know I'll always be there for you. So that when you're better . . ."

She threw it on the steps, and I heard it crack on the floor. I picked it up. The stone was glass. It now had a thin white line down its center.

Emma walked away, and I followed her outside. The cameras turned on us—I didn't care. I tried to shove the hamsa into her hand. "You have to take it. It represents luck. And healing." I followed her all the way to the street and the car that was waiting for her. "Her name was Karen Friedman. She died after a suicide bomber blew us all up."

Emma stood with her parents and stared at the cameras, but she wouldn't look at me. "Whatever happens next, I didn't want this. I should have been given a choice. You should have let me make that choice."

Then she turned around and sat in the back of her parents' car.

Her mother shook my hand. "Thank you."

I gave her the hamsa. "Please take it. It's for protection. I hope it gives Emma the healing hand she wanted." Emma looked small in the back of the car. She looked scared. I said, "I hope someday she will forgive me. Even if she can't, I will be glad she's alive."

She shook her head and finally looked at me. "It doesn't matter what happens next." Her eyes glared at my hands and made them burn. "You had no right. I will never forgive you." She slammed her door shut.

FORTY-TWO

On the way home, the phone didn't ring. We didn't talk. Every time Lo started to say something, I turned and looked out the window.

I didn't need a lecture. I knew what I did was wrong. But I couldn't imagine letting her die.

When we pulled into the driveway, Sharon stood on the grass. I ran past her, away from Lo, up the stairs to my room. I gathered up all my pictures—the ones of my parents as well as the shots of me, Abe, Miriam, and Dan—and put them in a drawer. Then I folded up my remnants and put them away, too. I shoved Annie into the closet. I covered the sewing machine with an old throw. I picked up the retrospective and ripped it to shreds.

Slow and heavy steps approached. Sharon said nothing about the mess. "Roxanne called." Emma was on her way to a hospital in Philadelphia. Her surgery was scheduled for first thing Monday morning. "It was the right thing to do," she said. "Your heart was in the right place." Hearing her say it didn't help.

I lay on my bed. There were clouds in the sky. One looked like an eagle. I didn't cry. Instead, I decided to walk to the farm.

***

All the equipment was gone. No one stood outside the nursing home. The streets were quiet. Already, I couldn't remember what it had looked like when there was a farm and a tree and my friends.

Now the land was clear. The vegetables were all gone. The tree was a stump. It was almost level with the ground.

I turned around and went home. I wanted to be close to the phone. Emma would be in surgery soon.

***

I tried to pray. I thought good thoughts. I almost wrote Emma a letter, but the only thing I could think to say was, "I'm sorry," and "I hope you get better."

I called the hospital, but no surprise, her parents wouldn't take my call. The nurse explained that it wasn't personal. Emma's family had left a message to tell all well-wishers that they would release a statement when the time was right. In the meantime, no visitors. No friends.

What felt strange (even though I shouldn't have been surprised): Dave wouldn't answer my calls either. And Miriam and Abe were totally AWOL. Her mother told me they were taking the week to look at colleges—a last-minute decision—nothing personal. She rambled for a while. She thought I knew.

On the third day with no news, four boxes from Israel

showed up on my doorstep. Three were addressed to me. One was for Lo. I brought them one by one to my room. They were heavy.

I decided to get it over with.

In the first box, I found my mom's jewelry and, wrapped in bubble wrap, a small glazed sculpture of a girl sitting on a stool with her legs crossed. She looked like she was thinking about something important. My mother's initials were carved into the bottom.

She also had a pretty impressive button collection. Mostly political things and ribbons for different causes. Some with those empowering sayings people like to post to pump themselves up.

Wherever you go, go with all your heart.
The truth will set you free, but first it will piss you off.

Couldn't disagree with that one.

In the second box, I found my dad's files. Photograph after photograph from his papers in New Jersey and Pennsylvania as well as national magazines. Some of them were boring, but some made me pause. Especially the faces.

There were also pictures of us. One was in a frame decorated by a few remaining stale Cheerios. There were glue marks where some of the Cheerios and decorations had disintegrated or fallen off.

Pretty soon, my entire floor was covered with ten years of bubble wrap, newspaper, and memories.

Lo walked up the stairs with some archive boxes and empty scrapbooks. She picked up some of the photos and sat in the window seat to look at them. She didn't ask about the sewing machine. Or Annie. Or where my fabric was. Later, she didn't make a single sarcastic comment when, lucky for me, the president made a major announcement about the economy, and Emma's story was reduced to a few words on the endless news crawl at the bottom of the screen . That happened sometimes. Sometimes your story broke at the right time. Sometimes it happened when there was something actually newsworthy to report. If that happened, it was forgotten.

At the end of the day, we sat in my room and talked.

Lo couldn't believe that my grandparents had collected so many clippings. Every story my mother ever wrote; every picture my father ever took. In the bottom of the second box we found an article about my mother's assignment and a notice announcing the event at the synagogue. It was circled in red pen. I said, "I wonder if they were planning to go see us?"

The house was really quiet. I looked up at the skylight. There was nothing to see. No moon. No stars. Just black sky. "Should I have kept my mouth shut? Let Emma die?"

Lo looked at the clippings all over the floor. We heard the doorbell ring, then the door slam. It was Sharon. "Okay to come up?" she yelled.

"Okay," Lo called back. Then she got up from the window and sat on the floor next to me. "I think there will be days when you'll regret what you did." (I was pretty sure she wasn't talking about Emma.) "But there will also be days when you can be proud that you did what you thought was right, even though it would have been easier to do nothing."

***

Something good must have happened, because when Sharon walked up the steps, I didn't recognize her. Usually, her footsteps were tired. Today they were quick.

She took her seat in the window. Everyone liked the window seat. It was comfortable and cozy at once.

"We need to talk to you," Lo said. They had an important announcement to make.

"Are you moving in?" I guessed.

They smiled. "Yes. If it's okay with you."

I said, "Of course it is," and "Oh my God," and "I'm so happy." As they hugged each other and me, I wondered if they had to do this, if they felt that they needed each other close to take care of me.

Then she looked around—at the empty boxes and memorabilia. "You guys have been busy."

I said, "We have one box to go. We can do it now. Or later. I'm not in a rush."

Lo said, "Let's do it now."

Together, the three of us opened the last box. This one looked like it was meant for Lo. It was filled with old clothes. A bunch of T-shirts with Hebrew lettering. Lo gave the orange one to me. "I think I stole that one out of your mom's closet." There were also pictures of both Mom and Lo when they were in the army. In most of the pictures, they stood to attention, but some were more casual. I found one picture of Lo cuddled up with a boy, which sent everyone into fits of giggles. She told Sharon, "That's Eitan." I was confused. Lo told me, "I almost married him. In a funny way, he was a lot like Abe. A good friend. But in the end, nothing more."

***

In the press, a week is an eternity. In high school, it's even longer. When I went back to school, everything seemed different. There were no reporters. Ms. Browning didn't say anything about my portfolio. No one asked me about Brian. I thought that was a good thing. A step in the right direction.

At the end of the day, I waited for Miriam at her locker. For her, time had changed nothing. She didn't want to talk. "You need to leave me alone," she said. "A lot has happened." We didn't need to make a list. We both knew what she was talking about. "Being friends with you—it's never been easy. You say you don't want to be famous, but if anyone ever—for one split second—forgets who you are and what you lived through—you make sure they remember."

My head spun. That was not what I was expecting. "I'm sorry, Miriam. Please. I'll change. I'm clueless. I need my tripod. I do want privacy. This is Samantha's fault. I think she's the one who leaked those photos of me."

She laughed. "It isn't *your* tripod. It's *ours*. It *was* ours." She grabbed her stuff. "And don't blame Samantha. She is a good friend. You should have given her a chance. I know for a fact she had nothing to do with those photos for the retrospective."

That got me. "How do you know?"

She dropped her arms and looked me straight in the eye, so I knew she was serious. "Because I was the one who gave them the pictures."

I shook my head. "No you didn't."

She said, "A few weeks ago, that reporter showed up at my house, and she showed me what she was going to print about you.

She said you were wasting your life; you were a disappointment to the world. She said that after being saved from the rubble, you owed it to the people who died to be a better person."

"It was a ploy," I said. "To get you to talk."

"And what if it was? If she was going to write an article about you, I wanted it to really be about you—the real you. The way she talked about you—she didn't know you." She looked tired—like she was explaining something easy to a child. "Maybe she was religious. Maybe she admired your parents. In any case, I gave her the pictures. I told her who you really were. A great friend. I told her that you were totally there for me and Abe." She paused, took a deep breath. "I wanted to tell the world that you were more than a survivor and that someday, the world would hear more from you—when you were ready. I wanted everyone to know that we don't care whether you're famous or not. You lost your parents. You were injured. I wanted that woman to understand that you didn't deserve what she was saying."

"You know me."

She slammed her locker shut. "I wanted everyone to know you. That's why I did what I did. But since, then, I've been thinking. I think I said all that, even though the truth was, you have never been that great a friend. What I said was as unreal as what she was going to write. I described the friend I want you to be."

I said, "I can be her."

Miriam turned to go. "I hope so."

FORTY-THREE

When I got home, I called the hospital for what felt like the fiftieth time—still, they wouldn't tell me. I called Dave—but he still wasn't picking up my calls either. CNN said he'd been released on his own recognizance.

So I called Roxanne. No matter what I did, she'd always pick up the phone. "Is she recovering?" I asked.

Roxanne sounded tired. Morose. I could hear a lot of noise in the background. People talking. Phones ringing. She told me she was putting me on hold so she could find a quiet place to talk to me.

Sappy music played. Then a voice: "Next week, be sure to watch Roxanne Wheeler as she tackles . . ."

"Janine. I'm sorry." Now I could hear her better. She still sounded upset.

"It's okay. I can stand being on hold."

That made her sigh. "No. It's not that. I thought you knew. I assumed Armstrong had called you."

"Knew what?"

Roxanne told me to sit down. I said, "She had the bone marrow transplant. Right? She should be in recovery. She should be getting stronger."

"That's not exactly true."

Bone marrow transplants were complicated things. Emma had been steadily improving until she contracted an infection. It was pretty common, but in this case, not good. Emma wasn't strong. She got weaker and weaker, so that the doctors had no choice. They induced a coma. Roxanne made sure to tell me that Emma's parents didn't blame me. She said, "There's no way to predict things like this."

I was confused. "What do you mean, I'm not to blame?"

Roxanne said, "If she dies." There was silence for a long time. "They are going to remove life support. She is very weak."

I asked, "Can I see her?"

Roxanne didn't think that was a good idea. "There is nothing more you can do. You don't need to come in. And forget about that exclusive—it won't be necessary after all." And then she hung up.

It might not be "necessary" for her, but right now, it absolutely was for me. I asked Lo, "Can you give me a lift to the bus?"

"What are you up to?" she asked.

When I told her, she wasn't happy. But she wouldn't stand in my way either. "Get in the car. I'll give you a ride."

I had something to say.

FORTY-FOUR

Roxanne Wheeler had one excellent poker face. When I walked into her office, she looked like she wasn't expecting me. Like she didn't know her little game of chicken would work like a charm, like she didn't think I was capable of getting myself down the Blue Route to Philadelphia.

"You're just like your dad."

"You knew my dad?" I wondered what she knew—what I could have known all these years.

She must have realized what this sounded like, because her voice got softer and kinder. "Right after I graduated, I interned for his magazine. When he walked into the room . . . everyone stopped and paid attention." She patted my shoulder. "He was bigger than life. A great, great man. His death was such a tragedy."

I asked her to tell me more about him—if he was a good boss or a hard ass, but her internship was short and that's all she had to say. She asked, "So what do you want? I told you . . ."

I told her not to bother pretending she didn't want me to show up. "I know what you said, but I need to make a statement." She didn't blink. I straightened out my shirt and skirt. "Are you game?"

She pulled out a notepad, and only then did I see what looked to me like the tiniest Cheshire-cat, snake-in-the-grass smile. "Of course I'm game. But first, can I send you to makeup? No offense." She sighed. "You'll thank me. The lights. They're harsh. This isn't high school."

She sent a quick text, then led me to a beauty parlor chair in front of a large mirror. The room was bright, and I looked washed-out. A man with long black hair pulled into a ponytail appeared. In his white jacket, and wielding various ominous-looking metal instruments, he looked like he was ready to deliver twins.

"Tommy, this is Janine. We're going to do a one-on-one in the red chairs," she told him.

Under any other circumstances, I would have complained. The make up was thick. My eyes looked too big. I was wearing blue, and this eye shadow was too green. "Trust me," he said. "Can I play with your hair?" Before I said yes, he whipped out a straightening iron and gave me a sleek look—the kind that a lot of TV stars liked. "You know, you would look awesome with a short blunt cut."

When I was ready, Roxanne led me back to the studio. She clipped a microphone to my lapel and barked some orders to the camera and sound people. Then she gave me a few pointers. "Just speak normally. When you're talking, look at me. The cameras will do their job. Try to be as natural as possible. If you mess up, we can always do a second take."

The cameraman raised his hand, and a huge light shined in my face. A man in jeans and a T-shirt said, "We're taping."

Roxanne smiled at the camera. "I am here today with Janine Collins, the Pennsylvania girl known as the Soul Survivor. As you know, ten years ago Janine was the sole survivor of a synagogue bombing that took almost seventy lives. Just in the past two weeks, she has been in the news for presumably healing two young men, but as we all know, one of them turned out to be a fraud." She nodded at me, and I tried to look relaxed. "Janine, tell us. You have been in the public eye for the last ten years. Tell me what that's like. How has your life been changed by the cameras?"

I cleared my throat.

"As you said, I was a survivor of a bombing. In that bombing, my parents died and my hands were badly injured. I spent more than a year in a hospital. People from all over the world sent me money and gifts and good wishes. And for that, I am grateful."

Roxanne started to ask another question, but I shook my head and focused on the camera.

"Over the years, some of you have wondered if there was a reason this happened to me. Some of you thought that because this happened in Israel, my hands might be a symbol of something more. I don't blame you. The magazines and newspapers and broadcasts that have followed me kept those rumors and my story alive. So did Dave Armstrong, the man who first found me."

I took a deep breath. I knew the words. I just had to say them.

"When people have asked me about God, I've always said

the same thing: I don't believe."

This was harder than I thought it would be. "I felt this way because I was bitter and angry. For a really long time, I felt used, maybe even persecuted. I wanted to be left alone. I didn't think that I could care about a God that would sit back and watch my parents—and so many other people—die. I didn't understand why anyone else would either."

***

It never made sense.

It still didn't. Not really.

***

"But then my friend was hit by a car, and I met people facing death and illness and hardship, and all of them—and I mean every single one of them—still believe. Not just that—they are grateful for what they have."

Roxanne raised her hand, one finger up, like she wanted to say something. Or maybe she was flipping me the bird.

I didn't wait to find out.

"You've heard about one of them. She was a girl who believed that faith would save her. She was so determined to stay out of the hospital that she hid from her family. When she told me this, I couldn't accept it. I didn't understand. I wanted to help her—I wanted to be what everyone had told me I was—a healer. So I betrayed her confidence."

This was so hard.

But it felt right.

"Even though she asked me not to, I told her family where she was. Maybe you saw it on TV. They brought her to the hospital, gave her the transplant she didn't want, and now she's in a coma." I swallowed hard. "She could die—because of me."

Even though she knew about Emma's condition, Roxanne acted surprised. "Is there no hope?"

I said, "Of course there's hope—ask Dave Armstrong. There is always hope, but she's in trouble because I thought I knew what was best. I forgot. I am not a healer." I stood up. "Do you hear me? I am not a healer. My hands are just hands."

Roxanne's face stayed still. She held out her arm and motioned me to sit down. "If she dies, will you feel responsible? Do you think Dave Armstrong should be prosecuted?"

I stared straight into the camera. My palms were burning, and all I wanted to do was rub them together hard. "I think we should pray. Pray for hope and faith. I don't care what religion you are or even if you don't really believe anything at all. I'm just asking you to think about her. Believe for her."

***

I took off the microphone. I smiled at Roxanne. I was pretty pleased with myself. "So, when are you going to air this?"

She looked at the cameraman, then at me—part annoyed, part shocked, part amused. "This isn't a church, Janine. You can't come here and make a confession and expect us to play it. Did you really think you have that kind of authority?" She told him to give me the disc, if I wanted it—for a souvenir. "I hate to disappoint you, but we can't run this. This is a news station. If you want forgiveness—or redemption—go to church. Or temple. Over here, our job is to report news. I thought you knew that." She told me to go home. "What you just said . . . no one wants to hear that."

FORTY-FIVE

As it turns out, even if the world stops caring about you, it does not stop turning. The next day, I took Annie out of the closet. I wiped off her makeup. I rethreaded my machine and made myself a brand-new dress. There was nothing else I could imagine doing.

It had short sleeves, a scoop neck, and a cinched waist—pretty standard for what they were showing in the stores—pretty much what most of my friends are wearing. For fun, I mixed a few fabrics against the grain. The effect was interesting, and yes, it was cute—really cute. Ms. Browning said she was happy to see me taking my time. She thought this dress looked great. Lo said she'd wear it in a heartbeat.

"I'm not sure that's a good sign," I joked, but when I wore it, I caught Dan checking me out. It was our "nothing is mutual" rule in action. The second I seemed over him, he missed me.

That's how things continued until the end of the school year.

Dan stared.

I dressed up.

The phone did not ring. We were beginning to think my story might finally have run out of gas, when Sharon told Lo to turn on the TV. Roxanne was scheduled to talk to Dave.

***

These days, no thanks to me, Roxanne had a regular spot at the evening show table. Some of her recent reports included: The upcoming heat and how to stay cool. Our local congressman and his fight for more jobs. The pros and cons of casinos. Lately, I thought she might still be happier doing her own thing.

But tonight was big. Tonight she was interviewing Dave.

He looked handsome in his suit. Emma's parents looked surprisingly good, too. They reported that even though Emma was still in a deep coma, there was so much reason for hope. The teddy bears and gifts and donations were greatly appreciated. They had every reason to believe that she would recover—they just couldn't say when.

I had a bad feeling about this.

But there was also good news. Dave told Roxanne that Brian's mother had been arrested for fraud; the district attorney and Emma's parents had decided not to prosecute him for kidnapping. He was very grateful for this. "Very soon, we will resume our mission." He smiled and put his hands together, palm to palm. He was good at this. He really knew how to look pious. He said, "Emma's faith is such a source of inspiration. Even in a coma, she has taught me many things."

Her mother seemed unnaturally happy about the situation. "Yesterday, she was visited by thirty-two people. Every single person who visited her said they felt euphoric—like they were touching a living, breathing angel. You could see it in their faces, and in hers. They came in feeling sad and low, but they left enlightened. Isn't that a miracle?"

They never said "healed," but they talked about Emma like she was no longer a living girl, like she didn't have the right to open her eyes and find her own story. They talked about her the way they used to talk about me, but they didn't mention me. Not once. No doubt, this was intentional.

Dave had a new story.

Of course, since they didn't mention me, they also didn't mention Mom's hamsa—I didn't expect them to—but somehow I sensed it was there.

I went back to the kitchen to drink tea with Lo and Sharon. I waited for the phone to ring—for someone to ask for a comment—but the house stayed quiet. "Do you think it's over? Do you think Dave will never talk about me again?"

Lo couldn't be sure, but she thought Emma's story wouldn't last forever. "I think we should just be grateful it's quiet," Lo said. She said Emma's situation was sad. It was terrible that Dave and her parents would use her this way.

I said, "People need to believe in something." That was one of the things I was sure of.

***

What I wasn't sure of is how I felt about it.

I asked Lo and Sharon, "Do you think I should have taken the opportunity to say something more to the world?" The truth was, I'd been so determined to disappear. Now that I had what I thought I wanted—freedom and anonymity—I felt more and more let down.

For the first time, no one was talking about me. No one cared what I thought. There were no reporters at my door. The believers were gone. No one cared that I survived the bombing, and maybe they wouldn't ever again.

"I blew it. I really blew it. I had a chance to do something spectacular, and all I did was make a mess."

They wouldn't say.

There wasn't anything they could say.

But I still wanted to believe that something good had come of all this. "I just hope Emma made peace with her parents. I hope they listened to her and that maybe she even agreed to the transplant. I hope that some day, when she wakes up—if she wakes up—she will understand why I did what I did."

I expected Lo to assure me that I couldn't have known what would happen, that I was not to blame, not at fault, but instead, she picked up the Dead Sea photo. I wondered if, for her, my parents were still a happy, devoted couple.

I wondered what her last memory of them was.

"Tell me the truth. What did you talk about when you saw my mom at the Dead Sea?"

She said, "I wanted to leave home. Your mother wanted to take the job. We talked about every possible scenario. You do know things were tense back then."

"You mean because of my mom, or because you were gay? My grandparents were that closed-minded? You couldn't get them to accept you?"

She sighed in a sad way. "This is not about my being a lesbian, although that wasn't exactly an easy thing to talk to them about." For a second, she almost smiled. "Janine, your grandfather can be opinionated, but I told you—he was never a religious zealot. It was just a fight between two stubborn people." When I looked confused, she tried to explain. "He thought he knew better. He hated feeling out of control. He had ideas about family and marriage that didn't exactly work out. But he had to have figured he had years to make it right." She said, "And then your mom died, and there was nothing he could say or do. It must have been terrible for them. To think their daughter died not knowing that he still loved her."

I thought about that. "That's terrible."

Lo nodded. "He lost a lot when your mom left. I wish they could have talked." She was sure they would have. "But then it was too late. They missed their chance."

She walked across the room and retrieved her favorite old photo album. She stared at a picture of the family— two girls in high-collared blouses and long skirts. My grandfather wore a suit. Everyone looked serious. "You need to know them. He is a good man. In his spare time, I think he still writes poems. But he is also a driven man. Strong but quiet—and extremely private. Living in Israel was his dream because he believed in a world that served the community first. With him, there was no such thing as ego. The individual always came second."

"A little like Emma?"

She pushed the hair off my face. "Just like Emma."

I wanted to hug her, but she wouldn't let go of the album. "If you want me to know them, why don't we visit?" I reminded her of the father and daughter in the story she told me. I said, "The way I see it, they had to stick together."

I closed my eyes, and from somewhere deep in my memory, I heard my parents fighting. I was in my bed, hugging my raggedy green blanket late at night. I heard terrible, ugly words about love and hate and work and me. I heard my name over and over again. The next thing I remembered, Dave Armstrong was lifting up the final rock. The pressure on my hands disappeared. He was in awe—amazed, I guess, that I was really, truly alive. Even though I was stiff and sore and mangled, I reached up to him and opened my hands to the light and the smiling faces and excruciating pain.

For a moment, I thought I saw my mother's face. But it wasn't her. The face that suddenly came into focus was never hers. Now I realized that the face I always saw, the face that comforted me when I was scared, was Lo's.

She said, "Your mother was not the first person to seek fame and a legacy. But then she died, and someone had to think about you. Someone had to decide what to do. Someone had to be . . ."

A parent. My parent. My mom. I said, "I'm so glad it was you."

She smiled. "I love you."

I nodded. "I love you too." I looked at a picture of her, my mom, and my grandparents. "It's not too late for us."

"Maybe." She looked sad. "When I decided to bring you here, your grandparents were hurt. And mad. And in mourning. They were mad at me. I was mad at them. I wanted them to live here. To help me. Back then, I wanted to be a lawyer." She and Sharon held hands. "You need to know, it took a long time just to get to the point we're at now. We argued over everything. We argued about where to raise you . . . and whether to destroy your mother's last journal. They wanted to erase the past. But I knew you would handle it. I knew it then, and I know it now. Nothing changes when we hide. Everything works out when we are honest with each other."

Before she could start lecturing about practice or contradictions or humility, I ran up the stairs to my room for the Book of Death. "This is yours," I said, handing it back to Lo. "Do you want it? I think it's done its job."

Lo turned to the back of the book, two pages before the end. It was a page I'd skimmed in a rage. My black magic marker made it hard to read.

Before they go back, we are going to do what I should have done—what Martin wanted to do—a long time ago. I am going to call my father. I am going to forgive him and tell him about my life, my marriage, and Janine. He needs to see us. He needs to know Janine. We need to make peace.

I need it too.

They will go, but I will stay. This land is too important to me. It is more than a job—it is in my gut. It is something I have to do. Someday, J will understand. Someday, when she is a little bit older, I will sit down and tell her everything and she will be proud. This is our homeland. My father was right. I need to do the right thing. Someone needs to step up and take a stand.

Lo brought out the box that was addressed to her. It was still unopened.

For every old picture I found, Lo told me a story about my mom and my grandparents. They weren't all bad stories either—my grandfather was a lot more than a tyrant. I said,

"He might not have been the best father, but maybe he could become a better grandfather."

She said, "That would be really nice."

At the bottom of the box I found a whole stack of high-school history papers. They are all about politics, women's rights, Anwar Sadat, and injustice. Held together by a rubber band were her Jewish studies papers.

She didn't have a computer, so most of them were written by hand with original handmade covers. I peeked at the corner. Leora Friedman. "Wait a minute. These are yours?"

Lo shrugged. "Your mom wasn't the only activist in the house."

I pulled out a blue-and-white book. It was called *Leora's Book of Prayers*. "Do you mind if I open it?"

We paged through it together. There was a Jewish prayer for just about everything—meals, bread, the first day of school, the first time for anything. Toward the back, I found the Kaddish, the prayer for the dead.

Her face looked the same way it did when she saw the hamsa. "I made this book when I was a little younger than you are now."

On the next page, there was a big heading: My prayer for peace. Underneath the title, I couldn't believe it—she had traced her hand. The prayer was written all over the hand.

"Lo, is this yours, too?"

"Yes," she said. "It's mine."

It was a pretty nice hand, but like most hands, it wasn't perfect. The little finger curved to the side, and the knuckles on the second and third bulged. I reminded Lo what my grandmother told me. "My mom had this dream. About people

281

holding hands. That's why they gave her the hamsa."

She said, "I remember. We used to talk about that image. Like one big long chain. Or maybe a circle." She smiled. "We all had that dream. When we go back to Israel, I bet you will have it, too."

Now I stretched my fingers until they hurt. I stretched them as straight as they could go. I started the chain, my hand on hers.

"Look at that," Lo said. Our hands matched.

Then Lo put her hand on mine.

Every finger was exactly the same.

FORTY-SIX

We flew to Israel the day after the last day of school.

As soon as we were through security, Lo hailed a cab. Before we did anything else, we had to see the Wall. This was the place my dad was going to take me the day my parents died.

It's where my story really began.

It's where we had to go before it could continue.

***

The plaza was huge. The Wall itself seemed to glow. Lo reminded me that people from all over the world came here to pray, and that it was important to respect their different customs. She explained, "This part is for observers." She pointed to other sections, closer to the Wall. "But if you'd like to pray, you can go to that section." There was one for men and one for women.

I wanted to get closer.

But not yet. First, I stood back and watched the crowd. There were young people, old people, tourists, rabbis, observant men in hats, soldiers, the women hovering around children. One woman sobbed. Near another corner, a bride and groom held hands and prayed. There were people huddled in groups. There were people studying. There were people praying. There were people kissing. One man chanted in Hebrew to a small group.

It felt like the center of the universe.

The beginning of everything.

For the first time, I saw what my grandparents came for, what my mother always wanted, what Lo served for. Peace. I thought about Miriam and what she'd said just before I left. "Have a great time. Meet the people. Don't be afraid. When you get home, we will talk."

"What do you think?" Lo asked.

"It's beautiful," I said. "And strange, too." The people who were praying didn't turn their backs to the Wall. When they were done, they walked backwards. They were completely focused on the Wall and God.

I also couldn't help feeling a little strange—a few weeks ago, I could've earned tuition to pose here. "The Soul Survivor Returns" would have made every cover on the planet. I could see it now. My hands clenched. The Wall. The entire world praying around me.

But now, no one recognized me. No one was looking at me or asking me to pray for them. I was one of them. A Jew. A person. A citizen of Israel.

Anonymous. Just what I always wanted.

A young man came up to us and asked if this was our first visit to the Promised Land. "Would you like a guide?" When Lo spoke to him in Hebrew, he said, "No problem" and handed us each a piece of paper. I'd read about this custom. When you stood at the Western Wall, you were supposed to stuff a prayer into the cracks. People said that God read every one. The young man winked at me. He said, "Make it a good one. The world is so crazy. We need as many prayers as we can get."

I had been thinking about what I was going to pray for. I had a lot of ideas: to make Emma wake up. To help me be a better person. Inspiration. Forgiveness. Friendship. To give me one more chance to do something good in this world. My mother had said, "Your story is not over," and it wasn't. But it was different.

Standing here, surrounded by all these people, I was aware I'd missed an easy chance to add to my story, to do something more than complain or run or nothing. I'd committed my mom's greatest sin—I missed an opportunity to make the world better.

I missed a chance to have my say.

I sat on the ground and traced my hand on the paper. There was one thing that said it all, one thing that we all needed. It was my private prayer for the world. It was the one thing I wished I'd always had.

In the middle of the palm, I wrote one word:
TRUST.

Then I folded the paper, closed my eyes, and said a prayer for Emma. And Dave Armstrong. I forgave my mother. I honored my father. I looked at Lo and thanked her for telling me the truth, for giving me this moment.

"Are you ready?" she asked.

"Ready."

I stuffed the prayer into the highest crevice, then backed

up to the visitors' area. Nearby stood a group of girls—Americans—chatting and laughing and talking about where they were going to do, if they thought they could really drink in a bar, if their fake IDs would work.

"Will you take our picture?" one of them asked me, holding out her camera.

"Sure. No problem." As she ran back to organize the group, she dropped her *People* magazine on the ground.

The cover showed a collage of familiar faces—actresses who'd graced the same magazine many other times. The headline read, "The Ten Stories that Made Us Cry." One of the girls looked terrible. Her hair was a mess. A small caption read, "What I'm learning in rehab."

"I hope she turns it around," the girl said, pointing to the famous face. When I shrugged, she said, "In *Glamour*, I read she wants to pose for *Playboy*. She really turned into a skank."

"Maybe she needs the money," I said. Or maybe that's the only way to stay famous. Brian's mom wasn't the only person who had trouble getting used to real life.

When they were still, I counted to three and yelled, "Smile."

Yes, I had lost a big chance to make a statement, and worse than that, I'd hurt my friends. But as sure as I was that they would give me another chance, I also knew that the news cycle would not discard me completely. It would file me away, like the ten stories that made us cry or the worst divorces or the most scandalous crimes, until the time was right and it needed to be fed. Maybe it would be the twentieth anniversary, or maybe when I got married or had a baby. I hoped it wouldn't be when I needed the attention or ended up in trouble. All I knew was that at some point, someone would find me and put me back on the cover.

I was still the Soul Survivor.

At some point, someone would care.

And when that day came, when they asked me to talk about my life or my opinions or my parents, I wouldn't tell them "no comment." Instead of running away, I'd pose for a picture. I'd have something important to say.

Next time, I would be ready.

ACKNOWLEDGMENTS

I started the first draft of this novel in my very last packet at Vermont College of Fine Arts. It was sort of a whim—a dare to write something outrageous and different—a reaction to four hard months of work on my creative thesis. With the encouragement of the faculty, I decided to honor the process and read that rough beginning at my graduation, the whole time, secretly hoping that it would force me to keep going (and show me what was supposed to happen next). Since then, I have read excerpts of later drafts at many retreats and events. I needed a lot of advice and encouragement.

When Grace Paley tells you she's intrigued, you don't put that thing in a drawer.

To my many writer-friends from VCFA, the Novel Retreat, and Kindling Words with special nods to Micol Ostow; Kathi Appelt; Kim Marcus; Kelly Carter Crocker; Elly Swartz; Marc Schulman; the late, great Norma Fox Mazer; and Laura Ruby, this novel's first cheerleader. Tami Lewis Brown gets kudos for discussing all my epiphanies. Tanya Lee Stone continues to offer me the unconditional support that every writer needs to be brave. (Hurray for a plan with unlimited minutes!) Big hugs and exclamation points to all my amazing writers.com writers for being brave enough to tell the teacher what she's doing wrong. I hope all of you are excited and surprised to read what this story ultimately became.

Kisses to Gail Marcus, Marjorie Rose, Lisa Silbert, and new friends Alex Sinclair and Bekki Harris Kaplan for all your support. To the ladies at Belleza Hair Salon in Lebanon, New Hampshire, for supplying me with fourteen years of tabloids, and to my fellow yogis in the Upper Valley and Evanston, Illinois: Namaste! The hot room offers many kinds of magic!

Thanks to my wonderful editor, Andrew Karre, who offered me vision and discipline and a new way to reimagine my stories. I'm so grateful you saw Janine's potential, even though she isn't always the most likable protagonist. It makes me happy to work with someone who likes pizza as much as I do. It makes me even happier to work with someone who speaks out for human rights and justice every chance he can.

Likewise, thanks to my agent, Sarah Davies, who offers guidance and support in an accent that makes me feel smarter. And she's a Glamour *Do*. Always.

To my parents, Rich and Judy Aronson, who could have stopped believing in me, but didn't. And to Ann and Jon Klein— you know what for. Writing is an incredible privilege, and I wouldn't be doing it if it were not for my wonderful husband and family. Thank you Michael, Rebecca, Elliot, Ed, Liz, and Gregg for unwavering support and humor and indulging me.

Chocolate and flowers for everyone! I'm so happy to finally be able to thank you!

ABOUT THE AUTHOR

Sarah Aronson holds an MFA in Writing for Children and Young Adults from Vermont College of Fine Arts. She is the author of several books for teens and young readers. She lives near Chicago. Visit her online at www.saraharonson.com.